MURDER
AMONG FRIENDS

THE ADAMS ROUND TABLE

BERKLEY PRIME CRIME, NEW YORK

MURDER AMONG FRIENDS

A Berkley Prime Crime Book / published by arrangement with the authors

PRINTING HISTORY
Berkley Prime Crime hardcover edition / October 2000
Berkley Prime Crime mass-market edition / November 2003

ISBN: 0-425-19265-2

Berkley Prime Crime Books are published by The Berkley Publishing Group, a division of Penguin Group (USA) Inc., 375 Hudson Street, New York, New York 10014.
The name BERKLEY PRIME CRIME and the BERKLEY PRIME CRIME design are trademarks belonging to Penguin Group (USA) Inc.

PRINTED IN THE UNITED STATES OF AMERICA

10 9 8 7 6 5 4 3 2 1

COPYRIGHTS

CONTENTS

INTRODUCTION
TO THE ADAMS ROUND TABLE
ANTHOLOGY
MURDER AMONG FRIENDS

"WRITERS help writers," my mother always said. As a pulp-fiction writer with romantic leanings toward the proletariat, this was one of her bedrock verities. Like college men play golf and vote Republican—not her idea of a compliment. My father on the other hand, patrician born and bred, avoided his fellow writers like the plague, detesting what he called "shoptalk" and preferring the company of the common man and woman found in a good saloon.

So I was not an unconflicted candidate for membership in the Adams Round Table when Dorothy Salisbury Davis and the late Tom Chastain invited me to join a group of mystery writers who met in a private room in the back of a restaurant the first Tuesday of every month to discuss their work.

Neither the "art of writing" nor even the process were subjects of conversation in my parents' house. They made their livings cranking out a couple of thousand salable words a day, every day. Discussing work-in-progress with anyone other than an editor empowered to write checks reeked of putting off the real job of sitting down at the typewriter—the "machine" in their parlance.

Perhaps they thought talk frivolous; perhaps they were afraid to undermine the magic they called upon daily. Or perhaps—like Rollerblading writers who wear wrist guards to protect their typing fingers but eschew helmets—they believed that writing didn't bear thinking about.

When I started writing mystery novels, friends who were writers had helped me with the basics like finding an agent and getting invited to publishing parties. But like my parents, my writer friends did not talk about writing. We talked a little about the publishing business and a little about books we were reading, and more than we should have about the movies. Sometimes after a poker game, or on a country walk while wives and lovers bounded ahead, we bounced a book idea off a friend. But mainly, we traded one-liners—sort of like sparring partners warming up for the main event. A main event fought in private.

So I dodged the invitation. To no avail. Tom Chastain, a gentleman of the old school, took me to lunch in a bar filled with beefily retired cops and asked me, again, to give it a try. Struck by his sincerity and remembering that Mom always said, "Writers help writers," I agreed to come to their next dinner as a guest.

I knew some of the dozen people there by their books or reputation and a few from hanging around New York and one or two by the sound of their voices echoing from mystery-convention panel discussions. Lucy Freeman and Mary Higgins Clark were there, and the short-story writer Joyce Harrington, and Warren Murphy, and Whitley Strieber, and the playwright Frederick Knott. None but Dorothy Davis were actual friends, that first night. Which mattered not at all as they got down to business.

After some brief small talk, they dealt with the menu. Then they started around the table, reporting one by one where they were at the moment and what they had done in the last month. Some related actual page counts. Others mentioned new ideas. Several admitted to being stuck in their book or displeased with the direction it was taking.

The group extended cheerful congratulations to the fortunate and got down to the business of leveling penetrating questions at the strugglers.

Did the struggler know how the book was supposed to end? Some thought that important, others advocated typing in the dark. Did the struggler know who committed the murder? Vital said someone, explaining why in convincing detail. Too constraining, said another, as persuasively. I was struck by the variety of approaches. Here were a dozen individuals each with a distinct work method. Some were outliners; some sailed through their first drafts on a wing and a prayer; several rewrote as they went along, others when it was all done; one lucky devil appeared to fax first drafts directly to the typesetter.

But time and again, the struggler's face would light with a vision from a shifting angle: Maybe *she's* the hero when I thought *he* was; or, my most interesting character doesn't appear until the end of Chapter Eight, which could be a problem; ditto for a distinct lack of urgency that allows my detective time off on weekends. Do I really need a subplot that occurs offstage? Would my character know how to do that? Could my character be so ignorant?

I noted a blessed dearth of generalities. And no more touchy-feelie "art of" talk than you'd hear from the pilots of a Boeing descending into a Third World airport. They were approaching each writer's problems as they would their own; it was all about specifics. And while most of the questions were questions that any professional would ask him or herself, eventually, wasn't it better to ask now than when the book was already in the bookstore?

Forgive me, Pop, I thought, when my turn came. Mom was right. Writers help writers.

I broke a lifelong habit of reticence. And was rewarded. Of the questions and suggestions flying back at me, several struck chords, or at least glancing blows, and I left with a feeling that tomorrow was going to start better than today had.

So I joined the Adams Round Table. It was reassuring to hear other writers' problems. Comforting to be reminded that other people writing novels are also struggling to reinvent the wheel every time. And that no matter how high you rise in the profession, you're not the only one who still feels like an amateur.

As the years go by, I continue to look forward to our monthly dinners. I often depart on a very satisfying high, owing as much to friends and colleagues as to good wine. When death and the vagaries of life thinned our ranks, we were replenished by Mickey Friedman and Judith Kelman and Stanley Cohen. Then came Peter Straub and Larry Block and, most recently, Susan Isaacs, who is publishing her first short story ever. Which brings me to *Murder Among Friends*.

Every now and then we write a collection of short stories. This is the sixth. And like its predecessors, purely voluntary. No member of the Adams Round Table has to contribute. Most do most of the time, but the short-story collections aren't why we get together. If anything, they're a *celebration* of why we get together. And *Murder Among Friends* strikes me as a most appropriate title for a collection written by the kind of friends a writer can count on when it counts, the first Tuesday of every month.

—Justin Scott

MURDER
AMONG FRIENDS

LET'S GET LOST

by Lawrence Block

WHEN the phone call came I was parked in front of the television set in the front room, nursing a glass of bourbon and watching the Yankees. It's funny what you remember and what you don't. I remember that Thurman Munson had just hit a long foul that missed being a home run by no more than a foot, but I don't remember who they were playing, or even what kind of a season they had that year.

I remember that the bourbon was J. W. Dant, and that I was drinking it on the rocks, but of course I would remember that. I always remembered what I was drinking, though I didn't always remember why.

The boys had stayed up to watch the opening innings with me, but tomorrow was a school day, and Anita took them upstairs and tucked them in while I freshened my drink and sat down again. The ice was mostly melted by the time Munson hit his long foul, and I was still shaking my head at that when the phone rang. I let it ring, and Anita answered it and came in to tell me it was for me. Somebody's secretary, she said.

I picked up the phone, and a woman's voice, crisply professional, said, "Mr. Scudder, I'm calling for Mr. Alan Herdig of Herdig and Crowell."

"I see," I said, and listened while she elaborated, and estimated just how much time it would take me to get to their offices. I hung up and made a face.

"You have to go in?"

I nodded. "It's about time we had a break in this one," I said. "I don't expect to get much sleep tonight, and I've got a court appearance tomorrow morning."

"I'll get you a clean shirt. Sit down. You've got time to finish your drink, don't you?"

I always had time for that.

• • •

YEARS ago, this was. Nixon was president, a couple of years into his first term. I was a detective with the NYPD, attached to the Sixth Precinct in Greenwich Village. I had a house on Long Island with two cars in the garage, a Ford wagon for Anita and a beat-up Plymouth Valiant for me.

Traffic was light on the LIE, and I didn't pay much attention to the speed limit. I didn't know many cops who did. Nobody ever ticketed a brother officer. I made good time, and it must have been somewhere around a quarter to ten when I left the car at a bus stop on First Avenue. I had a card on the dashboard that would keep me safe from tickets and tow trucks.

The best thing about enforcing the laws is that you don't have to pay a lot of attention to them yourself.

Her doorman rang upstairs to announce me, and she met me at the door with a drink. I don't remember what she was wearing, but I'm sure she looked good in it. She always did.

She said, "I would never call you at home. But it's business."

"Yours or mine?"

"Maybe both. I got a call from a client. A Madison

Avenue guy, maybe an agency vice-president. Suits from Tripler's, season tickets for the Rangers, house in Connecticut."

"And?"

"And didn't I say something about knowing a cop? Because he and some friends were having a friendly card game and something happened to one of them."

"Something happened? Something happens to a friend of yours, you take him to a hospital. Or was it too late for that?"

"He didn't say, but that's what I heard. It sounds to me as though somebody had an accident and they need somebody to make it disappear."

"And you thought of me."

"Well," she said.

She'd thought of me before, in a similar connection. Another client of hers, a Wall Street warrior, had had a heart attack in her bed one afternoon. Most men will tell you that's how they want to go, and perhaps it's as good a way as any, but it's not all that convenient for the people who have to clean up after them, especially when the bed in question belongs to some working girl.

When the equivalent happens in the heroin trade, it's good PR. One junkie checks out with an overdose and the first thing all his buddies want to know is where did he get the stuff and how can they cop some themselves. Because, hey, it must be good, right? A hooker, on the other hand, has less to gain from being listed as cause of death. And I suppose she felt a professional responsibility, if you want to call it that, to spare the guy and his family embarrassment. So I made him disappear, and left him fully dressed in an alley down in the financial district. I called it in anonymously and went back to her apartment to claim my reward.

"I've got the address," she said now. "Do you want to have a look? Or should I tell them I couldn't reach you?"

I kissed her, and we clung to each other for a long moment. When I came up for air, I said, "It'd be a lie."

"I beg your pardon?"

"Telling them you couldn't reach me. You can always reach me."

"You're a sweetie."

"You better give me that address," I said.

• • •

I retrieved my car from the bus stop and left it in another one a dozen or so blocks uptown. The address I was looking for was a brownstone in the East Sixties. A shop with handbags and briefcases in the window occupied the storefront, flanked by a travel agent and a men's clothier. There were four doorbells in the vestibule, and I rang the third one and heard the intercom activated, but didn't hear anyone say anything. I was reaching to ring a second time when the buzzer sounded. I pushed the door open and walked up three flights of carpeted stairs.

Out of habit, I stood to the side when I knocked. I didn't really expect a bullet, and what came through the door was a voice, pitched low, asking who was there.

"Police," I said. "I understand you've got a situation here."

There was a pause. Then a voice—maybe the same one, maybe not—said, "I don't understand. Has there been a complaint, Officer?"

They wanted a cop, but not just any cop. "My name's Scudder," I said. "Elaine Mardell said you could use some help."

The lock turned and the door opened. Two men were standing there, dressed for the office in dark suits and white shirts and ties. I looked past them and saw two more men, one in a suit, the other in gray slacks and a blue blazer. They looked to be in their early to mid-forties, which made them ten to fifteen years older than I.

I was what, thirty-two that year? Something like that.

"Come on in," one of them said. "Careful."

I didn't know what I was supposed to be careful of, but found out when I gave the door a shove and it stopped after a few inches. There was a body on the floor, a man, curled on his side. One arm was flung up over his head, the other bent at his side, the hand inches from the handle of the knife. It was an easy-open stiletto and it was buried hilt-deep in his chest.

I pushed the door shut and knelt down for a close look at him, and heard the bolt turn as one of them locked the door.

The dead man was around their age, and had been similarly dressed until he took off his suit jacket and loosened his tie. His hair was a little longer than theirs, perhaps because he was losing hair on the crown and wanted to conceal the bald spot. Everyone tries that, and it never works.

I didn't feel for a pulse. A touch of his forehead established that he was too cold to have one. And I hadn't really needed to touch him to know that he was dead. Hell, I knew that much before I parked the car.

Still, I took some time looking him over. Without looking up I asked what had happened. There was a pause while they decided who would reply, and then the same man who'd questioned me through the closed door said, "We don't really know."

"You came home and found him here?"

"Hardly that. We were playing a few hands of poker, the five of us. Then the doorbell rang and Phil went to see who it was."

I nodded at the dead man. "That's Phil there?"

Someone said it was. "He'd folded already," the man in the blazer added.

"And the rest of you fellows were still in the middle of a hand."

"That's right."

"So he—Phil?"

"Yes, Phil."

"Phil went to the door while you finished the hand."

"Yes."

"And?"

"And we didn't really see what happened," one of the suits said.

"We were in the middle of a hand," another explained, "and you can't really see much from where we were sitting."

"At the card table," I said.

"That's right."

The table was set up at the far end of the living room. It was a poker table, with a green baize top and wells for chips and glasses. I walked over and looked at it.

"Seats eight," I said.

"Yes."

"But there were only the five of you. Or were there other players as well?"

"No, just the five of us."

"The four of you and Phil."

"Yes."

"And Phil was clear across the room answering the door, and one or two of you would have had your backs to it, and all four of you would have been more interested in the way the hand was going than who was at the door." They nodded along, pleased at my ability to grasp all this. "But you must have heard something that made you look up."

"Yes," the blazer said. "Phil cried out."

"What did he say?"

" 'No!' or 'Stop!' or something like that. That got our attention, and we got out of our chairs and looked over there, but I don't think any of us got a look at the guy."

"The guy who . . ."

"Stabbed Phil."

"He must have been out the door before you had a chance to look at him."

"Yes."

"And pulled the door shut after him."

"Or Phil pushed it shut while he was falling."

I said, "Stuck out a hand to break his fall . . ."

"Right."

"And the door swung shut, and he went right on falling."

"Right."

I retraced my steps to the spot where the body lay. It was a nice apartment, I noted, spacious and comfortably furnished. It felt like a bachelor's full-time residence, not a married commuter's pied-à-terre. There were books on the bookshelves, framed prints on the walls, logs in the fireplace. Opposite the fireplace, a two-by-three throw rug looked out of place atop a large Oriental carpet. I had a hunch I knew what it was doing there.

But I walked past it and knelt down next to the corpse. "Stabbed in the heart," I noted. "Death must have been instantaneous, or the next thing to it. I don't suppose he had any last words."

"No."

"He crumpled up and hit the floor and never moved."

"That's right."

I got to my feet. "Must have been a shock."

"A terrible shock."

"How come you didn't call it in?"

"Call it in?"

"Call the police," I said. "Or an ambulance, get him to a hospital."

"A hospital couldn't do him any good," the blazer said. "I mean, you could tell he was dead."

"No pulse, no breathing."

"Right."

"Still, you must have known you're supposed to call the cops when something like this happens."

"Yes, of course."

"But you didn't."

They looked at each other. It might have been interesting to see what they came up with, but I made it easy for them.

"You must have been scared," I said.

"Well, of course."

"Guy goes to answer the door and the next thing you know he's dead on the floor. That's got to be an upsetting experience, especially taking into account that you don't know who killed him or why. Or do you have an idea?"

They didn't.

"I don't suppose this is Phil's apartment."

"No."

Of course not. If it was, they'd have long since gone their separate ways.

"Must be yours," I told the blazer, and enjoyed it when his eyes widened. He allowed that it was, and asked how I knew. I didn't tell him he was the one man in the room without a wedding ring, or that I figured he'd changed from a business suit to slightly more casual clothes on his return home, while the others were still wearing what they'd worn to the office that morning. I just muttered something about policemen developing certain instincts, and let him think I was a genius.

I asked if any of them had known Phil very well, and wasn't surprised to learn that they hadn't. He was a friend of a friend of a friend, someone said, and did something on Wall Street.

"So he wasn't a regular at the table."

"No."

"This wasn't his first time, was it?"

"His second," somebody said.

"First time was last week?"

"No, two weeks ago. He didn't play last week."

"Two weeks ago. How'd he do?"

Elaborate shrugs. The consensus seemed to be that he might have won a few dollars, but nobody had paid much attention.

"And this evening?"

"I think he was about even. If he was ahead it couldn't have been more than a few dollars."

"What kind of stakes do you play for?"

"It's a friendly game. One-two-five in stud games. In

draw it's two dollars before the draw, five after."

"So you can win or lose what, a couple of hundred?"

"That would be a big loss."

"Or a big win," I said.

"Well, yes. Either way."

I knelt down next to the corpse and patted him down. Cards in his wallet identified him as Philip I. Ryman, with an address in Teaneck.

"Lived in Jersey," I said. "And you say he worked on Wall Street?"

"Somewhere downtown."

I picked up his left hand. His watch was a Rolex, and I suppose it must have been a real one; this was before the profusion of fakes. He had what looked like a wedding band on the appropriate finger, but I saw that it was in fact a large silver or white-gold ring that had gotten turned around, so that the large part was on the palm side of his hand. It looked like an unfinished signet ring, waiting for an initial to be carved into its gleaming surface.

I straightened up. "Well," I said, "I'd say it's a good thing you called me."

• • •

"THERE are a couple of problems," I told them. "A couple of things that could pop up like a red flag for a responding officer or a medical examiner."

"Like . . ."

"Like the knife," I said. "Phil opened the door and the killer stabbed him once and left, was out the door and down the stairs before the body hit the carpet."

"Maybe not that fast," one of them said, "but it was pretty quick. Before we knew what had happened, certainly."

"I appreciate that," I said, "but the thing is it's an unusual MO. The killer didn't take time to make sure his victim was dead, and you can't take that for granted when you stick a knife in someone. And he left the knife in the wound."

"He wouldn't do that?"

"Well, it might be traced to him. All he has to do to avoid that chance is take it away with him. Besides, it's a weapon. Suppose someone comes chasing after him? He might need that knife again."

"Maybe he panicked."

"Maybe he did," I agreed. "There's another thing, and a medical examiner would notice this if a reporting officer didn't. The body's been moved."

Interesting the way their eyes jumped all over the place. They looked at each other, they looked at me, they looked at Phil on the floor.

"Blood pools in a corpse," I said. "Lividity's the word they use for it. It looks to me as though Phil fell forward and wound up facedownward. He probably fell against the door as it was closing, and slid down and wound up on his face. So you couldn't get the door open, and you needed to, so eventually you moved him."

Eyes darted. The host, the one in the blazer, said, "We knew you'd have to come in."

"Right."

"And we couldn't have him lying against the door."

"Of course not," I agreed. "But all of that's going to be hard to explain. You didn't call the cops right away, and you did move the body. They'll have some questions for you."

"Maybe you could give us an idea what questions to expect."

"I might be able to do better than that," I said. "It's irregular, and I probably shouldn't, but I'm going to suggest an action we can take."

"Oh?"

"I'm going to suggest we stage something," I said. "As it stands, Phil was stabbed to death by an unknown person who escaped without anybody getting a look at him. He may never turn up, and if he doesn't, the cops are going to look hard at the four of you."

"Jesus," somebody said.

"It would be a lot easier on everybody," I said, "if Phil's death was an accident."

"An accident?"

"I don't know if Phil has a sheet or not," I said. "He looks vaguely familiar to me, but lots of people do. He's got a gambler's face, even in death, the kind of face you expect to see in an OTB parlor. He may have worked on Wall Street, it's possible, because cheating at cards isn't necessarily a full-time job."

"Cheating at cards?"

"That would be my guess. His ring's a mirror; turned around, it gives him a peek at what's coming off the bottom of the desk. It's just one way to cheat, and he probably had thirty or forty others. You think of this as a social event, a once-a-week friendly game, a five-dollar limit and, what, three raises maximum? The wins and losses pretty much average out over the course of a year, and nobody ever gets hurt too bad. Is that about right?"

"Yes."

"So you wouldn't expect to attract a mechanic, a card cheat, but he's not looking for the high rollers, he's looking for a game just like yours, where it's all good friends and nobody's got reason to get suspicious, and he can pick up two or three hundred dollars in a couple of hours without running any risks. I'm sure you're all decent poker players, but would you think to look for bottom dealing or a cold deck? Would you know if somebody was dealing seconds, even if you saw it in slow motion?"

"Probably not."

"Phil was probably doing a little cheating," I went on, "and that's probably what he did two weeks ago, and nobody spotted him. But he evidently crossed someone else somewhere along the line. Maybe he pulled the same tricks in a bigger game, or maybe he was just sleeping in the wrong bed, but someone knew he was coming here, turned up after the game was going, and rang the bell. He would have come in and called Phil out, but he didn't have to, because Phil answered the door."

"And the guy had a knife."

"Right," I said. "That's how it was, but it's another way an investigating officer might get confused. How did the guy know Phil was going to come to the door? Most times the host opens the door, and the rest of the time it's only one chance in five it'll be Phil. Would the guy be ready, knife in hand? And would Phil just open up without making sure who it was?"

I held up a hand. "I know, that's how it happened. But I think it might be worth your while to stage a more plausible scenario, something a lot easier for the cops to come to terms with. Suppose we forget the intruder. Suppose the story we tell is that Phil was cheating at cards and someone called him on it. Maybe some strong words were said and threats were exchanged. Phil went into his pocket and came out with a knife."

"That's—"

"You're going to say it's farfetched," I said, "but he'd probably have some sort of weapon on him, something to intimidate anyone who did catch him cheating. He pulls the knife and you react. Say you turn the table over on him. The whole thing goes crashing to the floor and he winds up sticking his own knife in his chest."

I walked across the room. "We'll have to move the table," I went on. "There's not really room for that sort of struggle where you've got it set up, but suppose it was right in the middle of the room, under the light fixture? Actually that would be a logical place for it." I bent down, picked up the throw rug, tossed it aside. "You'd move the rug if you had the table here." I bent down, poked at a stain. "Looks like somebody had a nosebleed, and fairly recently, or you'd have the carpet cleaned by now. That can fit right in, come to think of it. Phil wouldn't have bled much from a stab wound to the heart, but there'd have been a little blood loss, and I didn't spot any blood at all where the body's lying now. If we put him in the right spot, they'll most likely assume it's his blood, and it might even turn out to be the same blood type. I mean, there are only so many blood types, right?"

I looked at them one by one. "I think it'll work," I said. "We'll want things arranged just right, and it'll be a good idea to spread a little cash around. But I think this one'll go into the books as accidental death."

• • •

"THEY must have thought you were a genius," Elaine said.

"Or an idiot savant," I said. "Here I was, telling them to fake exactly what had in fact happened. At the beginning I think they may have thought I was blundering into an unwitting reconstruction of the incident, but by the end they probably figured out that I knew where I was going."

"But you never spelled it out."

"No, we maintained the fiction that some intruder stuck the knife in Ryman, and we were tampering with the evidence."

"When actually you were restoring it. What tipped you off?"

"The body blocking the door. The lividity pattern was wrong, but I was suspicious even before I confirmed that. It's just too cute, a body positioned where it'll keep a door from opening. And the table was in the wrong place, and the little rug had to be covering something, or why else would it be where it was? So I pictured the room the right way, and then everything sort of filled in. But it didn't take a genius. Any cop would have seen some wrong things, and he'd have asked a few hard questions, and the four of them would have caved in."

"And then what? Murder indictments?"

"Most likely, but they're respectable businessmen and the deceased was a scumbag, so they'd have been up on manslaughter charges and probably would have pleaded to a lesser charge. Still, a verdict of accidental death saves them a lot of aggravation."

"And that's what really happened?"

"I can't see any of those men packing a switch knife, or pulling it at a card table. Nor does it seem likely they could have taken it away from Ryman and killed him with it. I think he went ass over teakettle with the table coming down on top of him and maybe one or two of the guys falling on top of the table. And he was still holding the knife, and he stuck it in his own chest."

"And the cops who responded—"

"Well, I called it in for them, so I more or less selected the responding officers. I picked guys you can work with."

"And worked with them."

"Everybody came out okay," I said. "I collected a few dollars from the four players, and I laid off some of it where it would do the most good."

"Just to smooth things out."

"That's right."

"But you didn't lay off all of it."

"No," I said, "not quite all of it. Give me your hand. Here."

"What's this?"

"A finder's fee."

"Three hundred dollars?"

"Ten percent," I said.

"Gee," she said. "I didn't expect anything."

"What do you do when somebody gives you money?"

"I say thank you," she said, "and I put it someplace safe. This is great. You got them to tell the truth, and everybody gets paid. Do you have to go back to Syosset right away? Because Chet Baker's at Mikell's tonight."

"We could go hear him," I said, "and then we could come back here. I told Anita I'd probably have to stay over."

"Oh, goodie," she said. "Do you suppose he'll sing 'Let's Get Lost'?"

"I wouldn't be surprised," I said. "Not if you ask him nice."

• • •

I don't remember if he sang it or not, but I heard it again just the other day on the radio. He'd ended abruptly, that aging boy with the sweet voice and sweeter horn. He went out a hotel-room window somewhere in Europe, and most people figured he'd had help. He'd crossed up a lot of people along the way and always got away with it, but then that's usually the way it works. You dodge all the bullets but the last one.

"Let's Get Lost." I heard the song, and not twenty-four hours later I picked up the *Times* and read an obit for a commodities trader named P. Gordon Fawcett, who'd succumbed to prostate cancer. The name rang a bell, but it took me hours to place it. He was the guy in the blazer, the man in whose apartment Phil Ryman stabbed himself.

Funny how things work out. It wasn't too long after that poker game that another incident precipitated my departure from the NYPD, and from my marriage. Elaine and I lost track of each other, and caught up with each other some years down the line, by which time I'd found a way to live without drinking. So we got lost and found—and now we're married. Who'd have guessed?

My life's vastly different these days, but I can imagine being called in on just that sort of emergency—a man dead on the carpet, a knife in his chest, in the company of four poker players who only wish he'd disappear. As I said, my life's different, and I suppose I'm different myself. So I'd almost certainly handle it differently now, and what I'd probably do is call it in immediately and let the cops deal with it.

Still, I always liked the way that one worked out. I

walked in on a cover-up, and what I did was cover up the cover-up. And in the process I wound up with the truth. Or an approximation of it, at least, and isn't that as much as you can expect to get? Isn't that enough?

HAVEN'T WE MET BEFORE?

By Mary Higgins Clark

WESTCHESTER County Assistant District Attorney Jack Carroll presented his credentials to the guard at Haviland Hospital for the Criminally Insane and waited for the gate to swing open.

It was the right kind of day to visit a place for psychopathic killers, he thought wryly: wet and raw, with a persistent dampness that chilled the spirit as well as the body. And in all probability, this was a fool's errand. It was the fourth time in as many months that he had come here to question William Koenig, who had been declared incompetent to stand trial for the attempted murder of twenty-four-year-old Emily Winters. His defense was that she had caused his death in another incarnation.

It was Jack Carroll's hunch that Koenig was more than a would-be killer. With every fiber of his being he was convinced that Koenig was responsible for the string of unsolved homicides that had plagued Westchester for the last eight years.

And there's not a shred of evidence, Jack reminded himself grimly as he pulled into the hospital parking lot. As usual, the frustration of that thought sent a dart of pure anger through him.

Fortunately, his boss, the DA, was willing to go along with him. "I think you're wasting your time, Jack," he'd said bluntly, "but in the three years you've been here, your hunches have been damn good. If you can manage to nail Koenig on even one of those homicides, I'll personally pin a medal on you."

Jack got out of the car, locked it and with rapid steps followed the path to the hospital's main entrance. It was a new facility, deceptively bland with windows that were barely more than slits. There were no bars, but even a monkey couldn't get through that amount of space, he decided.

Inside the building, the large reception area was tastefully decorated. He might have been entering an upscale business office. As always when he was here, Jack hoped the fact that tight security wasn't readily apparent was not a sign that it didn't exist.

Koenig was going to meet his new psychiatrist today. Rhoda Morris, the one who had been assigned to him since his commitment eight months ago, had left for the private sector. Jack was not sorry about the change. In his opinion, Koenig had had Dr. Morris buffaloed. He hoped the new psychiatrist, Dr. Sara Stein, was older and more experienced.

When he was ushered into her office, he immediately liked what he saw. Dr. Stein was a pleasant-looking, full-figured woman who looked to be in her late fifties, with gray hair and even features in a face dominated by warm and intelligent brown eyes. He felt her scrutiny and hoped her first impression of him was favorable as well.

He knew she was seeing a twenty-eight-year-old, sandy-haired six-footer with a boyish face. He only hoped she wouldn't mistake him for a recent college graduate, the way some people did.

She did not. "I'm glad to meet you, Mr. Carroll," she said briskly. "As you know, I haven't yet met William

Koenig. After reading the file and learning of your interest in him, I decided to have my first session with him with you present. Of course, he knows why you are here."

Jack drew a deep breath. "Doctor, I'm here because I think William Koenig may be the most dangerous inmate under this roof."

"We discussed him at the staff meeting this morning. The consensus is that his psychotic tendencies may have been fueled by his experimenting with past-life regression. But as you may have suspected, my colleagues do not agree with you that Koenig is a multiple killer."

"Dr. Stein, he may not be. On the other hand, if I'm right and we can get to the truth, the families of at least four homicide victims will have some sense of closure."

He paused for a moment and then continued: "Let me give you an example. Two years ago an elderly woman in Dobbs Ferry was asphyxiated during a fire that had been deliberately set in her home. Her family is making life hell for a twelve-year-old neighborhood kid who had started a campfire in the nearby woods a few days earlier. They're accusing him of being an arsonist."

"They need someone to blame," she observed. "But that will have a terrible effect on an innocent child. Let's get Koenig in here."

"Doctor, try to get him to talk about other lives he may remember. If we knew about them, I believe we could begin to understand why he might have selected other victims for retribution."

She nodded and turned on the intercom. "We're ready for Koenig," she said.

• • •

"William, Assistant District Attorney Carroll wants to talk with you."

"I've explained to your assistant, Doctor, that I will talk to him only through you," Koenig said patiently. "I will answer his questions through you. I understand that my

answers may be used against me. I do not want to have a
lawyer present. I also understand that I can stop answering
questions at any point. I do not expect the confidentiality
of a doctor-patient relationship in this matter. You are new
here, but I have met Mr. Carroll a number of times before.
I will not speak to him directly again. Is there anything
else?"

Dr. Stein glanced at Jack Carroll, who shook his head.

"No, nothing else, William," she said.

"Then I think we should proceed. The state is paying
you handsomely to probe my mind, Doctor. Why don't you
start earning your money?"

William Koenig smiled gently to take the sting out of
his words. He was quietly counting the hours until this evening but wanted nothing in his demeanor to suggest that
this was his last day here. His escape plan was foolproof.

William hoped that the weather would continue to be
gray and rain-filled at least through tomorrow. His mana-
cled hands clasped in his lap, a restraining strap across his
waist, the guard studying him through the heavily glassed
door, he sat in silent contempt across the desk from his new
psychiatrist, Dr. Stein, and his old adversary, Jack Carroll.

Behind his seemingly anxious-to-please smile, he was
thinking that Stein was dowdy, with her hair slipping from
where she'd twisted it into a bun. She didn't wear makeup,
either. His last psychiatrist had been pretty. He'd liked
her—she was so engagingly naive.

Carroll was a nice-looking guy, the kind who probably
had all the girls after him in school. He was smart, too, the
only one smart enough to wonder if maybe he, William
Koenig, was responsible for a string of unsolved homicides.

But all they could prove was that last February he had
tried to strangle Emily Winters.

"William, I hope you'll be comfortable with me and help
me to understand you. In your own words, will you tell me
why you attacked Emily Winters?"

William knew perfectly well that Stein had studied his

file backward and forward. Even so, it was flattering to see the interest in her eyes when he told her—in his own words, as she put it—that in 1708, in his life as Simon Guiness, he had been hanged in London because of the false testimony of Kate Fallow, a woman who had become obsessed with him.

"She killed her husband, then made it look as though he had been the victim of a random attack on the road to their estate," William explained gravely. "Then, when I rejected her, she went to the magistrate and claimed that I had stabbed her husband because I coveted her."

He shivered as he spoke, remembering the misery that followed. They had believed Kate Fallow. For months he had rotted in a damp and dirty prison until execution ended his life as Simon Guiness.

"When did you first know that you had a past life, William?"

"I learned that about myself when I was in high school. I became interested in parapsychology and succeeded in hypnotizing myself and finding my own path into all that had gone before."

William realized that Dr. Stein did not believe that he had the power to hypnotize himself. "It's not hard if you concentrate," he said impatiently. "You sit in front of a mirror in a dark room with just one candle burning. With a pen or crayon, put a dot in the center of your forehead to indicate your third eye. Then stare at that dot in the mirror." His voice lowered. "You will see the change beginning as you find your way into the past."

"Change, William?"

"You will see it in the mirror," he whispered. "Your present image will dissolve and disappear, as mine did. Other faces will evolve, faces of the people you were in previous lives."

He glanced over at Jack Carroll. "I've explained all this to him," he told the doctor. "I bet he's tried to see if he could hypnotize himself. Tried and failed. He's too sensible. He doesn't get it."

"Will I know what happened to those people in my past lives if I am able to hypnotize myself?" Dr. Stein asked.

"Oh yes, Doctor, you will remember all the details."

"How many lives do you remember, William?"

William stared at the green wall behind Dr. Stein's desk. Moss green. He was very proud that he understood shades, not just colors. They all tried to trick him into telling about the other lives he had lived, about punishments he had meted out to people who had hurt him in the past.

If you only knew, William thought. There were eleven others. A smile played around his lips as he recalled the first, the old woman he'd followed home from the railroad station because he realized she was the witch who had put a curse on him in Salem. He had waited until he was sure she was asleep and then set fire to her house. Fire for fire.

He chose his words carefully. "The face that was clear to me at the time I happened to come across the woman you call Emily Winters was that of Simon Guiness. Knowing the terrible fate I suffered as Simon, you can understand why the sight of a young woman with red-gold hair and wide blue eyes upset me so much."

"Did seeing a woman with that appearance always upset you, William?"

"Oh, no, it began a little over three years ago—after I had relived my life as Simon Guiness."

"Tell me about finding Emily."

He remembered how he had spotted her from the street. She was waiting on a window table in the restaurant. "I studied her, to be absolutely sure it was Kate," he reminisced. "Then I went into the restaurant. It wasn't very crowded, so I was able to observe her very carefully . . ."

William's voice trailed off as he remembered the thrill of realizing he had finally tracked down Kate Fallow. "When she passed my table, I touched her arm," he confided. "She looked startled, then frightened. I'm certain that she sensed danger, even though I apologized."

"Didn't you say something else to her, William?"

"I asked, 'Haven't we met before?' "

"Then you waited outside until she left the restaurant?"

"Yes, she began to walk home. I followed her from a distance. I saw her turn into a gated area. It was easy to climb the fence out of sight of the guard. I caught up with her at the driveway of a lovely home not unlike the mansion I lived in as Simon Guiness. I thought it was a rather inappropriate dwelling for a woman who makes her living as a waitress. Later I learned that she is a law-school student who works evenings and house-sits for a couple named Adamson, the absent owners of that dwelling."

"You broke into the house."

"That is too crude a word. I waited for hours and observed that an upstairs bedroom had an open window, which meant it could not be alarmed. It was easy to climb the tree nearby and slip inside from there."

"It was Emily's bedroom?"

"Yes. She was asleep. The moon was quite bright, and I was able to study her for a long time. The memories came flooding back of her persistent efforts to win my attention when we lived on neighboring estates in England."

Jack Carroll listened with mounting fury. Emily had told him that she'd seen Koenig when he came in the window. She knew she couldn't get away in time, that her only hope was to push the panic button on the side of the bed. The security-conscious Mr. Adamson had ordered that each bed be equipped with one. It was wired into the station of the private guards who patrolled the gated community. They knew instantly what room she was in, and they had a key to the house.

"I was so afraid, Jack," she'd told him, her voice a monotone. "I sleep with the lights on now, and I'm afraid to open the windows. I could tell he was going to kill me when he bent over and whispered, 'Haven't we met before?'—the same question he'd asked me in the restaurant."

Somehow Emily had managed to stay coolheaded, Jack thought. She'd told Koenig that she was sure they had met, but wouldn't he talk to her about it and refresh her memory?

"He was so scary," Emily had recalled. "His face got all red, the veins of his neck stood out. He told me how I'd tried to waylay him in the fields, how I'd bragged to him about killing my husband for him. Then he said it was time—and put his hands around my throat."

The security guards had burst in just as Koenig had begun to squeeze her throat. "His fingers were so powerful," Emily had whispered. "So many nights now I wake up feeling them."

At his arrest, William's hysterical rantings that Emily had caused his death in another life had resulted in a media circus.

"You attacked Emily Winters because she looked like Kate Fallow?" Dr. Stein prodded.

"She didn't *look* like her," William said with a touch of irritation. "She *was* Kate Fallow. I recognized her and immediately became my former self, Simon Guiness. Simon had a right to be angry—you should see the justice of that, Dr. Stein. How would *you* feel about someone who caused you to be executed?

"I will tell you that I regret I did not awaken Emily sooner. If I were doing it again, I would wrap a noose around her neck so I could enjoy seeing her experience the fear and anguish I experienced at my own execution. As I tightened the rope, I would explain to her exactly why she had to die."

He was rewarded by the visible tensing of Jack Carroll's body. He sensed that a personal relationship had developed between Carroll and the woman they called Emily Winters.

"Was Emily the only woman you saw who was Kate?" Dr. Stein asked.

"A few times after I recalled my life as Simon Guiness, I saw women with red hair and I got close to them. But one of them had dyed hair. Another didn't have the same shade of eyes. Kate's were very blue. A particular shade of blue. There's a name for it: periwinkle, a sort of blue-violet shade.

"You may be interested to learn that Kate has reappeared in other lifetimes, but obviously has managed to evade judgment. When I studied her that night, I knew she was Kate Fallow, but another name also kept running through my mind. Eliza Jackson. As that lifetime becomes clearer to me, Doctor, I will discuss it with you."

He's playing games with her, Jack Carroll thought. *He's managed to convince everyone here that he's crazy, and he is—but crazy like a fox. If we just had some indication of who he believes he was in other lives, we might be able to start matching victims to him.*

"You've seen yourself in other past lives?" Dr. Stein asked.

"I've seen faces and sensed that I lived as a knight in King Arthur's time, and in Egypt during the Roman occupation, and as a minister in sixteenth-century Germany, but none of those lives was filled with detail. I am sure that means that only my life as Simon Guiness was unjustly terminated."

William Koenig smiled to himself. His other lives had been very clear, and in all of them the people who had caused him injustices had been punished. Except for the woman they called Emily Winters, but he knew where to find her tonight. When his cousin had visited him in prison, Koenig had told him that he wanted to write a letter of apology to Emily. The cousin had checked and discovered she was in her last year of law school, still working at the restaurant, still living at the Adamsons'.

He felt Dr. Stein's eyes studying him. Jack Carroll's eyes were always impassive, but he knew that under the bland exterior Carroll was furious. Carroll wanted answers. Koenig wondered if Carroll would have Dr. Stein ask the usual questions:

Did you have anything to do with the fire in Rosedale that killed an elderly woman eight years ago?

Five years ago in March, someone of your description was seen leaving the York cinema in Mamaroneck, where a cashier was later found murdered. Did you ever encounter that cashier in another life?

Did you ever call yourself Samuel Ensinger and make an appointment with Jeffrey Lane, a real-estate agent in Rye?

The old woman was the witch from Salem. He'd recognized the cashier as the seventeenth-century pirate who had set him adrift in 1603. Lane had been his younger brother in Glasgow in 1790 and murdered him for the estate.

Dr. Stein could sense Carroll's frustration. As he had explained, "I refuse to believe it's sheer coincidence that someone of Koenig's general description was seen in the area where homicides of totally unconnected people took place."

General description, the doctor thought. *That suits him. Medium height, medium build, plain features, dirty-blond hair.* As Carroll had pointed out, different glasses, a wig, or even a cap or ski hat could alter Koenig's appearance. Only his eyes were compelling: not so much blue as almost colorless. And he was strong. Cords of muscles bulged in his neck and hands. He worked out in his cell for hours at a time.

According to his file, both his mother and his father had been brooding and reclusive. When he was growing up, other children were forbidden to play with him. There were too many accidents when he was around. He'd gone to high school in White Plains and been considered a creep by his classmates.

William had graduated from high school, left Westchester County, and drifted from job to job around the country. His records showed him to be highly intelligent but unable to control his temper. Outbursts of violence against coworkers had led to several brief confinements in mental hospitals. He had returned to White Plains, a time bomb ready to explode, and he did explode the night he attacked Emily Winters.

Dr. Stein noted that William was a voracious reader. Several of the psychiatrists believed that Simon Guiness, the person he claimed to have been in a past life, was a fictional character he had read about. But except for Assistant DA Carroll, no one believed that William was a serial killer.

It was obvious there was no information to be gleaned from him today. It was also obvious that he was baiting Carroll.

"Our time is just about up, William," Dr. Stein said. "I'll see you on Thursday."

"I look forward to it. You seem to be very kind. Who knows? Maybe in another incarnation you were my friend. I'll try to find out if that might be true. I wish you would try as well."

• • •

"How is Emily Winters doing?" Dr. Stein asked Jack after Koenig had been removed.

"She's gone to counseling a few times, but I think she should go regularly. Recently, she did something that I thought was dangerous. She went to a parapsychologist and had herself regressed to a former lifetime."

"She wanted to see if she really *was* Kate Fallow?"

"Yes."

"The power of suggestion would pay a great role in any memory like that."

"She didn't remember being Kate Fallow. But she tells me she has a tape of a life she described under hypnosis—when she lived in the South during the Civil War."

"Did she play the tape for you?"

Jack shook his head. "I told her I thought it was absolute

nonsense and that she should stick with the trauma counselor and not mess up her head."

"I understand she goes to Fordham Law School. But why waitressing?" Stein asked. "And why live in White Plains?"

"Emily's paying her own way through law school and doesn't want a load of loans on her back. She plans to be a public defender—which isn't the biggest paycheck a lawyer can get. Her rent is free because of the house-sitting job. She gets her main meals—and excellent tips—at the restaurant. Finally, the grandmother who raised her isn't going to live much longer. She's in a White Plains nursing home, so this way Emily can run in to see her almost daily."

Sara Stein did not miss the warmth in Jack Carroll's eyes when he talked about Emily Winters. "You're seeing her on a personal basis," she suggested, "which may, of course, affect your response to William Koenig."

"Enough to want to be very sure that if he's ever declared sane, he'll stand trial for enough homicides to need all the lifetimes he can find to serve his sentence."

• • •

THAT evening William made his carefully planned escape. The friendly and careless new guard was an easy target. William left him wrapped in blankets on the bed in his cell, his face turned to the wall. The elderly orderly in the locker room didn't live long enough even to glimpse his attacker.

He left the grounds in the orderly's car, dressed in the orderly's clothes and carrying his identification. On the way to Emily's house he made a stop at a hardware store to purchase a rope. The slipknot was in place by the time he abandoned the car in a municipal parking lot and went on foot to the exclusive neighborhood where a guard stood at the gate. A few hundred yards down, he scaled the fence with the ease of long practice and, sliding behind bushes and trees, made his way to the Adamson residence, where Emily was still living.

He had realized the elderly couple she worked for might have returned home, but a quick glance showed no car in the garage. *It will be just Kate and me,* he thought. She was due home anytime now. As soon as she opened the door, he'd push in behind her. If necessary, he'd kill her immediately. But he'd give her a chance to disarm the security system so they could talk. She'd probably do that. Of course, there was always the possibility she'd disarm it in a way that would send a panic signal, yet he'd be listening for anyone trying to get into the house. This time, no matter how fast they were, they would not find her alive.

• • •

"THE veal chop is wonderful," Emily assured the indecisive customer who could not make up his mind between the veal and the swordfish.

"Do you mean that it's better than the swordfish?"

Oh dear God, Emily thought. She didn't know why she was so nervous today. She had the feeling of something hanging over her, of something terrible about to happen. She felt in her soul that it was inevitable that one night she would awaken from sleep and again see William Koenig, his eyes glazed, his hands outstretched, his fingers reaching for her throat.

Or she'd hear footsteps behind her and turn and he'd be there. Once again he'd ask in that quiet, eerie voice, "Haven't we met before?"

"Maybe I will try the veal."

"I know you'll enjoy it." Emily turned, glad to get away from the window table, glad to retreat to the kitchen, where no one could see her from the street. She felt so vulnerable near the windows, ever since she'd learned that William Koenig had studied her from the dark.

Maybe I should have changed jobs, she thought. *But if he ever gets out, he'll find you anywhere you go,* a sub-

conscious voice whispered. This job, this situation suited
her. She'd be finished with law school in May and had
already been promised a job in the public defender's office.
Jack teased her about that. "You'll be trying to get people
out of jail, and I'll be trying to put them in. Should be
pretty interesting."

They were right for each other. They both knew it, but
it was unspoken. There was plenty of time, and he was
smart enough to understand that what with school, the waitressing job, house-sitting, and Gran, she wasn't ready for
another level of involvement.

She handed the order to the chef's assistant, smiling to
herself at what Jack had told her. "I feel as though we're
dating in my mother's era. The movies, dinner, bye-bye."

They'd had only one serious misunderstanding. She'd
been annoyed that Jack didn't want to listen to the tape that
had been made when she was hypnotized and regressed.
*Maybe it is the collective unconscious. Maybe it's some-
thing I read somewhere,* she said to herself. But it was
compelling to listen to her own voice claiming she had
lived in the South during the Civil War.

*Not that I put any stock in it, but you can see how people
get caught up in the idea of reincarnation,* she thought.

The last table of four finally cleared at ten-thirty. Jack
had phoned earlier. He'd been up to see William Koenig
and suggested meeting her for a nightcap. She was sorely
tempted, but she had an exam coming up in two days and
a lot of reading still to do.

Emily had said good night to Pat Cleary, her boss, and
smilingly agreed to stop by the restaurant tomorrow and
pick up a hot lunch to take to the nursing home for her
grandmother.

"I know you see her on Thursdays in the late morning,"
Pat said genially, "and we all know that nursing-home food
isn't the sort that comes from a good pub."

Her car, parked in the restaurant lot, started with its
usual protesting screech. *Maybe next year at this time, when*

I finally finish law school, I can actually get myself a car that travels on more than prayers, Emily promised herself.

Jack drove a Toyota. He'd told her that when he graduated from law school three years ago, his father had presented him with a Jaguar. "Broke my heart, but I thought it would look a little peculiar for an assistant DA to arrive at court in a Jag," he said.

The guard waved her through the security gate. It was a joke between them that with all the pricey cars that rolled through here, hers was the only one that qualified as a possible candidate for Rent-a-Wreck.

She always put it in the garage. The Adamsons had made it clear they did not want it in view of the neighborhood.

Emily walked quickly along the path from the garage to the kitchen door. This was the most frustrating moment of her day. Once inside, and with the instant-security button pushed, she knew that no door or window could be disturbed without the alarm blasting. That would bring the security guards to the house within seconds.

And besides, William Koenig was in a padded cell, or however they kept maniacs confined in that new facility.

She put her key in the door and turned it. As the lock clicked and the handle turned, she felt a firm hand cover her mouth. The door opened, and she was propelled inside the house. "Haven't we met before?" Koenig whispered.

• • •

JACK Carroll went back to his office, his mood angry and disgruntled. *Snap out of it*, he told himself. He had a case to prepare for trial, and the boss would hardly thank him if he messed it up because he'd been spending time on his hunch about Koenig.

It would have been nice to be able to look forward to meeting Emily for a drink, but he did understand that she had to burn the midnight oil. When Jack reflected on his privileged upbringing in Rye and the struggle Emily had always known, he felt humbled. Her parents dead. Raised by a grandmother who'd been ailing for years and was now terminally ill. Partial scholarships to good schools and lots of hard work. And now, instead of going for the big bucks, Emily wanted to spend her life taking care of people who needed legal assistance and could not pay for it.

And she's the one who had to have that nut attack her, Jack fumed to himself. He admitted that after seeing Koenig today, what he really wanted to do was to put his arms around Emily and make sure she was alive, close, safe, out of danger.

The hours passed as he immersed himself in preparing his opening statement for the trial that would begin next week. In other small offices, other assistant DAs were doing the same thing. Brothers all are we, they joked to one another.

And sisters, the woman assistant DAs would remind them.

At eleven-fifteen his phone rang. Dr. Stein sounded surprised when he answered. "Mr. Carroll," she said, "I didn't really expect to get you at the office."

The strain in her voice made Jack's throat close. "What's happened?"

"It's Koenig. The guard assigned to his unit has been found strangled in Koenig's cell. The orderly who cleans around the locker room was found in a closet. We're searching the grounds, but we think Koenig got away in the orderly's car. He's been gone at least two hours. Does he know where Emily Winters lives now?"

"He might. I'll call her and get protection around her." Jack jiggled the disconnect and dialed Emily's number. *Emily, answer, please answer,* he begged. As soon as he heard her voice, he'd tell her to bolt and lock the doors. Then he'd call the private security guards and have them rush over until he could get the squad cars there. Until he could get to Emily himself.

The phone rang twice. With a vast sense of relief he heard it being picked up.

"Emily?"

"No, Mr. Carroll, it is I, Simon Guiness. Kate is with me. She has just agreed with me that, yes indeed, we have met before."

• • •

THE panic button on the security panel was the star-shaped button. It would have been easy to hit it with the tip of her finger as she disarmed the system, but Emily had made an instant decision not to do it. He was watching her too closely. He'd have known, and the rope he had slipped around her neck would have been tightened.

She had only one chance, and that was to get him to talk. It would have taken him at least half an hour to get from the hospital to here. By now they must know he had escaped. By now Jack would be on his way to her.

"That was a wise decision you just made," Koenig said, "a very wise decision. You have bought yourself a few minutes' more existence in this lifetime."

They were in the kitchen. It was a large room with a fireplace at the far end, faced by a couch and two comfortable chairs, with a television set to one side. When the Adamsons were home, Mr. Adamson would frequently tell Emily that with all the rooms in this great barn of a house, this spot was his favorite. They often ate dinner there, with Mrs. Adamson doing the cooking. He would sit content, reading the paper and watching the news.

Emily realized that she was in shock. Why else would she be thinking of the Adamsons as William Koenig guided her to Mr. Adamsons chair and stood behind her? She felt the rough rope scrape the skin of her throat.

Please God, she thought, *don't let me show him how scared I am. He needs that. Let me try to keep him talking to me. Jack will be here. I know he will.*

She struggled to remember all that Jack had told her about Koenig. "I know you are going to kill me," she said, "and I know I caused your death. But it was because I loved you so much, Simon, and you rejected me. A woman scorned can surely be forgiven because of such great love."

"I did scorn you," Koenig agreed. "But that was no reason to lie."

Emily's mouth was so dry she didn't know whether or not she could force the words from her throat. "But you see, Simon, you encouraged me. Don't you remember? I know I flirted with you, but you said you desired me. You were the most handsome man in the village. All the girls wanted you."

"I didn't realize that." Koenig sounded pleased.

Keep him talking, she warned herself. *Keep him talking.* "Am I the first person you have punished for offenses against you in other lifetimes?"

"Oh no, Kate. You are the eleventh."

"Tell me about the others."

Jack is right, Emily thought. *He is a serial killer. If I can just get him to boast.*

The phone rang. When Koenig answered and spoke to Jack, Emily knew that she had only seconds to live. Jack would call the security guards and they would break in.

Koenig knew that, too. He hung up and smiled at her. "If you're wondering if I expect to get away, of course I don't. They'll take me back to Haviland. But that's all right. It's not a bad place, and you're the last one I needed to find. Now my revenge is complete. Stand up."

He pulled at the noose as she stood. Emily began to gasp. *Oh God, please,* she prayed.

"Stand on that chair." He indicated the kitchen chair under the cross beam.

"No."

She felt a vicious yank. *Do it!* she screamed to herself. *Buy another second or two. Maybe they'll get here in time.*

With a seemingly effortless movement he tossed the end of the rope over the cross beam. "Scared, aren't you? My sole regret, Kate, is that I believe I also knew you in another, different lifetime. Your name was Eliza Jackson. I'd like to have known what happened between us then."

Emily felt herself begin to black out. "I remember that lifetime," she whispered. "I *was* Eliza Jackson. I went to a parapsychologist. He hypnotized me, and when I regressed, I told him I was Eliza Jackson."

"I don't believe you."

"There's a tape in that drawer. The recorder is next to it. Please, listen. We did know each other in 1861."

"I'm not letting go of the rope. Even if they try to break in, it will be too late for you." He reached into the drawer and pulled out the tape recorder. With one hand he dropped in the cassette and pushed the on button.

Emily saw faces at the window: the security guards. But Koenig had seen them, too. With a lightning gesture he wrapped the end of the rope around his left hand, braced himself, and began to pull it toward him.

Emily couldn't breathe. Her hands clawed at the rope around her neck as she felt herself being pulled up, her feet rising from the chair.

"My name is Eliza Jackson." The tape was rolling, the volume high.

William Koenig froze, dropped the rope, and rushed to the recorder as Emily's voice, dreamy and reflective, filled the room.

"We *did* meet in another lifetime!" Koenig shrieked.

The second of hesitation was all that was needed. The window shattered. The guards were in the room.

One grabbed Koenig. The other gently lifted Emily from the floor, where she had tumbled when Koenig let go of the rope, and removed the noose from around her throat.

Koenig was being clapped into restraints. "I want to hear

the rest of the tape!" he screamed. "I need to know what you did to me as Eliza Jackson!"

Emily looked straight into Koenig's eyes. "I don't know what Eliza Jackson may have done to you," she told him, "but I do know this: She just saved my life."

A NIGHT IN THE
MANCHESTER STORE

by Stanley Cohen

I T all started one night as we were driving home from La Guardia. Wally said to me, "Whaddaya say we go to The Manchester Store on our way."

Out of the clear blue sky? I said, "Wally, are you serious? Now? What the hell for?"

"I want to check on something."

"Check on what?"

"Something. I might even buy it, tonight."

Or steal it, maybe? "Wally, it's almost nine now. And we're a good fifteen minutes away from there. Don't they close at nine?"

"Nine-thirty."

"Well, that still doesn't leave us much time. Can't it wait? Because I'd really like to get home. We've been away for three days. Is this something important?"

"Yes, it is, or I wouldn't have brought it up. And you'll be glad we stopped. You're going to have a great time. Count on it."

I'll have a *great* time watching him shop? Or I'll just have a *great* time? What the hell did that mean? ...

What was he up to? Was this going to be another one of his crazy-ass things? . . . It'd been a lot of years since the last one. A long time. Was there going to be some element of risk involved, this time? . . . I decided not to bother responding to his comment about the "great time." Just sweat it out and hope for the best. So we'd be a few minutes later getting home. And he *was* the boss.

And since *he* didn't say anything further about it, we just lapsed into a period of quiet as he continued driving. He loved to drive, usually very fast. He thrived on doing reckless things, taking chances of all kinds, challenging fate, it always seemed to me, and I don't recall his ever failing, or getting caught, at anything he'd decided to do. He simply never got caught . . .

Wally Hunter and I go back a long way. We'd worked together at the national lab in Oak Ridge. He was a brilliant engineer, and he did his expected work, more or less, but he was also a cynic, always spouting sardonic humor about everything around us, knowing, as I guess I also did, that the project to which we were assigned was never going to produce anything. An aircraft engine powered by a nuclear reactor was not a realistic objective and was never going to fly.

And so we joked and laughed a lot about it. And we attended the regularly scheduled progress meetings, listened to all of the optimistic feasibility reports, carried out our assigned tests and experiments, compiled our data, and wrote up our results. It was, as they say, a living.

But that was only part of what made life with Wally Hunter in Oak Ridge so fascinating. I never thought of him as a close friend. He really wasn't that likable. And he wasn't someone I ever saw or even expected to see socially. I never met his wife. I thought of him instead as a very intriguing fellow worker, a sort of "what will this nut come up with next?" kind of guy.

And what made my association with him so unforget- table was that he occasionally sucked me into some wacko thing to do, either on or off the job, but mostly off. A Saturday-morning adventure for two engineers with weekends free. I was always a little nervous about what he'd get me into, but somehow I was drawn to him, and I seldom resisted the opportunity to spend time joining him in one of the far from routine things he came up with, despite some element of risk or danger that was always involved.

Like the cave. He was, among a myriad of other things, a spelunker, someone who loved to explore caves, and he'd found one that contained this unique chamber he said I just had to see, so one Saturday morning we drove to it, parked the car, and with his waterproof flashlight, which he'd probably stolen somewhere, we plunged ahead, into the depths of the cave.

We came to a passage he'd known about, of course, but never mentioned, where we had to crawl through an opening no larger than our bodies, and which had water, very cold water, running through it. But it was summer, and our clothes would dry, so what was the problem? He went first and snaked right through the hole. Then it was my turn.

I started through and got stuck! I couldn't move in either direction! Although he was at first amused by this, I was in a state of panic, and despite having my belly in cold water, I began to sweat profusely. *I absolutely couldn't move!* Stuck in a hole in a cave? Who needed this? What kind of crazy business was this for a nice Jewish boy? Better I should have been in the synagogue, attending services with my wife! . . . Not that we went that often, frankly. But at that terrifying moment, wedged tightly in that hole in solid rock, blocking the passage of the freezing water, which was beginning to deepen under my chest and approach my face, my brain was also alive with poisonous snakes, water moccasins with dripping fangs, and all sorts of other fearful creatures, and with visions of being stuck there for who knew how long, wondering if I'd ever get out alive.

After he'd enjoyed his moment of amusement at my

panicked state, he finally began reaching under me, cleaning out the small stones and gravel, and then he grabbed me by the hands, told me to exhale, and pulled me through the opening, leaving my poor chest and belly, and a couple of spots on my back, rubbed raw.

He led me to the subterranean chamber he'd brought me to see, and I guess it was everything he'd promised it would be, but all I could think about at the time was the return trip through that hole to get back to the outside world. And to this day, I still shudder at the thought of having been stuck there.

And then there was the abandoned quarry, just a stone's throw off one of the main roads inside the government-restricted area. On another Saturday morning we went there with his .22 rifle and his .22 target pistol and all the bottles and cans we could scrounge up, and we set up our collection of targets on a rock, down in the quarry, and climbed up to the rim, sat there, and had a little target practice.

It was great fun but it was also very illegal. We were fooling around with firearms inside the government-restricted area and definitely had no business being there. We could have easily found ourselves trying to deal with the rotten local gendarmes, redneck deputy-sheriff types who were allowed access to the roads. Or maybe government security types, connected to the plants. But of course we didn't . . .

. . . And I still wonder where some of those shots might have gone as they ricocheted off that rock. What goes up must come down at virtually the same velocity it went up, it seems to me. Gravity is gravity. What if . . . ? But that was years ago.

And Wally was a master thief. He simply loved to steal. He was constantly taking things home from the lab. Tools, expensive instruments, electronic stuff, whatever . . . At times he could hardly lift his briefcase when he left work and walked through guard stations to the parking lot. And of course he never got caught. The same was true when he visited the various stores in town, satisfying his love for thievery. He never got caught. I was with him one afternoon in a small downtown department store, and when he began lifting things, I didn't quite know what to say or do. All I wanted was to get the hell out of there.

And being as smart as he was, he spent most of his time at the lab, on company time, writing for several technical magazines, articles totally unrelated to his job at the laboratory, and he was getting paid good money for them. And he was never questioned, even when he got our company secretary to type them. Because he never got caught at anything.

He left the job in Oak Ridge several years before I did, and I never expected to see him again. Finally, years later, when my wife and I decided we'd spent enough of our life in that unique community, we, too, decided it was time to leave. I went to an employment clearinghouse at a convention, got several offers, and took one which brought us to Connecticut. Senior engineer at Metals and Materials Technology, Inc.

On my first day on the new job, the personnel director said to me, "I understand you already know the section chief you'll report to."

"I do?"

And in walked Wally Hunter. "Welcome to 'Met'n'Mat Tech,' " he said with a wide grin. And he was wearing a suit and tie. All those years in Oak Ridge he'd worn nothing but jeans or suntans and sport shirts, while most of the other professionals around him, including me, "dressed for business" and wore jackets and neckties to work.

He led me to his spacious office, and after we'd gabbed a few minutes about whether things had changed much in Oak Ridge since he'd left, he advised me that he'd been able to get me a separate office, and with a window, no less. "I refused to let them toss you into the bullpen where most of the fresh meat gets thrown," he said.

Then he added, "And the salary offer they made you?

The one that you accepted? I insisted on having it increased a hundred a month. They don't do that too often, around here, once they've gotten an acceptance, but I told them you had special skills that our section needed badly, and I didn't want to take any chances on losing you." Listening to all of that, I was rapidly getting over the shock of running into him again and discovering that he was my new boss. I was even beginning to feel a little pleased about it.

The first year of working with him went by fast. He was still the same old Wally Hunter in most respects, entertaining to be around for his total cynicism, but a little more scary than I remembered. He'd become much more intense in his attitudes toward the world around us, and the fact that it owed us a living. His cynicism could at times become almost incendiary.

Since we were no longer both living in the same small Southern town where there wasn't much to do, the "Saturday-morning adventures" were ancient history. All of that small-town stuff was behind us. We were out of the sticks and into upscale areas in the civilized world, living in widely separated Connecticut towns within commuting distance of the plant.

But, occasionally, when on the road together, we'd do things I considered a little strange. One night in Chicago he insisted we go to a notorious gay bar and have a couple of drinks so we could observe how "that other ten percent" lives. In offhand comments about his own sexuality once, he'd suggested that he was into "limited," or "mild," sadomasochism, from the sado side, of course. I'd still never met his wife.

At the end of my first year at Met'n'Mat Tech, he called me into his office one day for my "annual review," and rather sternly asked me, as an opening remark, how much salary increase I felt I deserved. I was hesitant. "Whatever you can get me, Wally. Seven, eight percent, hopefully something over five. I'd feel very good about ten."

He broke into a broad grin and said, "I got you fifteen."

And that was the end of our so-called annual review, a type of corporate activity he considered to be total bullshit. One of his favorite forms of larceny was getting me, and I suppose others in our small section, as much money from the corporation as he could manage. He signed my expense accounts, and when we traveled together, he'd often say, "You lie and I'll swear to it." It was these attitudes toward company funds which probably explain the strong sense of loyalty we all had to him . . .

. . . When we arrived in front of The Manchester Store, he didn't pull into the store's private lot, but parked instead on the street, around the corner from the store's main entrance. I asked him why.

"I like this better," he said in a familiar tone of voice he used once in a while when he didn't want to be questioned further about something. We got along well, but on the occasions he used this tone, I'd learned to just cool it.

Before getting out of the car, he opened his briefcase and took out his cell phone, dropping it into his jacket pocket.

"Just curious, Wally, what do you need with that?"

"Why not take it with us? The company pays for it. If I decide I want to make a call, I'll have it handy. I don't want to have to use a public phone or go through the store's switchboard."

Knowing Wally, that somehow had a little bit of a scary sound to it. What call would we want to make some fifteen minutes before the store was closing? Why were we even going in there when all the clerks would be anxious to leave? But what the hell? This was Wally.

The Manchester Store was unique. It was large and complete, with huge, tasteful spreads of just about everything a department store could offer. In addition to extensive, major-name-brand departments for clothing and footwear, and of course, perfumes and cosmetics, it also specialized in furniture, appliances, fine jewelry, toys, and sporting goods of every description, including a widely respected department of everything needed for hunting and fishing, and finally, a rather nice restaurant.

But it wasn't its size and completeness that made The Manchester Store unusual. It was its style and character. The Manchester Store was an old, long-established family business, and the Manchester family was dedicated to preserving the store's venerability, maintaining the special charm and ambience of earlier years. Only recently had its management made such radical changes as installing escalators, while still maintaining those ornate old elevators with the filigreed silverish doors. The store had even finally started accepting credit cards other than those issued exclusively for use in the store. The Manchester Store, an ageless example of period architecture among other things, stood alone in all respects, including location. It was a very popular alternative to the fancy New York chain department stores and the gigantic malls where they were usually found.

We walked around the first floor for a minute or two, among other customers still milling around, and then went to the fancy jewelry department, where Wally shopped for an expensive string of cultured pearls, presumably for his wife. A very proper elderly lady waited on us, unlocking the glass case and taking out the one he pointed to, and it became quite clear that he knew more about pearls than she. But this didn't surprise me. He knew more about most things than most people.

As he discussed them with her, I glanced at my watch and saw the store was to be closing in a matter of minutes. The saleslady was growing impatient. He asked her about gift cases and she hurriedly pulled one out of a drawer and showed it to him.

Finally, he told her he'd think about it, and led me away. "Let's go up to the fifth floor, to furniture," he said.

"Wally, the store's closing in a couple of minutes."

"Come on."

"For what?"

"Because I want to go up there. And I'm driving. Come on. We'll have a ball."

A ball, now? What the hell kind of a ball? It was no use. It had been a long time, but once again, I sensed that I was being sucked into one of Wally's things. And this time I had no idea what the hell it was. But this one clearly smelled of trouble, serious trouble, and I was beginning to feel more than a little damp around the collar.

We took the escalator to the top floor, strode toward the furniture and bedding area, and as we arrived there, the earsplitting bell rang for some twenty to thirty seconds, announcing that the store was officially closed. We looked around and there wasn't a salesperson in sight.

"Wally, they're closed. We've got to get the hell out of here, now, or we're going to get in trouble."

"Relax, for Christ's sake. Follow me. There's a men's room right over here, and I've got to go bad."

"Can't we just leave? Can't you wait until you get home?"

"No way. Come on!"

I followed him. We went into the men's room and I stood there while he calmly pulled a paperback from his jacket pocket, went into a stall, hung up his jacket, dropped his pants, and sat down. The paperback was a spy novel he'd been reading on the plane. He consumed paperback spy stuff. But was this the time to be doing it? I looked at my watch. Minutes were ticking away and I was sweating heavily. What the hell was this? The reading hour?

When he finally came out, he asked, "Don't you have to piss or anything?"

I wasn't sure I wasn't too nervous to perform any bodily functions, and I was getting worse by the minute. But I figured it was probably a good idea, because I had no idea what was going to happen next, so I fronted up to a urinal and, with considerable concentration, managed to get it done. "Wally, you want to tell me what the hell's going on, here?"

"I thought we'd spend the night here in the store. Do a little easy unhurried shopping."

Had I heard him right? "Wally, did I hear you right?"

"Relax, man. I've done it before. We'll have a ball."

He was serious! I felt a little dizzy. This topped anything from the Oak Ridge days by a couple of quantum leaps. "Wally, we've got to get the hell out of here! Now! Before they shut the place down and turn on their security setup! If we don't, we're going to be in a lot of trouble."

"Will you relax? I told you, I've done this before."

And he *was* relaxed. Completely. I couldn't believe it. "Well, look," I said, "I want to get on home. I told my wife I'd be home around ten, ten-thirty, and that's what I want to do. I don't want her worrying."

He pulled the cell phone from his jacket pocket and handed it to me. "Here. Give her a call. Tell her we missed our flight and she'll see you tomorrow."

"What if I just leave now and I'll go look for a cab home? You can stay if you want. I can get my suitcase from you tomorrow."

He looked at his watch. "You're too late, pal. The front door's already shut. Nobody's down there. And if you start looking around for somebody to let you out, you're going to run into some rather tedious problems . . . Why don't you relax? We'll have a great time here, tonight. I told you before, this is not my first time doing this."

"What do you do?" I asked, partly as a joke, "sleep in the furniture department?"

"Of course," he answered with his usual cynical grin, "and then be the first person in the coffee shop for a great bacon-and-eggs breakfast in the morning." Then he handed me his phone. "Call your wife and tell her you'll see her tomorrow."

"I don't believe you. I don't think you've ever done this before. You can't walk around this store at night. They must have some kind of fancy electronic security system, motion detectors, closed-circuit TV, some damn thing, that'll pick us up and start ringing bells and have police coming in here like gangbusters. What I do think is, you've gotten me in a lot of trouble, and I have to tell you, Wally, I'm sweating bullets. How in hell are we going to get out of here?"

"Will you take it easy? First of all, they *don't* have any fancy electronic stuff here. In The Manchester Store? Never. It wouldn't be in keeping with the store's image. What they do have is a night watchman who walks the store once an hour, on the hour, and sticks his key in one of those old time clocks on every floor, and then returns to his little office in the basement, where he does have closed-circuit TV monitors covering all the outside doors to the building."

Then Wally looked at his watch. "Keep an eye on that middle aisle of the floor. He'll go walking down it in about five minutes to go to the time clock on the back wall, back there in appliances. We'll stay down, out of sight, but I'll bet he doesn't even look in this direction."

"Well, when he shows up, I hope you don't mind, but I'm going to tell him I accidentally got caught in here after the doors closed, and ask him to let me out. And I'll look for a taxi to take me home."

"A taxi ride from around here to where you live, even if you could get one, which I doubt, could cost you a couple hundred bucks. Have you got that kind of cash with you, hotshot? I doubt it. And taxis don't take credit cards. And even if you do have cash, you can't put *that* on your expense account. Whether I sign it or not, it won't fly."

"I don't care. Wally, I'm a nervous wreck. What I want to do is leave."

"Well, you can't. If you do, he'll call the cops to come and investigate, and the cops'll write it up. And you don't want that. Do you hear what I'm saying? Why can't you just relax and have some fun doing a little *shopping*? It's great not having a bunch of stupid clerks trying to wait on you."

My shirt was getting damper by the minute and clinging to my body. "Wally, I'm scared out of my head being in here like this, now."

"Jesus, I thought you'd love it." He looked at his watch. "It's just about time for the night watchman to come traipsing through. Let's sit here on this sofa and keep our heads down and we can watch for him. You can call home after he's gone."

I did as I was told. I had no idea what else I could do. And I was shaking. What if the guard decided to come walking over to the furniture department to browse? He could. He could be in the market for a sofa. Maybe even the one on which we were slumped, watching for him. "Tell me, gentlemen," he could say, when he came strolling over, "how does this sofa sit? Nice? Comfortable? And try to keep your dirty shoes off of it. I may want this particular one. And by the way, you're under arrest."

And just as Wally had said, we heard elevator doors open, followed by footsteps, and finally, there he was. The area had been darkened from what it had been during sales hours, but from our crouched position, peering over the back of the sofa, we could still see him clearly. Wally had picked us a spot where we could watch through a maze of lamps and stick furniture, and easily go unnoticed. The guard was a big man, middle-aged, burly, tough looking despite a potbelly.

He walked slowly along the middle aisle of the floor, glancing in all directions. He moved out of our view as he reached the back of the floor, in appliances, and, in the quiet, we heard the small mechanical sound of his key being inserted into the time clock. He then walked back toward the elevators, and we kept our heads down until we heard the elevator door open and close.

"That's a different watchman from the one I saw the last time I was here," Wally said.

"It is?"

"This one's a *big 'un*. The last time I was here, the guy

was so old and puny he looked like a good strong fart would knock him down."

"Wally, you're not making me feel any better."

"Oh, for Christ's sake, relax. We're not going to be seeing him up close. We'll be seeing him just like we did, then. From a distance. Every hour on the hour. And in between his hourly visits, we'll do a little shopping."

"He thinks he's alone in this store, Wally. What makes you so damn sure he won't do something different?"

"Because that's his job. He's gotta hit every one of those clocks at a specific time, and he spends the rest of his time sitting on his ass in that office in the basement. They provide him with a television to keep himself occupied."

"How do you know that?"

"I've been down there. I talked to the other guy down there one night, just before closing. I started picking his brain and he was more than happy to spill his guts. He told me everything about his job. They provide him with a TV to watch while he's keeping an eye on all those closed-circuit screens monitoring the outside doors."

I was impressed, as usual, with Wally's research. Almost as much as with his nerve. He was a crazy man. But he never got caught at anything. Never.

"Here," he said, "take the phone and call your wife."

I couldn't think of an immediate alternative. I told her the flight had been canceled because of mechanical problems, and I'd be home the following day. Then I returned the phone to him. "I guess you can call *your* wife now."

"She'll see me when she sees me." He stuffed the small phone into his jacket pocket. Then he said, "Let's go do a little shopping. We've got a good forty-five minutes before he gets off his ass again."

"How about if I wait here for you?"

"Are you kidding? Come on. I'm going to help you with your Hanukkah shopping. Make a real hero out of you. Let's go."

I reluctantly got to my feet and went with him. I guess

it was out of a long-established habit of letting him talk me into doing things that I was absolutely sure I'd regret doing. This was crazy. This was no cave exploring or deserted-quarry target practice. This was big doings. Felony-sized . . . So what else was new?

We walked to the escalator, which was silent and unmoving, turned off for the night. Then it was cautiously down the steps, tiptoeing just far enough to be able to survey the next floor before continuing down into it. I followed behind him, gradually becoming a little more relaxed. I had to marvel at the fact that he really seemed to know what he was doing. He'd never gotten caught at anything. Despite his almost deranged driving habits, he'd never to my knowledge even gotten so much as a ticket.

We approached the first floor, and after surveying it longer than any of the others, we moved toward the fine jewelry area. Despite the subdued lighting, visibility was still adequate. Wally stepped behind the counter where he'd seen the fancy pearls, and it was at this moment that I knew for sure he'd been planning this. He reached into a pocket and pulled out thin, plastic-film gloves! As he slipped his hands into them, he whispered, "You keep *your* hands in your pockets."

I understood perfectly. He and I had come to Oak Ridge during a time when all new employees were fingerprinted on being hired, and those prints were still on file somewhere. I was more than glad to do that. I had no desire to touch anything. I wanted no part of the whole business. But I did have a question: how was he going to get into those jewelry showcases? They were all locked.

And as quickly as I wondered about the question, I got my answer. He poked his hand into his pocket and came out with a bunch of those little metal things that locksmiths use to open locks.

"I'll bet you were wondering how I'd get into this showcase without breaking any glass," he said with his cynical smile.

"As a matter of fact, yes, I was."

"You think I want to smash the place up? That wouldn't be any fun. I'm not here to rob the store. The challenge is just to do a little shopping without their help. And if they do notice that something's missing, which I doubt will even happen, they'll maybe ask a few questions and then write it off to employee pilferage and get the loss reimbursed by insurance."

"And those lock picks? Where'd you get those?"

"I've got a buddy who's a key-and-lock guy, and he's been checking me out on this particular skill. These little locks on the jewelry showcases? Shit! These are kid stuff."

Another of my firmest beliefs shattered. Locksmiths sell absolute security. It's their stock-in-trade. So it goes. "And The Manchester Store is your favorite store," I said. "Right?"

"A fine old store. Everything is of highest quality." And with a flourish, a smile, a wave of his hands, and a softly whispered musical "ta-da," he opened the display cabinet.

He reached inside and from an extensive array of pearl necklaces, he carefully lifted out a necklace, a double strand of large cultured pearls, priced at thirty-five hundred dollars. It was not the same one he'd looked at before. That had been a single strand, and much cheaper. He avoided disrupting the arrangement of necklaces in the black velvet tray, pushing the others together just enough to eliminate the gap left by the missing one.

He next opened the drawer in a side cabinet, the drawer opened by the saleslady earlier, and took out one of the black gift cases. He laid the necklace into it and smiled. Then he began opening other drawers until he found a small box made to contain the gift case. He put the case into this box and slid it into his jacket pocket. Then he looked at me. "Which one would you like?"

"What?"

"Pick out one. Come on. We haven't got all night."

"Uh, no. Really. No thanks."

"Come on, pal. Don't be a schmuck. We're standing here. Pick something."

"No. Really, Wally. Forget it. It's not necessary. Actually, to tell you the truth, my wife's not much into jewelry." And what a whopper of a lie that was. But I'd made up my mind.

"Shit! For Chrissakes, will you pick out something? This is last call."

"Nothing for me, Wally, but thanks." I backed away a few feet from the showcase. He was hot, but somehow, I just couldn't make myself be a party to it.

"Schmuck!" Wally snapped. "What the hell's the matter with you? That's why I brought you here." He relocked the showcase. "Come on, then. Let's get back upstairs."

We made our way back up the escalator steps to the fifth floor, and furniture. I still couldn't believe what was happening. Did he really think I was going to be able to sleep through the night up there? But it was still early.

We just sat and stared at our watches until eleven o'clock approached, and then we began to anticipate the next pass by the guard. And he appeared, as expected, just as Wally had assured me he would. He walked the length of the floor, this time, hardly looking around, until he entered the appliances area, where he disappeared. He looked even larger this time than I'd remembered from his first pass. We heard the sound of his key in the time clock and then he reappeared as he made his way back to the elevators.

After we heard the elevator door open and close, Wally said, "How about that? Everything right on schedule." There was still a trace of annoyance in his voice, but he was cooling down.

I asked, "And he just sits down there in an office and watches the tube for an hour, and then repeats his rounds?"

"If he doesn't key those clocks on schedule, *he's* in a lot of trouble. Maybe one of these days, during store hours, I'll take you down there and show you around. There's a lot of stuff going on down there." Wally smiled. "If he's there, we'll get him to give us a tour."

"And are we supposed to just go to sleep now, and wait for morning?"

"First, I've got one more little item to shop for, as soon as he's had time to get back to his office, and after that we can think about getting a little rest. Matter of fact, I could use some sleep. It's been a long day. We got up early in Chicago this morning, did a day's work, drove to O'Hare, and flew home. And we were up late last night, running around . . ." Then he looked at me and grinned one of his familiar teasing grins. "How about you, hotshot? Think you'll be able to get to sleep after all this excitement here tonight?"

He'd read my mind. I felt a little weak at the knees every time I remembered just where the hell we were . . . But I had to hand it to him. He was right at home. How many times *had* he done this, before?

Then he said, with his playful smile, fully aware of my state of unrest, "Okay, let's go. One more little purchase and then we can turn in." He chuckled. "I'm a pretty good customer here, you know? My wife loves this store. She spends a fortune here. She'll love getting this gift, knowing it came from The Manchester Store. She doesn't much like all the New York stores they have around, up this way."

"What floor this time?" I asked.

"The fourth."

"What department?"

"Sporting goods."

"Oh? Whaddaya need?"

He glanced briefly in my direction and gave me one of his special, wait-and-see smiles. "Be surprised."

As soon as we entered the sporting-goods area, he walked directly to a large, glass-topped showcase filled with handguns.

"A gun, Wally?"

"I've been thinking that I need a good handgun for protection at home."

"Don't you already have handguns? I remember that day in Oak Ridge when we went out shooting, you had a handgun. I remember shooting it."

"That was a twenty-two target pistol. They're strictly for recreation. You'd have to hit a man right in the eye to stop him with that. If it was on the line, I wouldn't want my life depending on the protection I'd get from that." Before touching anything, he once again slipped on his plastic-film gloves and then brought out his lock picks. It took him a matter of seconds to open the cabinet.

He looked through the glass top of the cabinet at the array of guns inside and the first thing he lifted out was an ornately engraved, oversized revolver with a very long barrel, probably the kind of thing only a collector would think of buying. He broke it open to see that there were no cartridges in it, then snapped it shut again, aimed it at the middle of my chest, and clicked it a couple of times. "How do you like this cannon?" he said. "Shit, I'd be Wyatt Earp with this thing. Hit a guy in the chest with a slug from this baby and you could send him right through a window." He put it back and continued studying the selection.

While I was nervous just being there, I was fascinated with what he was doing. I didn't own a gun of any kind. Not even a rifle. He wanted to be prepared to win a shootout involving heavy artillery right in his own home. I couldn't imagine such a thing. But watching him was like watching a movie. "Well?" I said. "See the one you want?"

"You bet your ass." He picked up a heavy-looking handgun that appeared to be like one of the new guns cops carry these days. He played with it for a moment, getting the feel of it, aiming it, examining it . . . He pressed something on it, allowing the clip to drop out of the handle, into his hand. "Nice," he breathed. "Very nice." He was a baby with a new toy. He snapped the clip back into place. Then, without warning, he abruptly tossed it at me. "Here, hold this in your hand and see how you like it."

I clumsily managed to catch it and then took it and played around with it for a moment as he had done. It was kind of a kick. But I couldn't possibly imagine owning something like it. "This is a pretty high-caliber weapon, isn't it, Wally?" What did I know about such things?

"Yes, it is."

"Wouldn't it have a lot of recoil when you shoot it?"

He nodded. "Quite a bit. It'd tear a big-ass hole right through you, too."

"I'll bet it would." I handed it back to him. And then the thought occurred to me that my fingerprints were on it. But if that was the one he kept? . . .

He surveyed a glass-doored cabinet behind the counter that was filled with boxes of cartridges and finally located the match for his new toy. He pulled on the knob and this cabinet was also locked. But that posed no problem. He took out his little picks and had it open in seconds.

He lifted out a box of the shells, dropped the gun's clip, and began loading it.

"You're loading it now?"

"What good's a gun if it's not loaded?"

What? . . . But I decided not to ask any further questions. No point in sounding any more naive to him than I already did. What the hell? He wasn't planning to shoot *me*. At least I didn't think so.

"You want to pick something out for yourself?" he asked. "How about it? While we're standing here with the showcase open. I'll help you pick out something if you want."

"No thanks, but thanks for offering."

"How about just a twenty-two target pistol? You had a great time that day at the quarry back at the Ridge. You did pretty good with it, as I remember."

"I'd shot twenty-twos years ago, Wally, when I was just a kid at camp."

"This is last call, pal."

"I don't want anything, Wally. But as I said, thanks anyway."

"Listen, nobody should be without some kind of protection in their home in today's world."

I didn't respond.

He was amused at my skittishness. I could see it in his eyes. But this was nothing new in our relationship, which had existed over a lot of years, and after the scene an hour earlier in jewelry, I guess he decided it wasn't worth the trouble of knocking himself out trying to do me a favor.

He moved the guns around in the showcase until it no longer looked as if one was missing, and relocked it. Then he locked the cabinet behind the counter. *And then,* he stuck the gun into his belt, just like he was one of the "wiseguys," and stuffed the box of shells into a jacket pocket. "What say we go turn in?"

• • •

I was dead asleep when I felt the hand shaking my shoulder. I hadn't expected to be able to sleep, but after we dropped ourselves onto beds in the furniture department, I disappeared into a world of dreamless slumber with remarkable swiftness. It *had* been a long day. Driving from our hotel to our customer's offices in Chicago, making our pitch, taking them to lunch, with drinks, getting to O'Hare, flying to La Guardia, driving to Connecticut, and then, a late evening of "shopping" at The Manchester Store. A full day.

And as I began to wake up, I felt I had slept long and well. I felt rested, but still a little groggy. It was apparently time to get up and get moving. Wally had set the alarm on his fancy-schmancy watch, which he'd probably stolen somewhere, so we could get up at the exact right moment to swing into action, Wally-style. But why was he shaking me so damn hard?

"What in the name of holy hell are you guys doing in here?"

That voice! I looked up at . . . It *wasn't* Wally! . . . He looked like he was nine feet tall, standing over me! It was the night watchman! With his huge shoulders and arms, and his slight paunch, he looked like he weighed three hundred pounds. He had a handlebar mustache and a bulbous nose, and graying, light hair. He gripped my upper arm in his ham hand and he was still shaking me, shaking my entire body, in fact, like I weighed nothing.

I got up on one elbow and looked around. Wally was lying there, apparently still asleep. I sat up, rubbed my eyes, and asked, "What time is it?"

"It's six in the morning," the man answered, "and I want to know what in hell you two are doing here."

As I hesitated, trying to think of something intelligible to say, Wally stirred, rolled over, and sat up, dropping his legs over the side of his bed, and I wondered what *he* was going to do at this point. Would the man see the gun in his belt? I muttered, "Uh, what happened was . . ."

"What happened was . . . ?" the watchman snapped, mocking me. He was hot! And I could see that he was a man who could rightly be called one big, tough, mean, son of a bitch! I glanced at Wally again, and he had buttoned his jacket. The gun was hidden. "Uh, what happened was . . . what happened was . . . uh . . . we were in the men's room, up here on this floor, when the bell sounded, and by the time we got down to the main floor, all the doors were locked, and nobody was around, and we couldn't get out."

"That must have been one hell of a leak you took, because the bell rings at nine-thirty and the main door doesn't get locked and left until at least nine-fifty, nine fifty-five."

"Well, that's what happened." I tried to look as straight at him as I could. "I have this intestinal problem, which—"

"I don't need the bullshit! I don't know what you two are doing here now, but it ain't kosher, and it'll have to be written up. We'll have to get the police in here on this."

"Oh, come on," I pleaded, "it was nothing. Really. I promise you." Then I looked at Wally, and he had the gun out, leveled at the watchman. I suddenly felt dizzy.

Seeing my expression, the watchman turned to Wally, and shock registered on his face. "Where'd you get the gun?"

"Downstairs in your gun department."

"Is it loaded?"

"Of course it's loaded. What good is a gun if it's not loaded?"

The watchman knew he was in trouble. He held out his hand. "Look," he said, "if you'll just give me the gun, I'll let you guys leave outta here, no questions asked, no police, no nothing. We got a deal?"

"Sorry," Wally answered flatly.

"All right, then," the watchman said, "keep the gun. Just put it away. And I'll let you two out, and you can go on about your business, no questions asked, no police, no nothing. We got a deal now?"

"I don't think so."

"Why not?"

"Because we have no way of knowing what you'll do after we walk out the door."

"I'll do whatever you tell me to do."

"But after we leave, how will I know that?"

"Look. You tell me whatever it is you want me to do. I'll go along with whatever you say. Okay?"

"You can say that, but I'll have no control over it."

I was listening to Wally's mind working, his very sharp, analytical mind. And if I'd felt stricken when I first saw that he'd drawn the gun, I was suddenly feeling light-headed.

The watchman saw it coming, too. "Then what do you want me to do?" he asked.

"Nothing," Wally answered.

I looked at Wally's hand and saw his grip tightening. "*No, Wally! Please God, No!*"

"Sorry," Wally said, to the man, almost in a whisper. "Nothing personal." He fired twice, point-blank, into the man's chest. The shots were deafening and echoed around the huge display floor. The man's body jerked from the impact of the slugs, one of which exited from his back, splashing out a little blood and stuff with it as it shattered the base of a table lamp across the area. The man crumpled to the floor, ending up in a contorted heap, his eyes still open and glazed.

"Wally?" I gasped, looking back and forth between him and the dead man on the floor.

"It was the only way we were going to walk out of here, completely clean," he answered quietly. "Think about it."

His analytical mind.

Wally squatted next to the watchman's body and disconnected the man's loaded key ring from his belt loop. "One of these'll open one of the doors to the street. It's early. There won't be any traffic outside. We'll go to the diner near the plant and spend a couple of hours having some breakfast and then go into the office. If anybody asks, just say we caught the five A.M. out of O'Hare. That works out about right."

Shortly after leaving the vicinity of the store, we drove onto a bridge over a river. There was no traffic at that moment. Wally slowed down, lowered his window, and tossed, first, the man's keys, and then the gun, into the water.

• • •

I don't know how I got through that day at the office. I could still hear those two shots ringing in my ears. I felt sure everyone could see in my face that I was beyond just a little disturbed about something, but, bless them, nobody inquired. I avoided spending time with Wally the rest of the day.

I took off a little early and drove home in my own car, which I'd left in the company's parking garage. And of course, I heard all about it on a local radio station as I drove. The watchman had a wife and four children.

I was sure I'd find two men in suits, two of our small town's detective squad, waiting for me when I arrived home, to lead me away in handcuffs. But when I got home, they weren't there. And they didn't come the next day or the day after that, or the day after that. And the thing I wondered was, if they finally did come, would they believe *my* story? Would anybody? Ever?

But the two men haven't come looking for me . . . And it's been quite a while . . .

. . . And neither Wally nor I has ever again mentioned our night at The Manchester Store.

HANK'S TALE

by Dorothy Salisbury Davis

I T was a gray raw day when we buried Billy Baldwin. The wind turned the women around on the church steps, tugged at their skirts, and tossed their hair. The Reverend Barnes, who'd begun to show his years, didn't seem sure of who he was talking about or when he died, and he was usually at his best at funerals, knowing everybody in Webbtown. But he hadn't been called to the Baldwin house till Billy was cold and some time dead. Of a heart attack, according to the coroner, who had a doctor-of-medicine degree, which I guess entitles you to work on dead people if that's your preference. He'd come from Ragapoo City, the county seat, routed out of his bed at four in the morning. Even at that, he'd got there ahead of Reverend Barnes.

But everything got worked out by the time of the funeral. The sheriff examined Billy's trap at Lookout Point, where he always stopped on his way home from work to pick up whatever small animal was waiting for him to put it out of its misery. There was a fair amount of trapping done in the Hills that time of year. Still is. Nancy Baldwin is famous up and down the valley for her hasenpfeffer. Never had much stomach for it myself. The sheriff brought the trap down with him. Had to spring it and break the lock. Billy was working on it, it looked like, when he slipped and tumbled halfway down the hill. It was scrambling up again and getting himself home safe, the coroner reported, that brought on the heart attack. I sure thought about those words, home safe. Dead. I asked Prouty what he thought happened. Prouty's the undertaker and my friend. It was in his cold room they did the autopsy. But Prouty didn't want to talk about it. In fact nobody in the whole town did, including me.

I did pay attention to who was at the funeral and who was not. Mostly women were there. They take to funerals better than men, certainly to this one they did. Mary Toomey was sitting next to Nancy in the front pew. Big Mary sat in the front pew of most things, especially since she'd been made president of Webbtown State Bank. First woman to hold the job. Nancy looked mighty frail and kind of scared. Every once in a while she'd let out a big, wet sob that started the little one in her arms wailing. Big Mary—we'd called her that since she was a bulging-out teenager—would clamp her hand on Nancy's and you'd have thought it was a tourniquet, the way it stopped the tears for a while. If the baby didn't let up, Mary took hold of her and gave her a shake that must've cured her of everything but breathing. I'd heard it was Mary who'd called Prouty from the Baldwin place. Said she'd been with Nancy when Billy died. I guess you could call that the truth if you wanted to and I didn't know of anyone who didn't. Across the aisle, next to the plain coffin he'd steered into the church, was Prouty, as pale as any corpse he ever got ready for a last viewing. In the next pew back were the four pallbearers Mary Toomey recruited on Nancy's behalf. I was one of them. During silent prayer I heard Mrs. Prouty clear her throat. Prouty gave a little flex to his shoulders when it happened, so I assume it was Mrs. Prouty sending some kind of message he picked up. Alongside her was the pastor's wife, Faith Barnes. She sat straight and solid as a farm silo. She'd always stood for what the pastor preached, even ecumenism when it came along. It was a word most of us found hard to say, but we swallowed it. Didn't mean much except to Pastor, who tried to keep up with what was going on in the world. We're a one-church town unless you count the itinerant hallelujah sayers who show up regular and get us hollering. I mention them now because one of them was going to show up before long, though we didn't know it then.

One person who wasn't at the funeral was Clara Mc-Cracken. I might as well say now, I don't think I'd have lived as long as I have if it wasn't for Clara McCracken. I'm a lawyer and I've practiced in Webbtown ever since I first hung my shingle upstairs of Kincaid's drugstore, some six decades ago. I don't have much of a practice left, but I've played the fiddle for pleasure all my life, and if I'm not better known for fiddling than I am for the law, I'm sure better liked for it.

McCrackens have run the Red Lantern Inn since the first of them came west after the War of Independence. One story says they were on the run from the revenue men during the Whiskey Rebellion. That sounds about right. The McCrackens almost died out twenty years ago, down to two sisters, Clara and Maud, maiden ladies. Maud, twice Clara's age, was determined to marry her sister to a paint salesman who put in at the Red Lantern whenever he came through the Ragapoos. Clara wanted nothing to do with him. She wanted to run wild in the hills with young Reuben White until the day he cornered her in the sheepcote. Maudie was accidentally shot dead that day and Clara tumbled Reuben headfirst into the well. I defended her when she was tried for murder. She wouldn't have any outside lawyer, and she wasn't much use in her own defense, taking the jury to the well and showing them how she did it. She did fifteen years.

Reuben's family didn't get much sympathy from the town. They moved away—deeper into the hills—I suppose more in shame than sorrow—when most of the townspeo-

ple drove up to the county jail to see Clara off to prison.
The one member of the family, a first cousin to Reuben,
who did not move away, was Mary Toomey, Big Mary.

I brought Clara home after she'd done her time, and
allowed myself to be made a silent partner so she could
reopen the Red Lantern. Not much business but it's been
going since.

If you wonder what all this has to do with the funeral
of Billy Baldwin, I'll tell you now. I'll swear to the Al-
mighty I saw Billy stoned—I think to death—on the veranda of the Red Lantern the night Big Mary and Nancy
said he died at home after coming down from Lookout
Point.

I woke up sudden that night and looked out my window.
It was moonlight, cold and past midnight. A dozen or so
women of the town passed under my window, silent except
for their whispering feet. I knew where they were headed.
There had been shenanigans, and as soon as I could get
there I followed them and lay down in the hollow alongside
where Billy Baldwin's car was parked. The women were
standing like statues beneath the steps, tinted pink from the
light of the Red Lantern sign. I heard the commotion upstairs and saw lights going on. I heard Billy yelping and
scrambling down the stairs, Nancy after him, yelling and
beating at him as he plunged outdoors, naked as birth
and his clothes in his arms. The women blocked the steps
and picked up stones from the walk, which they handed
round among them. Then out from a side door came Clara,
wispy as a ghost in a negligee the likes of which no woman
of Webbtown had ever seen before. The women stood,
stones in hand, until Clara went down the steps and got
one, too. Billy by then was on his knees, pleading with
them, and one of the women took Nancy away. Clara threw
the first stone and Billy went down in the barrage that followed. Didn't move even when Clara went back up the
steps and kicked him like he was a dead calf. The women
picked up more stones and flung them at Clara. They hissed

at her like snakes. When she made it into the inn I took off
and never looked back.

• • •

AFTER the funeral nobody, even at Tuttle's Bar and Grill,
where most of the men hung out, ever mentioned Billy. I
felt things were hanging in a kind of delicate balance, but
I could've felt that way because of what I'd seen. I didn't
know for a fact about Prouty or Reverend Barnes, but I was
pretty sure I was the only man in town to know what really
happened to Billy. It bothered me a lot at first, but after a
while I got to thinking maybe I dreamt the whole thing. I
sure liked it better that way.

There was a thaw in early January. It made the three-
mile exit off the interstate almost impassable. I'd just come
up from the town and waited on the veranda when a car
and trailer pulled up in front of the Red Lantern. Both vehicles looked as though they'd had a long and hearty life.
Which was more than I could say for the driver. He got
out of the car and scraped his boots at the bottom step. He
was tall and thin as a string bean, the eyes of a zealot, I
thought. I'd seen his like among mountain preachers. His
smile was practiced, on and off. His clothes were a dusty
black, a topcoat that flapped open, trousers tucked into his
boots. He tipped the brim of a high-crowned hat, and the
first words out of his mouth were, "Are you a Christian?"

I didn't like him asking that. "I am when I have to be,"
I said.

But he took my words at their best value. "I'm the Reverend Isaiah Teague, but I'm not a prophet. I'm only a poor
evangelist." He offered his hand and I took it. I could feel
the bones.

"I'm Hank," I said, hoping it would be enough to get
him on the road again. I didn't offer him the hospitality of
the inn. To tell the truth I was afraid if I let him in, I
wouldn't be able to get him out and Clara would kill me.
I was glad I hadn't been too hospitable when next he asked

me if I knew of a lady named Mary Toomey in the town,
and where he'd find her.

I looked at my watch. "I think you can find her at this
hour at the bank."

"She works at a bank?" he questioned, and nodded ap-
proval.

"She's president of the First State Bank of Webbtown."

The smile came and went, and so did he.

Before he was out of sight Clara came out to me. "What
was that all about?"

"Looking for Big Mary. He's a clergyman of some sort."

"They know where the money is," she said. Which was
more or less what I'd thought of him myself.

But Mary took to him from that first day. She helped
him in more ways than we knew at the time. First, she did
two good turns at once by getting him room and board at
Nancy Baldwin's. Billy hadn't left Nancy more than a rab-
bit's skin, and she hadn't been the same since his death.
The baby, too, was sickly. It cried most nights through,
according to the neighbors. That stopped whenever the reverend was there. If you listened close you could hear him
sing gospel at all hours, Annie Pendergast said, as sweet as
any you ever heard on the radio. He'd go off for days at a
time and come back weekends. He was laying out a summer tour of the campsites, it was told, and on one return
when he stopped first at the bank, Big Mary came out and
climbed into that woebegone vehicle of his and rode with
him past the inn and up over Lookout Point. You had to
say his attitude toward Mary was gallant, not exactly
bowing and scraping, but so respectful it could turn your
stomach. We didn't begrudge her such attention, you understand. I suppose we even pitied her, the way you would
anybody you thought was being taken advantage of.

• • •

WHAT happened to me that winter was that Tom Kincaid
sold the drugstore to a chain company, and the first thing

a chain company does is renovate. Clara suggested I move my office into the first-floor parlor of the inn. Pointed out it had a separate entrance. After hemming and hawing and looking her straight in the eye to see if I could tell what was going on with her, I agreed. I knew that was the door Clara had come out of in the negligee. But I also knew that moving my office into the Red Lantern, I might help spread a little goodwill where it was needed most. Clara didn't go into town much, just for what shopping she had to do, and some of that she shunted onto me. The women were cold toward her, crossed the street when they saw her coming, things like that. She never was sociable. Loving people didn't come natural to her. She'd learned a lot in prison, but not about loving.

The day after I moved my office in, she was watching me put things away where I could find them. She was being lazy, which was unusual for Clara. I put my violin case on the top of the shelves for my law books. I never played it at home. Too lonesome.

"Fiddle us up a tune," Clara said.

"I'm getting terrible arthritic," I told her, but I got the fiddle out and tuned it. I don't get asked so often anymore.

Clara, sitting half off, half on the side of my desk, the sunlight playing round in her hair, looked prettier than I'd seen her since she went to prison. Not a bit like her sister Maudie, who I'd thought she was getting to resemble more every day.

"Anything special you got in mind, Clara? You know my repertoire."

She grinned at me and gave her nose a crinkle. "How about a lullaby, Old Hank?"

• • •

IT was going on ten o'clock when I got a call from Clara. She wasn't feeling so good and wanted me to take over the desk. I asked her if she wanted me to get in touch with a doctor for her. I hadn't mentioned it till then. She hadn't either. Now she exploded.

"What in hell for? Go to bed, Hank. You're getting to be a nag, a nanny. You're more old maid than I am."

I guess that was the truth. There was a storm coming sure, that dead quiet when even the crickets stop to listen. They're better forecasters than radio or television, closer to home. I still live in the house I was born in, and going out, I locked the door. I wasn't sure when I'd get back.

Clara was sitting in the lobby, sweating and bubbling gas. Like I'd thought, all eight room keys were hanging in a row. Nobody was coming off the interstate that night. Webbtown wasn't even on the interstate, three miles from the nearest exit.

"I'm going upstairs now," she said, and lifted herself out of the chair, real careful. Didn't show much, but she was a big woman, and a heck of a lot stronger than I was.

"I could fix that storeroom off the kitchen for you, Clara. I could set up a bed in there. You'd be more comfortable."

"Think so, Hank?" Real sarcastic.

She went up the stairs one creaky step at a time. From the landing she called down to me. "Better fire up the hot water. Feels like we're going to need it soon."

No point in going into details here, but my first trip upstairs she warned me if I tried to call a doctor she'd get up and pull the hall phone clear out of the wall. When she got to moaning and twisting the brass rungs of the bedstead, I couldn't take any more of it. I started out of the room and said I'd come back soon.

"You better, Old Hank. I did fifteen years on account of you."

You don't take serious what people say to you at a time like that, but I sure felt it.

"I didn't mean to say that ever. It's this ornery little son of a bitch inside me trying to get out."

I just nodded and went on, but I'd been standing there long enough to notice that fancy negligee draped over the chair like somebody invisible was sitting in it.

The wind was rattling shutters like they were castanets when I got downstairs. The telephone operator got the County Hospital for me, but there wasn't anything they could do if I didn't bring her in, baby and all if it got born on the way. The one doctor on duty was already in the delivery room. They'd try to hold him till we got there. I knew I could get a mountain to Mohammed a lot easier.

I called Faith Barnes, the pastor's wife. Pastor was having an asthma attack. This weather brought it on every time and she wasn't going to leave him. "Are you sure it's a baby, Hank?"

I just asked her who she thought I could call.

"I can do that much for you. I'll try and find someone willing to go up there. People are scared of her. And now this . . . She's got to be near fifty years old."

I'm not much for quoting Scripture, but I said to think of John the Baptist's mother, how old she was when he was born.

"She at least had a husband," Faith said, and hung up.

The phone was crackling and the lights flickered whenever there was a big gust of wind. I got two hurricane lamps and a couple of farm lanterns from the storeroom. I'll say this for Clara, they were on the ready, chimneys clean, wicks trimmed, and a big can of kerosene with a funnel. I took one of the lamps upstairs with me in a hurry. When she was quiet it was almost worse than when she was hollering. She looked like something done up for Halloween, her hair in strings, her eyes popping, her face in a kind of green sweat.

"It's recess time," she said, "unless he's got himself tied up in there. Come here, Hank." She took my hand and put it where she wanted it over her nightgown. "Feel anything?"

I did feel a tiny pulse. It could have been my own, but I said yes. I could feel her heart pumping like an oiler.

She let go my hand and groped for the brass rungs behind her head. "Here he comes again, the little bulldozer."

I suppose I was thinking, What if it's a girl? But what I said was, "Who is he, Clara?"

"Jeremiah McCracken."

The wind kept whistling at the window, and Clara howling every time the pains hit her. She told me to bring up two buckets to haul water from the bathroom and told me where to find more towels. I was to bring the kitchen scissors she used to cut up chickens. The light hanging over the bed would swing and stay off longer every time. I put the kitchen matches by the hurricane lamp and what flashed through my mind was when my mother was dying and I came home from law school. She went so quiet when I got there. That was over sixty years ago, and it was just as though it happened yesterday.

Clara went quiet and stared at me like she was listening with her eyes. "There's someone in the house."

"I'll go see," I said.

"You stay here. I got Pa's shotgun under the bed." And at the top of her lungs she shouted, "Get out! Whoever's there, get out!"

The lights went down again and then went off. I'd left a lantern burning on the desk below, and now through the bedroom doorway I could see its wavering light move up the stairs. When the electric light came on again, there was Big Mary Toomey already in the room.

"Hank, get her out of here! You hear me, Mary Toomey, I don't want you here."

"I'm not asking for hospitality. I'm doing my Christian duty. Hank, we need more light. I don't care where you get it. Get it now." She put what looked like a tool kit on the commode and untied it. It was medical instruments. I knew the midwife in town, but it wasn't Big Mary.

Clara kept tossing her head and biting back crying out. I did everything Big Mary told me to. She was a born top sergeant. I'd been in the army long enough to know one when I saw one. When I'd done what she told me, she sent me downstairs and told me to stay there till she called me. Then I was to come running.

I sat in the lobby and wished the wind was louder so I wouldn't have to hear Clara giving birth. I tried to think about Big Mary and how she'd battered her way to the top job in the bank. Nobody thought she'd make it, and she wasn't going to do it by women's wiles, so you had to give her credit for hard work and taking correspondence courses. And now this business of the traveling preacher—she gave us a real surprise. You had to wonder which of them had the other in the palm of their hand. I'd have thought Mary Toomey was the last person Faith Barnes would send to Clara—and maybe she was, nobody else willing. And Big Mary practicing Christian charity on Clara? I couldn't believe that.

I didn't even notice when the storm died down. I must've fallen asleep. I woke up sudden to what I thought was crows, first birds up in the morning. It was dawn and what I was hearing was Jeremiah. The next I heard was a terrible squabble between the women. When I got upstairs both of them were pulling at the baby, him wrapped in a towel and sputtering like he'd choke. The tiniest, reddest thing I ever seen alive.

"She's trying to kill my baby! Hank, take him away from her!"

Mary left Clara with a towel and held the creature by the feet, bare as a plucked chicken. She whacked him until he was crying again. Then she put him in a clean towel and handed him to me. I saw for sure he was a male child.

"You better get him baptized soon," Mary said. "I don't think he's going to last long."

"He'll make it," Clara said. "He's a McCracken." She was trying to get to the side of the bed.

"Can't be more than half-McCracken, can he?" Big Mary said. She was packing up the instruments where she'd dip them in the bucket of water and dry them on whatever she found to do it with. When she'd tied the strap, she stood, hands on her hips, and looked down at Clara. "Why don't you let me have him, Clara? I'll raise him in a decent Christian house. I won't say where I got him. Sent away to the Indian reservation—I could say that. Looks kind of like one. Old Hank won't tell what happened here tonight."

"Shut up! Just shut your rotten mouth." Clara was sitting up by then and getting her feet over the edge of the bed. I knew she was aiming to get hold of the gun.

I put the baby in her arms and pushed her back in bed. He kept her busy for the minute. "You better go now, Mary," I said. "Folks'll be out and around cleaning up. You did a good deed, but no point advertising it, if you want my opinion."

"Mind who you're talking to, Old Hank. I'm running Webbtown these days, didn't you notice?"

"You're doing a fine job," I said. Pure babble. I got her out the bedroom door and closed it. Clara lay back on her pillow, with that little red body making sucking noises. His mother knew what to do about it. When I went 'round the room, trying to tidy up where I could, I knew I should be fixing coffee and oatmeal. But being me, I had to neaten things up a bit first. That's how I noticed Big Mary'd used the negligee to wipe up the instruments on. I just took it down the stairs with me and put it in the furnace.

Jeremiah got more human looking every day. He sure knew where his next meal was coming from. Clara was up and doing in a day or two. She spent a lot of time filling in and scratching out the Sears-catalog order forms. You could almost hear the silence come up from the town. People drove by without looking our way. I could be standing out on the veranda and nobody seemed to notice. Even at Tuttle's they didn't ask if there was a baby at the Red Lantern. You'd expect that, but it was another thing they didn't want to know. A couple of big boxes of baby things was delivered by the Pendergast twins, who said Miss

Toomey sent them. Clara hid in the storeroom with the baby until the kids were gone. When I told her where they'd come from, she said to burn them. "Pour kerosene over them and put a match to it."

I told her not to be a darn fool. He was going to puke and pee in them anyway. I did some threatening and we had words you didn't hear from me very often, but she gave in. Didn't have anything herself to put him in but swaddles. She called the county nurse a couple of times, and when Jeremiah was two weeks old, I drove them both to the clinic in Ragapoo City. Clara wanted to drive—she always did—and me to hold the baby, but I wasn't ready to be seen in public doing that. They gave her such good marks at the clinic she thought she wouldn't need to go there anymore. I figured that was why they gave her such good marks.

. . .

FALL came on as beautiful as I'd ever seen it. The rain from that summer storm had something to do with it. Or just having a child around made a difference in how things looked. Some of the same harvesters came through as last year and didn't mind too much going down to Tuttle's for their main meal. Just so they could come up and finish off with the beer we still called Maudie's Own. I kept looking at one and another of them and at Clara, just wondering. Nobody but Clara would count on a one-night stand to make a baby. I knew now, if I ever doubted it, she wanted him bad.

. . .

IF I'd been paying less attention to Jeremiah those days, I'd have known better what was going on in the town. I heard that Reverend Teague had taken his trailer on a camp tour that summer, and then parked it by River Junction, where he preached from a platform that was part of the old county fairgrounds. Prouty and Mrs. Prouty and some others went to hear him, watched a couple of baptisms. They thought he was pretty good. He knew the Bible a lot better than they did. But most of them thought they'd stick with Pastor Barnes. Big Mary went up and gave him a few amens, and he came down now and then for a meal at her house or Nancy's, but he wasn't living there anymore. And when he walked in town with Mary, he wasn't just sidling along with her the way he did at first. He walked with his back straight and he always wore his hat and was sure to take it off to anyone they met. He'd turn and smile to those who didn't stop, even if it meant showing his back to Mary. Mary was as proud and patient with him as if he was a child. When I heard this, what went through my mind, in and out, mind you, was her asking Clara to give Jeremiah to her. I never thought it was a serious proposition, just something she said to rile Clara. But where did it come from? Anyway, like Nora Kincaid said, Isaiah Teague was beginning to feel his oats.

Halloween passed with nothing worse happening at the inn than the rain barrel being toppled. I was rolling it back into its place when Reverend Teague drove up, parked, tried to help me, and was no help at all. He followed me into my office. "I hear you have a baby here in need of baptizing."

"That's something you'll have to take up with his mother," I said.

"I've never met Miss McCracken," he said.

"Well, why don't you go around and introduce yourself? She'll know who you are."

"A friend of Mary Toomey's." He cleared his throat. He'd said something that could be taken for a joke.

"I'd just ask her about getting the baby baptized," I said.

Isaiah quick-smiled at me. "She'll never know, unless you're the one to tell her—I was with Miss Mary when the call came from your parson's wife. I persuaded Mary to come and help. I'd have come myself, but Mary said she might become violent, seeing a man. But I've delivered a baby or two in my time."

"That a fact?" I said. I knew now where Big Mary got the instruments she'd brought along. He'd softened me up a little, telling me. But why tell me, except he wanted me to tell Clara? I didn't like him much better than the first time I'd laid eyes on him. "I'll take you 'round and introduce you. Then you're on your own."

I gave Clara ten minutes at most to send this tent Christian on his way. Two hours later, when I went in from my office, there he was in the lobby, rocking Jeremiah in his basket and mumbling, singsong, something like, "You're going to be a Christian boy." Jeremiah was burbling with pleasure.

Clara was almost as perky as her son. "Hank, we're going to have another christening. Remember the last one?"

I tried to remember if there'd been one in the last forty or so years.

"I don't remember it either," Clara made fun of me. "It was me, Old Hank, and you played the fiddle. You're going to be the godfather, aren't you, Hank?"

I knew I was too old to be anybody's godfather for it to do him much good while he was growing up, but I didn't like the way Jeremiah took to Reverend Teague. "I guess I can handle it," I said.

After Teague was gone and she'd quieted Jeremiah down, I said to her, "You know Big Mary's gone kind of sweet on him, don't you?" I always took whatever news I could of the town up to her, and I might have had in mind to dampen her interest in him by mentioning Big Mary. But it was about as foolish a notion as I ever had. You could've said her smile was angelic if you didn't know how much wickedness was in her. "We got a parson of our own in Webbtown," I snapped. "It ain't right trusting Jeremiah's christening to an outsider."

"Something I learned when I was away, Old Hank, it

don't matter who dishes it up, it's what's on the plate that counts."

I left her to manage her own doggone inn and her own doggone baby, closed up my office, and went down to Tuttle's. I hadn't been there much lately. Prouty and Tom Kincaid were resting their elbows on the bar. Tuttle drew me what used to be my usual, said it was on the house, hospitality to a stranger. It wasn't as good as Maudie's Own, but I sure liked drinking in their company. I took a long pull before I even said "thank you." Then, like I had a chip on my shoulder, I said, "You know we got a baby up at the Red Lantern."

"Congratulations, Hank, you old son of a gun," Kincaid said.

Not much of a laugh from the other two. It ought to have come off funnier than it did. But then they'd have had to forget that it was in this very room they'd all chipped in to send Billy Baldwin up to proposition Clara: they were so doggone sure she was running a house and maybe coaxing doves from among their women. So now you know why no one was talking about Billy Baldwin. Maybe I was the only man to know how he died, but every married man in town had a hunch why.

"The visiting preacher came by today, looking to do a baptism," I said. "And I guess there's going to be one. I put in a word with her for Pastor Barnes, but the evangelist got to her first. Don't know what's wrong with Barnes. Isn't it his job to gather in the lambs?"

"He's about to retire, Hank," the barkeep said. "That's what we were talking about when you walked in."

"He's getting kind of old," Prouty said.

"I know what's old and what isn't," I said. "When's this going to happen?"

"Soon as we get a replacement. He's going east. Him and Faith's got a son back there and grandchildren they've never even seen."

"And this Isaiah Teague—what kind of a name is that

anyway?—he's first in line. Is that what's happening?"

"Big Mary's been working on it," Tuttle said.

"Tell me something I couldn't guess. Is she running the church now, too? Ain't the bank enough for her?"

"Take it easy," Tuttle said. "You'll get your say when the time comes."

"Looks to me the time's already past." I was getting myself madder by the minute. "Prouty, you know what's going on with the church. Is this all her doing?"

"She petitioned the Convention, him being a different kind of Baptist. They're going to meet on it first of the year."

"Hold on one damn minute," I said. "I've supported the Webbtown church for over sixty years. What's this petition you're talking about? Who all signed it? I thought we were a congregation, not a Holy Roman Empire."

Finally Prouty admitted, "Mrs. Prouty signed for both of us, signed it Mister and Missus."

"And you let her do it?"

"Well, she didn't exactly ask me. You've not been around much lately, Hank. There's some who like him. They think he's a good man."

"And a good man's hard to find," I said, sour.

"Specially when he's still alive," Prouty said, and pushed over his glass to Tuttle for a refill.

I went straight home from Tuttle's instead of going back to the inn and relieving Clara. I was spending a lot more time at the Red Lantern than I was in my own house. I could write down a phone number in the dust on my hall table. I knew there was a lot of bluster in what I had said at Tuttle's. My edgy feeling about the situation had to do with how Clara felt about Big Mary, and me telling her how Big Mary felt about Teague. Even so, when I went up the next day and she asked what was doing at Tuttle's— she knew by instinct that's where I went—I had to tell her about Pastor Barnes quitting and Teague lining up for the job. She'd have found out anyway.

You could have heard her cackle all the way to the interstate. "Queen Mary! Rattling the gates of heaven, ain't that right, Hank?"

I hadn't even mentioned the petition business. I didn't say anything. I watched Jeremiah pee straight up in the air.

"Ain't he a devil?" Clara said, busting with pride. "I hate to put a dappy on him."

• • •

SURE enough, the following Sunday, Reverend Barnes announced he was going to retire in early spring. Retirement isn't something we go in for voluntarily in the Hills, but he was trembly again and Faith said at coffee hour they wanted to spend time with the grandchildren while they were still children. Nobody asked what they were going to live on—or off—but everybody wondered. I wasn't at church myself. I'm not regular, but I'm dependable when they need me. And when I heard that Parson had invited his friend Reverend Isaiah Teague to preach the next Sunday, I made up my mind to be there.

Reverend Teague preached as though he wanted to make us feel good about ourselves, and I must say that hit me just right. He told us about the Campbellite roots of our denomination and the pioneer spirit that brought them west and settled this evangelical Christian group in the Ragapoo Hills. We'd almost forgotten that. And I could see what he'd meant with that "Are you a Christian?" introduction. There was a time that's what we were called, just plain "Christians." I felt foolish for what I'd said back to him about being one when I needed to be.

"I don't mind listening to sinners," he said at one point in the sermon. "That's what I'm here for. But like Jesus Himself, sometimes I'd like to hear about these transgressions over a good meal. And by transgressions, I don't mean fibs and nickel-and-dime meannesses. I want something I can get my teeth into before the devil gets there ahead of me."

It went something like that, and I could see he was going to get several Sunday dinner invitations. Might even get "the Call" if we came to a vote on it. I thought I might have made a mistake measuring him on my early impression. And then there was the way Jeremiah and him took to one another.

Clara couldn't wait for me to come up to the Red Lantern to tell her about it. I told her what I could remember. She was disappointed, expecting hellfire and brimstone. "Where was Big Mary in all this?"

"She was there in her pew. And pouring coffee afterward, come to think of it."

"Pouring coffee, la-di-da." She'd seen that on the television, but I didn't say so.

"She was kind of holding back. She'd done what she could for him, getting the petition to the Convention," I said.

"And pushing poor old Barnes off the cliff."

"Where'd you hear that?"

"I know human nature better than you do, Old Hank."

She'd ought to, I thought, having all that time to think about what she'd done to Reuben. And to poor Billy. Then she said the craziest thing: "I don't think she could have a baby, do you?"

I wasn't going to answer that one.

She pouted for a minute or two. Then: "Hank, you know where he's living now. He's got his trailer on the fairgrounds by River Junction. People come miles to him for real baptisms. I want you to drive over there and arrange Jeremiah's before the weather gets any colder."

"You mean you're going to let him plop your baby like a duck egg in the river?"

"It's called immersion, baptism by immersion, and I want him done right."

"Then get yourself another godfather. I ain't going to stand out there and get pneumonia." Which wasn't what I meant to say at all.

"Hank, just go over and let him show you how he does it. Real quick and into a warm blanket. All the praying's done ahead of time."

I guess I don't have to tell you, I went to see Isaiah Teague just as I was told to, and the next Tuesday, after all the school buses had driven by the junction, Jeremiah Henry McCracken was dipped into a Monongahela inlet and came up Christian, smiling.

We went back to the Red Lantern and fired up the furnace. A couple of oil inspectors were signing in that night. Phoned to make reservations, which tickled Clara. The Ritz. Isaiah stopped on his way in town and I brought the bottle of Old Kentucky from the back bar into the kitchen. I made hot toddies for Clara and me, and Clara put a drop of watered whiskey on the tongue of Jeremiah.

"Me, too," Isaiah said, which sure made us laugh.

But Clara took a tablespoonful and poured it into his mouth, forcing him to open up. "Hank, you won't tell Big Mary, will you?" she said, a spark in her eye.

"I wish you hadn't said that," Isaiah said. "I'm supposed to be a peacemaker."

"I say what's on my mind and do what I have to do."

"We must have a discussion about that someday, Miss Clara."

"Hank, go get your fiddle."

Isaiah looked at his watch. It was getting on toward noon, but he didn't say anything. I noticed from my office window he'd parked his aging vehicle right alongside mine at the back of the inn. You wouldn't notice it just driving by. Nothing could stop me from remembering—in and out of mind again—where Billy Baldwin parked his car the night of the stones. I'd wondered which woman drove it home, with him in it, Nancy or Big Mary. It had to've been Mary who transported him. Nancy was falling-down frail that night.

• • •

IT was Big Mary herself who asked me to head a committee to make a farewell purse for Parson Barnes. She came out to where I was at the cashier's window in the bank and invited me into her office. It was plain but tidy—some rubbery plants and a picture of her father, one of those paintings a traveling artist paints from a Brownie snapshot. I guess you'd say it was a lady's office, but the smell of cigar smoke was going to last till they tore the building down.

I protested that the only way I could raise money was with my violin and a tin cup on a Saturday night. But she got her way with flattery and a first contribution. It wasn't diplomatic of me—in fact, it was kind of sly—when I asked her if there was any word yet from the Convention on how Reverend Teague stood with them.

"Better than you'd think, Hank, but they feel they have to make conditions." She was blushing like a schoolgirl. She gave a funny little toss of her head, as though maybe she had a fly on her nose. "We'll just have to wait and find out."

I realized I was seeing Big Mary in love and I was as embarrassed as she was. I thought one of those conditions would want the parson to be a family man and she was working on it. I was trying not to say anything like that, so I said something worse, meaning money for the retirement purse: "I'll be doing my best, Mary, but you can't get blood from a stone."

We could've choked on the silence.

"Good old Hank," she said then, and gave me a cold smile. She ought to have known I wasn't smart enough to make that insinuation on purpose. But what she'd be pretty sure of now was that I knew what the women did that night, and how her and Faith had got Billy home where they could say he died in his own bed.

• • •

WHAT made Christmas special that year was Jeremiah.
There hadn't been a tree at the Red Lantern since before
Clara went away. She wanted to know if I thought he'd
understand if we got one for him. I said we'd be lucky if
he paid it attention at all, and I told her about the Christmas
I remembered most. I'd have been five years old. My folks
didn't have much money and what Ma and I did, we went
out in the woods back of where we lived, picked out a tree,
and made Pa come and chop it down. I told Clara the whole
story, how we stuck it in a bucket of coal and decorated it
with pictures of toys and bicycles and sleds we cut out of
the Sears, Roebuck catalog. I'll be darned if she didn't
make me do the same thing and herself got out the Sears
catalog and cut it up. They don't make catalogs like they
used to, but Jeremiah didn't know that, and he kind of liked
the whole celebration.

On Christmas Eve, a dozen or so youngsters with Isaiah
leading them and Anne Pendergast, Mrs. Prouty, and Faith
Barnes a kind of rear guard against defections came up
from the town and sang carols below the Red Lantern sign.
I stood out on the veranda and waved my hands like I was
directing them. I wanted to take Jeremiah out but Clara said
no and took him into the storeroom again till they were
gone.

There wasn't going to be a better time to ask Clara a
question that'd been nagging at me since Jeremiah's arrival,
so I just blurted it out. "What are you going to tell him
when he starts asking about not having a father like other
kids?"

"I'm going to tell him about a hunting accident," she
said, and got a dreamy look in her eyes. "It was way up
north in Canada, bear country, during a terrible blizzard.
His pa was hurt bad and his partner went looking for help.
Got somebody but they got lost on their way back and
couldn't find him. They looked and looked and they called
and called, and all they could hear back was their own
voices. They never found him. All they found was bear

tracks in the snow. Ain't that beautiful, Hank?"

I figured there was no point in reminding her about bears hibernating in the winter.

By Groundhog Day, no word had come from the Convention. Faith Barnes, who was trying to pack up a lifetime, invited Isaiah to board with her and Pastor for the last months of winter, but he said no, but thank you kindly. He called the trailer his hermitage, said the solitary life was good for him. He stopped by most times he came to town, pinched Jeremiah's toes, and talked real soft to Clara. Left her a Bible I never caught her looking at, but maybe she did. Even a good baby gets tiresome when you don't know what he's saying back to you.

I did better than I thought I would collecting a retirement purse for Reverend Barnes, and we decided to give it to him early so him and Faith would know what they could count on. Easter was coming mid-April that year and we decided that was when we'd hold the party for them. Nobody was pushing things except maybe Big Mary. Most of us, even me by that time, didn't see why Convention had to make a theological issue of it, if that's what was happening. After all, Pastor had preached ecumenism to us and it could be stretched to fit. But Isaiah himself was for due process, as he put it to me, the lawyer.

It was Clara, squinting into the early dark, noticed Big Mary going by most nights when the snow was cleared, driving up past Lookout Point. If I was behind the bar, Clara'd call out—whether I had a customer or not—"There she goes!" An hour or two later, Mary'd come down again. Clara was clocking her. I wasn't. She figured Mary was taking him up a warm supper and looking for a little cuddling. I thought it'd be easier to cuddle with a giraffe, but I didn't say so.

Spring always comes if you believe in it. The cardinal's song was almost musical, the willow trees were getting yellower, and Isaiah Teague took to dropping by the inn late of an evening—well after Big Mary had come

down from whatever she'd gone up for. We included customers if there were any, me fiddling and the reverend
singing out the words of hymns we'd heard since childhood. Now and then I'd lapse into country, and once
Clara picked up her skirts and skipped into a solo performance of the Virginia reel. I remembered how she first
got into trouble dancing wild with Reuben. The switch
Maudie took to drive him out with was still in a corner of
the bar. Sometimes Isaiah would tell us what it was like
preaching and singing gospel and when he got carried
away with the message, dancing for God. He showed us
a step or two and you could tell he'd been a real prancer
in his youth. Clara made bold to ask him right out if he
didn't have a wife and kids somewhere. He gave her that
quick smile I'd almost forgotten and said, "Don't you
have a husband somewhere?"

Mind, all this congeniality didn't go on for very long.
The days were getting longer and I thought it a miracle Big
Mary hadn't walked in on us. I don't suppose I'll ever
know how she'd've taken to it. She was a blood relative of
Reuben White, and he was a live one. Alive, that is. I had
a little legal business I could only put my mind to after
Jeremiah was laid down for the night, and I must've missed
the stories Isaiah told of preaching on the open road, stories
that went to work on Clara's imagination. She asked me
once if I'd ever known of any women evangelists and I told
her what I could remember hearing about Aimee Semple
McPherson. She was even before my time.

I don't like to say it had anything to do with April Fools'
Day, but on the first Sunday in April Pastor announced he
had a letter to read us from Convention. I was in church
because of a meeting afterward of the retirement committee.
There was a rumble of satisfaction at the dispensation they
granted us to hire the Reverend Isaiah Teague. Isaiah sat
up there alongside Pastor, stiff and straight, and kept that
come-and-go smile under control, though I could see a
twitch getting loose now and then.

What Pastor didn't read out was the Convention's consideration that Reverend Teague expected to marry soon. The word got out almost as soon as if he'd read it. I guess we all knew who we thought leaked it, but we didn't say so. We just congratulated Isaiah on coming through and thanked Mary Toomey for getting the petition to Convention in the first place. But it set me to wondering what else Pastor had kept from us over the years. I was thinking of how late he was called that night to Billy Baldwin's and how he kind of groped his way through Billy's funeral. And then I thought of how natural he took to the idea of retiring. If it was me, I thought—after all those years of ministering—I'd've straightened my back, spit in the wind, and stayed till they carried me out. It was as though he had something on his conscience he'd not been able to hand over to the Lord. It made me feel guilty, and then when I thought how much money people had come up with for the retirement gift, I was pretty sure a lot of Webbtown folk felt the same way I did.

I dreaded telling Clara the news, thinking how it meant an end to those cozy evening visits from Isaiah. We'd never talked to one another about why he came. We'd made fun of Big Mary's courtship—I guess you'd call it that—never believing for a minute—I know I didn't—that she'd win.

"Won't make any difference," Clara said. "He ain't going to abandon us, Hank. We'll just be his hermitage and she won't ever know."

"Clara, this ain't New York City or Paris, France." Where I'd been once after the war. The very idea of him coming up to us, a married man, made me feel guilty, even though there was nothing sinful in those visits. That I knew about anyway.

"I know what it's like to be in prison, Hank. That's what Maudie wanted to marry me into—and what I had fifteen years of when the only green I ever saw was when I stood on the toilet and looked out the window. He's a wild bird,

Hank. Big Mary's crazy if she thinks she can keep him in
a cage."

I felt the same. I didn't know what was coming, and I
didn't want to know.

• • •

ISAIAH was to preach the morning of the retirement party.
He invited Clara to attend, even threatened to come and
get her himself if she didn't come with me. I was of two
minds, at least two minds, knowing how unpredictable
Clara was, but thinking it'd be as good a time as any to
introduce Jeremiah to the congregation since he was already a Christian boy. When Clara said they'd be there, I
went up to Ragapoo City and bought him a nice outfit out
of my own pocket. Clara let me. She had money since the
state bought a section of McCracken land, but she was
saving every penny now for Jeremiah. I was nervous helping get him dressed on Sunday morning, even more when
Clara came down wearing a dress I hadn't seen for over
fifteen years. It was black and fit her snug, and just the way
she wore it at her trial, she had a red handkerchief at her
throat.

The ones in church ahead of us fell silent when we were
ushered down near the sanctuary, Clara holding Jeremiah
out front of her like he was a little king. I don't remember
much about myself, except that I was wearing my good
suit.

When Isaiah stepped up to the pulpit, he was carrying a
bundle of letters. He made a little bow toward Pastor, who
sat in his usual place aside so the pulpit didn't block him
from the congregation's view, and said he had in hand the
tributes of a grateful parish, which he'd present to Pastor
by and by. I guess he said how grateful he was to all of us
for promising to call him, and I know he did mention Mary
Toomey by name. She was on the other side of the aisle
from us. I saw heads turning her way, but I didn't look and

Clara didn't look, I don't think even at Jeremiah, just straight at Isaiah.

Then he told us what brought him to Webbtown.

He'd been preaching in a town he'd never heard of in the mountains to the south, and a woman stood up and told him of her terrible pain—she'd lost a son to murder and his name was Reuben White. Isaiah told us how he was able to help her and her family heal a wound festering a whole generation. They didn't expect any peace in this world unless they got revenge. That's what they lived for. I think this is what he said: "With God's help I persuaded her family, one by one, to bring their anger to Jesus and their suffering, and let go of their bitterness." And I know he said this: "Shall I tell you the Lord's message to me? He told me there was healing to be done in the town they moved away from, a whole town that needed healing but needed first to tell its sins and sorrow." He preached for maybe an hour, straight out of the Bible, things we'd never heard just that way before. Even Jeremiah seemed to listen. Clara seemed dead alive, if you know what I mean, frozen.

But he wound up thanking us again and saying he was going to preach this coming week at River Junction, starting a new tour. "I thought I had the makings of a pastor," he said, "but I'm only an evangelist trying to make straight the way of the Lord."

The party went on, but neither Clara nor Big Mary stayed for it. It turned out to be a pretty good welcome to Parson Barnes, asking him and Faith to unpack.

I went back after taking Clara and Jeremiah home. The only thing Clara said that I remember, "I ain't going up to River Junction." She kept saying it now and then for the next day or so.

Finally I said, "Well, maybe River Junction will come down to you."

"Better not," she said, and then brightened up. "It won't be coming down to Big Mary, will it?"

I didn't say anything. I didn't like that "Better not."

Then, as I was going home that night, and I hadn't been home much lately—home was getting to be where Jeremiah was and maybe needing me—as I was going out the door she called me back. "I want you to take Pa's shotgun with you, Hank. And you'd better hide it somewhere good in case I ever ask for it back."

THE DIAMOND G-STRING

by Mickey Friedman

I

HER name was Gigi Dahl, but the Lobby Lizards called her The Sexpot. When Gigi flitted through their domain in her short shorts and tight tank top, with her even briefer costume (sequins, tassels, a filmy pink wrap trimmed with ostrich feathers) on a coat hanger, Marva Trout would raise her eyebrows and murmur, "There goes The Sexpot." Lilith Gervase would close one eye in a fluttery wink.

As far as anyone could remember, petite, tousle-haired Gigi was the first exotic dancer to live at the Estelle Peavy Residence for Women. The neighborhood was raffish, to be sure. The Marvelous Mile section of Cape St. Sebastian, Florida, was a collection of honky-tonks, cheap carnivals, video arcades, and hot-sheet motels strung along the shore of the Gulf of Mexico. In the midst of it all, the Peavy Residence recalled a more refined era in the history of this Redneck Riviera resort.

Marva Trout, chronicler and observer of that era, could expound on it by the hour to those few with the time and patience to listen. Marva remembered when the Peavy Res-

idence was the Hacienda Hotel, a small jewel of stucco and
red tile set amid cabbage palms and oleanders. Estelle
Peavy, a wealthy citizen who never recovered from her dis-
may at the excesses of the flapper days, had rescued the
place from decrepitude and endowed it in her will. As the
Estelle Peavy Residence, the former Hacienda provided
cheap, long-term accommodation for women of slender
means who were willing to do without male companion-
ship—on the premises, at least. From its vantage point on
the Marvelous Mile, the Peavy Residence maintained a
slightly seedy gentility in the midst of neon gaudiness.

Even though Gigi Dahl spent her evenings gyrating at
the Stowaway Lounge, Marva and Lilith, the self-styled
Lobby Lizards, didn't dislike her. Far from it! Gigi had a
personality as bouncy as her anatomy. She struck a pose
and allowed Lilith to sketch her for Lilith's book of "character studies." She listened patiently while Marva ex-
pounded on the Union blockade of Cape St. Sebastian
during the Civil War. Gigi lent a bit of flash to life at the
Residence, which on the whole tended to be on the boring
side of placid. In a milieu where finding a smudge on a
fresh tablecloth could provide conversation fodder for days,
Gigi was a godsend.

Her disappearance (if indeed she had disappeared) was
perplexing. Could sweet Gigi have come to harm?

The answer was unclear. Gigi was a flighty young thing
who kept irregular hours and often wasn't seen in the lobby
or dining hall for days on end. It took a while before anyone
got worried about Gigi Dahl.

As so often happened, Marva Trout sounded the alarm.
Wandering through the corridors in an effort to keep abreast
of events, Marva passed the door of Gigi's room. She noticed, barely protruding from beneath it, a sliver of fluores-
cent pink paper. That particular paper had been used for
flyers announcing the Residence Arts and Crafts Festival,
flyers that had been slipped under everyone's door at
least—Marva calculated back—at least four or five days

ago. Surely, had Gigi been in her room since that time, she would have picked up the flyer? Yet there it lay.

Marva removed a hairpin from the coils of her gray bun. With the tip of the pin, she speared the corner of the pink sheet and pulled it toward her. It was indeed the Festival flyer. Marva knocked, then rattled the knob of Gigi's locked door. Getting no response, she marched straight downstairs to the office of the resident manager.

When Emily Pye, deep in paperwork at her desk, looked up to see Marva in the doorway, her rabbity face fell. Marva noticed, of course. She said, "Yes, it's me again."

Emily sighed and tugged the bow at the neck of her blouse. She said, "Marva, the answer is still no. If I do it for you, I have to do it for everyone."

Marva was writing an epic poem. Her request to use the office photocopier to reproduce *Legend and Legacy: The Saga of Cape St. Sebastian* was a constant bone of contention. Annoyed at being mentioned in the same breath with "everyone," she said, "You're being very shortsighted, Emily. I hope you won't regret it later." She did not add, "When my poem is recognized for the masterpiece it is," but the thought was in her mind. Instead, she waved the pink flyer and said, "Have you seen Gigi Dahl lately?"

Emily shrugged. "I don't believe so. Why?"

"I think she may be missing."

Emily Pye, being Emily Pye, was uninterested in "upsetting the applecart," as she put it after Marva explained her concern about Gigi Dahl. Emily pointed out that Gigi was an adult with a life of her own. If she chose not to return to her room, that was not a problem until her rent was in arrears, which it would not be for another three and a half weeks. Emily suggested, in pointed terms, that Marva turn her attention to her own concerns. Marva left the office, steaming.

As usual, Marva's friend Lilith Gervase was in the lobby, sitting on the centrally placed rattan sofa the Lizards had appropriated for their exclusive use. From this vantage point they were able to monitor the comings and goings of all residents and visitors, greet their friend Jonah the postman, inspect and speculate about floral bouquets and other deliveries, and be prepared to exit quickly in case something exciting happened outside.

Marva harrumphed loudly to signal her approach, but Lilith did not look up. Lilith, like Marva, was a widow and a retired schoolteacher. She was also an artist. Today she was working in watercolor, her dreamy study of seagulls and sand dunes propped on a small easel.

Although the women were about the same age—i.e., not spring chickens—the two were dissimilar physically. Marva was buxom, solid, and sensible, her wardrobe running to seersucker shirtwaists and styled-for-comfort sandals. Lilith, on the other hand, decked her spindly frame in Indian-print skirts or natural linen shifts with macramé insets, and wore brightly patterned African leather thongs on her feet.

Marva plopped down on her end of the sofa, dislodging her carelessly strewn notebooks and research materials, and proceeded to tell Lilith that Gigi Dahl had disappeared and Emily Pye was an idiot. As she listened, Lilith nibbled the tip of her brush handle and stole looks at her painting. When Marva ran dry Lilith said, in her tinkly voice, "Do you suppose Gigi's gone away with her boyfriend?"

Marva stared. "Boyfriend? What boyfriend?"

"She had a boyfriend. Someone special." Lilith dabbed at her watercolor scene.

"She never said anything about a boyfriend to me." By Marva's standards, this was a serious lapse of decorum.

"She mentioned him a few weeks ago," said Lilith in an absentminded way. "I could see she was very pleased. She made me promise not to say anything to anyone." Her eyes widened, and she put her fingers to her lips. "Oh, dear," she said.

Now Marva was truly steamed. It was maddening enough that Gigi had confided in Lilith. It was even worse that Lilith, up until now, had respected Gigi's confidence, leaving Marva completely out of the loop. In frosty silence Marva stood up and stalked to the telephone booth in the hall, where she thumbed through the directory and found the number of the Stowaway Lounge.

A man answered. Loud music was playing in the background. Marva asked to speak to Gigi Dahl, and the man said, "What?"

"Gigi Dahl!" Marva raised her voice. "I want to speak to Gigi Dahl!"

"She's not here."

"Well, can you tell me where—" There was a click, and the connection was broken.

Marva slammed down the receiver and glared at it. Hang up on Marva Trout, would he? Marva didn't think so. Filled with resolve, she returned to the lobby.

Although Marva loved to hold a grudge, circumstances dictated that she must mend her fences with Lilith. The reason was straightforward: Lilith had a car, and Marva didn't. Mending fences turned out to be easy, however, since Lilith had no idea she and Marva had been at odds. She consented readily to Marva's suggestion that the two of them take a drive along the beach to the Stowaway Lounge.

II

IT was a blazing afternoon in May, the height of the season. The Marvelous Mile was choked with traffic. Pedestrians in various states of garish undress flocked to and fro buying seashells, T-shirts, sunblock, and cotton candy. Beyond the commercial strip was the beach, strewn with sunbathers, and the gleaming bay. As Lilith maneuvered her ancient Chevy into the flow of vehicles, Marva gave secret thanks for the slow pace. When driving, as at all other times, Lilith was in a world of her own, as likely to pay attention to cloud formations as traffic signals.

They reached the Stowaway Lounge without incident. It was an unprepossessing beige concrete-block establishment with a flat roof, surrounded by a cracking asphalt parking lot. Only when Lilith pulled into a space and turned off the coughing motor did Marva begin to have qualms about their field trip. Despite her long tenure in the neighborhood, she had never actually visited a strip joint.

The two of them got out of the car, trailed across the baking asphalt, and went in the front door. There were no windows in the Stowaway Lounge, and it took a few seconds for Marva's eyes to adjust. The two women were standing in a room that smelled of beer and cigarette smoke. Music of no discernible melody thundered and thumped. There was a bar near the door, and beyond it an array of tables and chairs. Perhaps a third of the seats were occupied, all by men. At the end of the room, on a small raised platform, a red-haired woman writhed as if in the grip of severe appendicitis. Her outfit consisted of spike-heeled sandals and a fluffy white boa.

Marva wiped her palms on her khaki skirt. Her intention was to speak with the manager and demand to be told the whereabouts of Gigi Dahl.

"Can I help you, ladies?" The bartender leaning toward them was a pudgy, mustachioed man wearing a hibiscus-print shirt.

Marva began, "I'd like to speak to—"

"A gin and tonic, please," Lilith put in.

Lilith didn't seem to notice Marva's reproving look. "Coming right up," the bartender replied, and busied himself fixing Lilith's drink. When she had it in hand, she drifted nearer the stage and took a seat at one of the tables.

Giving up on her, Marva said to the bartender, "I'd like to speak with the manager, please."

"He isn't here," the bartender said. "Is it about that zoning ordinance again?"

"No, it is not." The music was getting on Marva's nerves. How could anyone concentrate in this racket?

"Well, what's it about, then?" the bartender said, and added, "ma'am," as an afterthought.

"I'm looking for one of your dancers. Gigi Dahl."

The bartender shook his head. "She's not here."

Marva was unsatisfied. "Where is she?"

"You got me."

Marva didn't care for this fellow's attitude. Raising her voice to make sure he could hear her over the music, she bellowed, "Young man, I asked you a civil question and you owe me a civil answer! *Where is Gigi Dahl?*"

While she was speaking, the music reached a crescendo and then stopped abruptly, as the throes of the dancer onstage came to a halt. Marva's question about the whereabouts of Gigi Dahl reverberated through the suddenly silent room, causing heads to turn and sending a ripple of comment through the audience.

Gripping his crimson forehead with his fingertips, the bartender said, through clenched teeth, "Ma'am, I'm telling you I don't know where she is. She quit last week. No forwarding address. All right?"

Marva glowered at him. Out of the corner of her eye she caught a glimpse of Lilith, who was chatting with the red-haired dancer.

"You're causing a disruption. Don't force me to ask you to leave," the bartender was saying.

Marva was nothing if not stubborn. "I want to speak to the manager!"

"I am the manager, dammit," the bartender growled. "Now go."

When they had exited to the parking lot, Lilith sighed with contentment. "That was lovely, Marva. Thank you so much for suggesting it."

"I'd better drive. You had that gin and tonic," said Marva grimly.

"If you like." Lilith surrendered the keys and climbed in

the passenger seat. While Marva endeavored to get the motor started, Lilith mused, "That dancer is such a beautiful girl. She promised to let me sketch her sometime."

Marva was having no luck with the Chevy. As the motor failed to catch for perhaps the fifteenth time, a figure loomed at her window. She turned her head to see the red-haired dancer, who was now dressed in shorts, a "Souvenir of Cape St. Sebastian" T-shirt, and sunglasses.

"I heard you asking about Gigi in there," the dancer said.

"Did you?" Marva said. The girl had excellent hearing, to go along with her other attributes.

"Just thought I'd tell you she left last week. She quit."

Marva gave her a thin smile. "So I understand."

"She was getting married. She was so excited."

"How wonderful!" Lilith trilled.

Marva gave up trying to start the car. "Married? Really?"

The redhead leaned down to rest her elbows on the window frame. "She had a rich boyfriend. She was crazy about him. They eloped last week."

"Goodness me," Marva said. This was unexpected. Fleetingly, she wondered, Why wouldn't Gigi have come back to her room for her things? Why wouldn't she give notice at the Residence, if she was leaving? Why wouldn't she tell anyone her good news? "Do you know the man?" she asked the dancer.

The dancer shook her head. "Gigi wouldn't let him come into the club. She never even told me his name. She would meet him out here in the parking lot after she got off work."

"Did you ever see him? When they met out here?"

"No. I admit I was curious, but they met way over there in the far corner." She sighed. "Gigi's a lucky girl. I just hope it happens to me one day."

"It will, dear, don't you worry," Lilith said, and the dancer smiled, waved good-bye, and ran back to the lounge.

Eventually, Lilith had to move over and start the car. While she did so, Marva stood in the parking lot, thinking.

So Gigi Dahl had gotten married. Perhaps she was still honeymooning, besotted by love. One day, she would come back to pick up her possessions. In the meantime, Marva had spent enough time on this nonsense. She had an epic poem to write.

Marva got into a minor fender bender on the way home, but there was no real damage. Lilith, unconcerned, thanked her again for the outing. The mystery of Gigi Dahl, it seemed, had been solved.

III

THE next day Marva was sitting on the rattan sofa in the lobby, pen in hand and open notebook on knee. She was unaccompanied, since it was the hour of Lilith's yoga class. A few other residents read or worked crossword puzzles, and in a secluded corner there was a bridge game going, as usual. Marva was always ready to reprimand the players if their conversation grew loud enough to disturb her concentration.

Marva was about to begin a new section of her Cape St. Sebastian poem. Canto IV was to be "Dreams of Steam: The Coming of the Railroad," and Marva was trying to think of words rhyming with "steel." There was "wheel," of course; and "reel," and "feel," and "congeal," and—

"Excuse me just a moment, ladies, please!"

Marva blinked. Emily Pye was standing in the middle of the room. Beside her was a man who looked to be in his late forties. He had thinning brown hair of a conservative length, and the tortoiseshell-rimmed glasses he wore gave a professorial air to his broad, pale face. His ears stuck out. His potbelly was putting a strain on the buttons of his short-sleeved plaid shirt. "Ordinary" would have been a flattering assessment of his looks. "I'd like to introduce Rex Ogden, our new desk clerk," Emily Pye said. "Rex will be working the night shift five evenings a week." She gestured at Rex, who smiled and raised a hand in a Queen Elizabeth wave around the room. "I hope we'll all welcome Rex to the Estelle Peavy family and give him any help he needs. Thank you."

Before Emily Pye and Rex Ogden were out the lobby door, Marva had forgotten their existence. Let's see, there was "feel," and "congeal," and "spiel," and—

Within a couple of days, Rex Ogden had established himself as a great favorite at the Peavy Residence. Part of his appeal, to be sure, stemmed from the all but total lack of male competition. Beyond that, Rex had a rambunctious joviality that made stopping at the front desk for a key, or picking up mail, a more personal encounter than it normally was. "Room twenty-five! Yes sirree-bob!" Rex would cry, rolling backward in his chair to retrieve the contents of a pigeonhole behind him. "There you go, madam! All righty-roo!"

In addition to greeting the public and manning the antiquated switchboard, Rex took a special interest in the mail. He made it a point to re-sort the letters, magazines, and junk communications distributed, often haphazardly, by the day clerk, and he scrutinized the daily intake of packages to make sure they reached the correct recipients. Since Lilith received a constant stream of mail-order vitamins, minerals, and herbal supplements from a company called Fountain of Youth, Inc., she and Rex were soon on the best of terms.

Marva was standing by one evening when Rex, with mock gallantry, took Lilith's hand and brushed his lips over her fingers while giving her her latest shipment of zinc capsules. "Fountain of Youth! If you get any younger, we'll have to buy a cradle for you!" he joked.

Watching her friend's face go pink, Marva snorted. Rex Ogden had never taken Marva's hand, or gotten anywhere near her fingers with his unimpressive lips, and he'd better not try. As she and Lilith proceeded to the dining hall for supper, Marva said, "I'd wash my hand if I were you. That's a good way to pick up germs."

"Such a darling man," said Lilith, clutching her Jiffy bag to her scrawny chest.

Marva dropped it. "Spaghetti night," she said, referring to the upcoming evening meal. "I hope they've adjusted the sauce. I don't want to have to tell them again."

The kitchen staff, however, had ignored Marva's suggestions and used far too much oregano. In retaliation, Marva left her spaghetti untouched after the first taste, eating only her roll, salad, and chocolate pudding. As a result she was awakened, in the small hours of the morning, by overwhelming hunger pangs. Her stomach rumbling, Marva told herself her blood sugar would plummet to dangerously low levels if she didn't get something more to eat. Another chocolate pudding, perhaps two, would hold her nicely until morning.

Raiding the kitchen after hours was against Peavy Residence rules, but Marva had concluded long ago that rules existed to keep others in check while Marva did exactly as she pleased. She put on her tartan robe and terrycloth slides, stuck her head out the door to make sure the coast was clear, and slipped out into the dimly lighted corridor.

The most direct route to the kitchen was via the musty and little-used back stairs, rather than the grander wrought-iron staircase that curved down to the lobby and the front desk. On her way Marva passed, once again, the room formerly occupied by Gigi Dahl.

Marva stopped in her tracks. There was a light under Gigi's door.

Or was there? It had been a brief, pale glimmer, nothing more, a sweeping flashlight beam, perhaps. Now, a mere instant later, all was darkness.

Marva stepped to Gigi's door and tapped. In a low voice she said, "Gigi? Are you in there?" After a pause she tried, "Is anybody in there?" Neither question got a response. As she had done before, Marva tried the knob. The door was locked.

Marva rarely doubted herself. If she truly believed she had seen a light she would stick to her guns until Judgment Day, trampling all evidence to the contrary. In this case, though, she felt uncharacteristically uncertain. Her famished condition could well have brought on a mild hallucination. If this was the case, the important thing was to get some food into her stomach before she fell deeper into delirium. She continued along the corridor toward the back stairs.

Once in the kitchen, however, she felt uneasy. Suppose she was not hallucinating, and the light had been real? She should alert someone, make sure she was the first to report it. Without even stopping to check the refrigerator, she pushed through the swinging doors into the dining hall, and crossed to the passage leading to the lobby.

Rex Ogden was at his post, in his chair behind the front desk. He didn't see Marva, who was approaching from behind. When she was fairly close, Marva intoned, "Rex, I have something to report to you."

Rex started violently. He whirled toward Marva and said, "Yikes!"

Marva Trout might not be a vision of loveliness in her tartan robe, but she considered "yikes" a rude and ungentlemanly comment. It didn't help when Rex took out his handkerchief and, mopping his brow with a shaking hand, amplified his remarks by saying, "My God, you nearly scared me to death."

"I apologize," Marva said in her coolest tone. She went on, "I was in the upstairs corridor just now. I thought I saw a light in the room of Gigi Dahl, who has been away for a week or more. Has anyone had occasion to go in there?"

Stowing his handkerchief, Rex crossed his arms over his ample chest and settled his palms in his armpits. He was flushed, and a bit breathless. He said, "What room number would that be?"

"Forty-two."

Marva's eyes strayed to the Peg-Board mounted on the wall of Rex's cubicle, where room keys were hung. There, in the fourth row, hung the key to number forty-two. Marva would swear that it was swinging, ever so gently, on its hook. She was staring at it so hard she almost missed Rex's assurances that not a soul could have been in that room during the evening and all had been completely quiet until Marva showed up.

The key *had* been swinging. Marva would almost swear it. Almost. If she was right, the person poking around in Gigi Dahl's room had been Rex himself.

Marva returned to the kitchen, where she discovered that after all there were no leftover chocolate puddings. She had to make do with a jelly doughnut intended for breakfast a few hours hence. Chewing the gooey pastry, she thought about Rex Ogden.

IV

LACK of sleep and a touch of indigestion put Marva in a cranky mood that day. She took it out on Lilith, who was doing sketch studies for an oil portrait of Rex Ogden. Rex had refused point-blank to sit for her, claiming to be too busy, but Lilith had sneaked enough looks at him to reproduce his image from memory.

Marva, meanwhile, kibitzed and criticized. "Who's that supposed to be? Rex Ogden or Clark Gable?" she said, craning her neck at Lilith's sketchbook.

"Rex does resemble Clark Gable, just a bit," said Lilith serenely.

"Ha! You mean because his ears stick out like Gable's did?"

Lilith continued drawing, maddeningly impervious.

The front door banged, and Jonah the postman trundled by, laden with his stuffed leather mailbag. Jonah, a spindly

young man the color of café au lait, was a longtime chum
of the Lizards. When he saw them he waved and said,
"Hey, Lilith! I got some more vitamins for you! You want
me to give them to you now, or leave them at the desk?"

Marva beckoned him over. "Take a look at those draw-
ings, Jonah," she said, gesturing at Lilith's sketch pad.
"Who do they look like to you?"

Stroking his chin, Jonah studied the sketches. "I'm not
sure," he said at last. "Harrison Ford, maybe?"

Marva rolled her eyes. Lilith smiled. "There is a suggestion of Harrison Ford," Lilith agreed.

Jonah, meanwhile, was rummaging in his mailbag. "This
is for you, and this and this—" he said, pulling out Jiffy
bags and handing them to Lilith. "This one, too, I think—
no, wait a minute. That one's for Gigi Dahl."

Marva did not hesitate, even for a second. "Gigi's out
of town. She asked me to pick up her packages and hold
them for her," she said smoothly. She held out her hand
for the innocuous-looking cardboard mailer, about the size
and shape of a videotape box.

How simple things could be sometimes! With no ado,
Jonah gave Marva the package. "I thought I hadn't seen
Gigi around lately," he said. He hitched his bag higher on
his shoulder and, saying good-bye, continued to the front
desk.

Gigi's package was light, almost light enough to be
empty. Her name and address were typed on a printed label
for something called DRU, Inc., with an address in New
York City. There was no indication of what sort of business
DRU, Inc., was in. The package was taped up so tightly
there was little leeway for it to come unwrapped accidentally, which was a shame. Marva shook it. There was no
rattle, or tinkle, or any other clue as to what might be inside.

Lilith seemed completely absorbed in rendering the cleft
in Rex Ogden's chin, but after a few minutes she said, with
the schoolmarmish intonation she got sometimes, "Marva,

Gigi didn't really ask you to look after her packages."

What difference, Marva wondered, did that make? "Something strange is going on. Something strange about Gigi," she said. "I intend to find out what it is."

Lilith sighed. "Rex has worked so hard to organize the mail distribution. You're going to ruin all his good work if you take packages that don't belong to you."

Rex's good work. Marva had never heard anything so ridiculous. She showed her opinion of Rex's work by raising her meaty shoulders in a contemptuous shrug.

The tip of Lilith's nose was pink. "It's wrong," she said, beginning to sound shrill. "You lied, and you interfered with the U.S. Mail. Interfering with the mail is a crime, Marva."

Marva Trout had been furious in her time. Frequently, in fact. But rarely had she been as furious as she was with Lilith Gervase at this moment. To keep herself from scratching Lilith's eyes out, she rose majestically and said, "I see no point in continuing this idiotic discussion." With Gigi's package firmly in hand, she swept out of the lobby and up the stairs to her room.

Dinner that night was not a congenial occasion. Marva and Lilith ate their chicken à la king and banana cake in total silence. When Marva had finished eating, she spoke for the first time, saying, "Excuse me," as she rose to flounce out of the dining room. Instead of going to the television lounge to watch the British Parliament on C-SPAN, as she would normally have done, she returned to her room to sulk.

Gigi Dahl's package lay unopened on Marva's dresser, where it had been all afternoon. Marva picked it up and studied it again.

Lilith's accusations rankled. Marva had lied, she said. Well, that was true, but it had been in a good cause, the cause of satisfying Marva's curiosity. Lilith also said Marva had interfered with the U.S. Mail, but how could you call it interference when the postman himself had handed her the package? If anyone got in trouble for that, it should be Jonah.

So, up to this point, Marva was innocent of all charges. It had never been in Marva's character, though, to quit while she was ahead. She would, therefore, proceed with the next obvious step and open the package.

She had imagined doing it in such a way that the package could be rewrapped, but that proved impossible. The tape was extremely strong, and was not about to let go without being cut to pieces. At last, Marva uncovered a lightweight Styrofoam container. Nestled snugly inside, in a niche shaped to fit it exactly, was an oblong box made of midnight-blue velvet. She opened the velvet box.

It was a necklace. A delicate chain of some silvery material—platinum, Marva supposed—was hung with six dangling charms, each a letter *G* created out of glittering diamonds. It was breathtaking, and Marva could imagine how lovely it would look around Gigi Dahl's tanned and seamless neck. She removed the necklace from its box and held it up to the light. Gigi, Gigi, Gigi, it seemed to say.

There was something else, she noticed, a small white envelope tucked in the curved top of the box. She retrieved it. On the outside was scrawled, *To Gigi Dahl, my precious Doll.* Inside, on the plain white card within, was written, *Here's a G-string from your very own Boopsie.*

Hmm. This must be a present from the rich boyfriend, the one Gigi had presumably married a week or more ago. It seemed odd that the happy couple hadn't made arrangements to have this very expensive gift intercepted, instead of leaving its fate to chance and Marva Trout. Or to the mail-conscious night clerk, Rex Ogden. For that matter, why had the bauble been sent by regular mail, and not even insured?

The G-string necklace shimmered under the lamp on Marva's dresser. The sight of it did not gladden Marva's heart. Marva was worried, very worried, about The Sexpot, Gigi Dahl.

As further cause for concern, Marva had now well and truly tampered with the U.S. Mail. Until Gigi turned up, or Marva found out what had happened to her, it would be just as well to conceal the evidence of her infraction. This was no problem. When Marva sold her modest suburban bungalow and came to live at the Peavy Residence, she had been nervous about the trustworthiness of her neighbors. She had engaged her nephew, an enthusiastic amateur carpenter, to construct for her a secret compartment in the headboard of her bed. In this small hidey-hole behind a section of bookshelf she had secreted bits and pieces of jewelry, various significant documents, and a packet of letters from a certain gentleman with whom she had once carried on an intense correspondence. Although in latter years she had rarely used the hidden space, this seemed a perfect occasion for it.

Marva took out a short row of books in front of the fake shelf back, removed the back by pressing on one corner, and stashed Gigi Dahl's necklace in its packaging within. She replaced everything and dusted her hands. That would do very well until she decided on her next move.

V

THE following day brought no thaw in relations between Marva and Lilith. Each sat on her prescribed end of the sofa, stiffly pretending to work while covertly peeking to see what the other was doing. Communication was minimal and stiff. By the time the dinner hour arrived, the strain had so exhausted Marva she could eat no more than three servings of creamed corn along with her country-fried steak.

It didn't help matters that after dinner Lilith immediately draped herself over the front desk, giggling with the abominable Rex Ogden. To spare herself this display, Marva went upstairs, determined on an early night.

In her room, the tribulations continued. Somehow, one of the charming Hummel figurines on her whatnot shelf had fallen to the floor. He lay facedown on the carpet, a large chip knocked out of his Alpine hat. Marva did not remember bumping against the shelf, but she had been distracted all day by Lilith's outrageous behavior and perhaps had not noticed. She added the damaged Hummel to the list of Lilith's transgressions and, in a foul mood, climbed in bed. Worn-out by the stresses of the day, she fell instantly asleep.

Later, much later, her eyes flew open. Something terrible was happening. A hand was clamped over her mouth. A cold metallic object was tickling her ear. A voice, unpleasantly familiar, said breathily, "This is a gun, Ms. Trout. I'm going to let go of your mouth, and you're going to tell me where you put the package that was sent to Gigi Dahl."

It was—who else?—Rex Ogden. Marva shuddered at the chilly presence of the gun barrel at her ear, but it was not in her nature to capitulate easily. When he removed his disgusting hand from her mouth she said, "What package?"

The cold pressure increased markedly. Marva felt his breath on her hair. "You know what package. Lilith Gervase told me you took it from the postman."

Lilith! How could she! She had tattled, and thrown Marva to this slavering wolf of a desk clerk. If Marva got out of this alive, she would break Lilith's stringy neck.

"You outsmarted yourself by hiding it so well," Rex was saying. "If you'd put it where I could find it, this episode could have been avoided."

Rex had searched her room. The idea was revolting. "You broke my Hummel!" Marva said indignantly.

"I'll break more than your Hummel if you don't produce that package. Now."

He sounded as if he meant it. With a gun in her ear, Marva was not in a position to argue. She turned on her bed lamp, removed the section of books from her headboard, and opened her hiding place. When she handed him the Styrofoam container, Rex said, "You opened it, did you? Dumb, dumb, dumb."

Marva was stung. She despised having her intelligence impugned. "At least I don't call myself Boopsie," she said in a withering tone.

Rex ignored her. He slipped the necklace in his pocket and muttered, "All righty-roo." He waved the gun at Marva. "Let's go," he said.

"Go?" Marva was in her nightgown, white cotton batiste printed with pink roses. "Don't be absurd. I'm not going anywhere."

But she was. She barely had time to shrug on her tartan robe and slip her feet into her terrycloth slides. As a further indignity, Rex tied her hands roughly behind her back with her own tartan sash. Shoving her in front of him, the gun nudging the small of her back, he led her along the somnolent corridor to the back stairs, and out the kitchen door into the alley.

There was a car in the alley, a large black Mercedes sedan. Rex pushed Marva into the passenger side and buckled the seat belt across her. Since her wrists were still tied behind her back, this made for a terrible strain on the arms. Marva pressed her lips together tightly. She would not give Rex Ogden the satisfaction of hearing her cry out in pain. When she was secured Rex slammed her door and walked around to the driver's side, stowing the gun in his jacket pocket. He got in, started the car, and they purred down the alley, around the corner, and out onto the neon-washed Marvelous Mile.

The dashboard clock told Marva it was two-thirty in the morning. Even pleasure-seeking tourists have to sleep sometime, and the streets were mostly deserted. Marva doubted anyone would hear her if she screamed, since the car was closed and the air conditioner running. She began to face the fact that she was presently at the mercy of Rex Ogden.

A beeping sound, shrill and unexpected, caused Marva

to jump. Rex detached a cellular telephone from its cradle near the gearshift lever, punched a button, and answered. After a moment he said, "Yes, hello, Lois. No, dear, I'm afraid I'm still working." He glanced at Marva. "I won't be home for another hour, at least."

This information did not seem to please Lois. Rex's side of the conversation deteriorated into a litany of "Yes, dear," and "I'm so sorry, darling." In the end, he said, "If you'll bear with me, I promise we'll go on a long vacation as soon as—" Marva saw him wince. Without speaking again, he replaced the phone in its cradle. Under his breath he said, *"Gosh darn it."*

Marva was never one to remain cowed and silent for long. "Sounds as if your wife is annoyed," she said.

Rex drove on, his jaw clenched.

"That's why you couldn't marry Gigi. You were already married," Marva continued. "What happened? Did Gigi find out the truth?"

Marva thought she saw Rex's eyes moisten. "Gigi," he murmured brokenly.

They had left the Marvelous Mile behind, and were driving along the beach highway outside of town. Civilization thinned as Cape St. Sebastian receded in the distance.

Marva understood it all now. It was an old, tawdry story. "You strung Gigi along by pretending you'd elope with her. You tried to pacify her with fancy presents, like the diamond G-string."

"I ordered it custom-made for her in New York, when I was there on a business trip," Rex said, his voice hoarse. "It was going to be a surprise."

"But things came to a head before the necklace was delivered. Gigi found out what a rat you are, didn't she? What did she do? Threaten to tell your wife?"

"Lois would kill me if she found out. Kill me," Rex Ogden whispered. He blotted his damp eyes with his knuckles.

"So you killed Gigi instead." Marva said. Poor, poor Gigi Dahl!

"She said I was a lying scumbag," Rex whimpered. "I just—I didn't mean to hurt her."

The highway whizzed beneath them, a gray blur. On their left was the vast expanse of the Gulf of Mexico, with its breaking waves and twinkling buoys. Where oh where, Marva wondered, where will I be this time tomorrow? Will I be with Gigi in a shallow grave? She stared out the window morosely, Rex sniveling at the wheel.

"You had the necklace sent by regular mail so it wouldn't attract attention," Marva went on at last. "By the time it was due to arrive, Gigi was dead. You had to get the necklace back before her body was found, because it could be traced to you through the company—DRU, whatever that means."

"Diamonds R Us," Rex said. "They know me. It was a custom order. Nothing but the best for my Gigi."

"So you took a moonlighting job as our desk clerk for a few weeks, until you could intercept the package. But I intervened."

Rex gave her a poisonous look. "You mean you interfered, you nosy old bag."

"I'd rather be a nosy old bag than a vile, vicious killer."

There was nothing left to say. Marva shifted her weight, trying to ease the pain in her arms and shoulders. She thought about her Cape St. Sebastian poem. She had been making headway on Canto IV. The thought of *Legend and Legacy: The Saga of Cape St. Sebastian* remaining incomplete sent a jolt of fury through her. She would not succumb easily to Rex Ogden. If he wanted to deprive the world of *Legend and Legacy* he would have to struggle to do it.

Rex slowed down. He turned off the highway onto a narrow track leading into a tangle of live oak and palmetto scrub. Spiny branches waved in the headlights and scratched the sides of the car. He pulled into a clearing where, Marva could see, a patch of sand had been disturbed. Her eyes prickled. That must be Gigi Dahl's final resting place. Rex Ogden wanted it to be Marva's as well.

Rex turned off the engine and got out of the car. When he came around to the passenger door, the gun was once again in his hand. He opened the door and reached across Marva to unhook the seat belt.

This was Marva's chance, maybe the only one. Released, she heaved herself forward as hard as she could into Rex's soft, pendulous belly. She heard him say, "Oof!" as the breath left his body, felt him lose his footing and stagger backward. She surged out of the car and, her hands still bound, took off through the underbrush.

She heard wheezing behind her. A shot rang out. She ignored the brambles tearing at her robe and gown, ignored the fact that at the first step she had stumbled out of her slides and was charging over the unforgiving vegetation barefoot. She put her head down and pressed forward.

Something unexpected happened.

Headlights. Headlights visible through the branches and leaves, headlights bumping down the road from the highway.

A siren growled. Doors slammed. She heard voices, saying something about freezing and dropping weapons. Behind her, a cry of frustration and anguish from Rex Ogden.

Suddenly it was over. Marva would live to compose Canto IV.

Later, when Rex had been bundled into a car and driven off with sirens wailing, Marva asked one of the deputies, a rawboned young man who found her slides for her and called her "ma'am," how the law happened to turn up at the critical juncture.

"We'd been looking for you, and we just caught sight of you when he turned off the road," the deputy said. "A woman called and alerted us. Mrs. Lilith Gervase. She said she was a friend of yours."

VI

MARVA Trout and Lilith Gervase, the Lobby Lizards, sat on their chosen sofa at the Estelle Peavy Residence. Shock and horror at the murder of Gigi Dahl had rocked the place. Emily Pye, who had hired the killer as a desk clerk, was hinting at taking early retirement from her job as resident manager. Rex Ogden had retained a good lawyer. Marva was eagerly anticipating her appearance on the witness stand.

Lilith was recounting, for the umpteenth time, her role in what was nearly Marva's last night on earth. "I couldn't sleep," she said. "I was upset about our disagreement, and miserably guilty that I had told Rex about the package. I tossed and turned, and tossed and turned, and finally I decided I would simply have to go to your room that very minute to wake you up and beg forgiveness."

Finding the room empty, and knowing Marva's penchant for raids on the refrigerator, Lilith had gone down the back stairs to the kitchen, glancing out a window just in time to see Rex put a gun in his pocket, get in the Mercedes, and drive off with Marva. The scales had dropped from her eyes, and she had rushed to call the police. "You really do forgive me, don't you, Marva?" Lilith pleaded.

"Certainly I do. You saved my life," Marva replied for the umpteenth time. She forbore to mention that had it not been for Lilith her life would not have been in danger. She forbore to mention that Lilith had been taken in by a loathsome murderer, while Marva had despised Rex Ogden from the outset. Marva could let it go. She could overlook Lilith's many failings and flaws. That was, after all, what friendship was about.

COMPLIMENTS OF A FRIEND

by Susan Isaacs

ON a chill and sodden Tuesday in March at one in the afternoon, the awesomely slender Deirdre Giddings, founder and CEO of Panache, the largest employment agency on Long Island, slipped into a chair in the designer-shoe department in Bloomingdale's in Garden City cradling a black snakeskin Manolo Blahnik slingback in her hands. She closed her eyes. A few minutes later, when Oliver, her usual salesman, gently tapped her shoulder and murmured, "Ms. Giddings? Seven and a half, right? *Ms. Giddings?*" he got no response. That was because she was comatose.

She passed from the world before the gray dawn of the following morning. The Nassau County medical examiner ruled her exit self-inflicted—an overdose of barbiturates. The Nassau County Police Department's spokesman (elbowing aside the ME so he could stand squarely in front of the microphone) announced that a suicide note had been found among her personal papers. When I came home from work that Wednesday evening and heard the first of four messages about her death on my answering machine— "Judith, did you hear . . . ?"—I wasn't just surprised. I was shaken.

Deirdre, of all people! So alive. Now, when I say "alive," I'm not talking about congenitally perky. I mean alive as in seemingly invulnerable. Dressed for success in a Prada suit and Gucci shoes, though I admit my grasp of fashion is a little iffy and it could have been the other way around. Anyway, her shoes were those clunky things that make me look clubfooted. However, on women like Deirdre, they look not merely stylish, they also make already slender legs appear even trimmer. Deirdre's hair? Blond, the expensive kind that gave off glints of platinum and gold. Her lips—outlined in burgundy, lipsticked in Chianti, glossed with a daring touch of strawberry—showed she was so much the captain of her fate that, while recognizing her own mortality, she could go for her mammogram without her guts in a knot.

Whenever I saw her at the semiannual meetings of the board of trustees of the Long Island Heritage Council, a group dedicated to preserving the region's historical sites, she was all business, never wasting even a microsecond. She'd stroll around the Peconic-Deutschebank's conference room exchanging power handshakes and networking with her fellow and sister hotshots—whereas I hung out with the other academic, an anthropologist from Southampton College, and watched while he wrapped the titanic bagels and raisin-glutted muffins on the hospitality table in napkins and stuffed them into his backpack.

But it would be inaccurate to think of Deirdre as a stereotypical career crone, hard-eyed and tight-lipped. Her face was peaches-and-cream pretty, with all-American apple cheeks. Her eyes were true blue. She had a pink rose petal of a voice. Further, she was unfailingly polite. Still, it was easy to understand how people could call her aloof. She seemed to hold back not from shyness, but as if getting to know you too well would inevitably be disappointing, and she truly preferred to think well of you. Not at all the brash glad-hander you'd expect from an employment-agency type.

That reticence not only made her stand out, but made people assume that the housemaids from Panache Home, the bookkeepers from Panache Office, and the pharmacists from Panache Professional were somehow endowed with Deirdre's cool professionalism.

At her funeral, the minister had called her "caring" because not even the most charitable Christian soul could go so far as "warm." However, for some reason, Deirdre was always cordial to me—so if not actually warm, at least tepid in the nicest possible way. She'd walk toward me with both hands outstretched. "Judith Singer." Then she'd grip my shoulders and stick out her head to bestow a kiss on the cheek. All right, so not an actual kiss: as her satiny, alpha-hydroxied cheek grazed mine, she merely made a chirping sound. But then she would draw back and regard me with something like satisfaction and inquire, "And how is my friend Judith doing?"

I hadn't the foggiest notion of how I rated her friendship. Outside of Council meetings, we never saw each other except in casual situations—coming out of Shorehaven Hardware on Main Street, or at the harbor band shell at the Sunday-night concerts each summer. Perhaps it was because we both lived in Shorehaven, a Long Island suburb which, despite being twenty-six miles from mid-Manhattan and filled with a fair number of urbane business types and cutting-edge professionals, had the aggressive neighborliness of an Andy Hardy movie.

To be honest, Deirdre's special treatment might have been pity: I was—am—a widow. For the past two years, since my husband, Bob, died half a day after finishing the New York Marathon in four hours and twelve minutes, I'd noticed that the same people who would treat a middle-aged divorcée with the same *tendresse* as they would a rabid dog could be surprisingly compassionate toward a woman who had lost her husband—as opposed to one who somehow sloppily allowed her man to slip through her fingers.

Or perhaps Deirdre was merely grateful to me. I am a historian who works two jobs. Half the time I'm adjunct professor of history at the formerly all-female, formerly nun-run, formerly first-rate St. Elizabeth's College across the county border in the borough of Queens; the other half I head my town's oral-history project at the Shorehaven Public Library. A few years earlier, Deirdre had come to me for help: a potential client, the president of Kluckers, a kosher-chicken distributor, wasn't sure if Long Island had the right "vibes" for his new corporate headquarters. I'd worked with her to compose a lively *précis* of the history of poultry farming on Long Island. Apparently, our effort wowed the guy. Naturally, I wouldn't take the money she offered for my work. So she'd sent the library a generous contribution and, to me, a gorgeously bound copy of *Leaves of Grass,* somehow having learned I'm a fool for Walt Whitman. Now she was dead.

"This Deirdre business has really gotten to me," I declared to my true friend Nancy Miller two nights later. "Not that I actually was her friend, even if that's what she called me, but . . ." Nancy was eagle-eyeing the waiter as he opened a bottle of Rosso di Montalcino, so I demanded, "Are you listening to me?"

"How can I avoid it?" We were in a new restaurant, La Luna Toscana. For some reason I cannot explain, whenever a new culinary trend gets under way in Manhattan, such as Tuscan cuisine, it gets out to Kansas City—with a side trip to Emporia—before it can manage to schlepp the twenty-six miles east to Shorehaven.

"About Deirdre . . ." I went on. "I'm upset . . . but not really touched . . . Shit, I wish I could find the right words to express what I feel."

"How about 'shocked and saddened'?" Nancy suggested. "Tell me, when Bob died, did you get one single note that didn't say, 'I was shocked and saddened to hear of your loss'? I mean—" Her "I mean" came out "Ah main." Although Nancy hasn't been back to her native

Georgia in thirty years, she has clung to its syrupy accents, convinced, correctly, that it adds to her charm. "I mean, did anyone even have the originality to say 'saddened and shocked'?"

"Of course not. But someone like Deirdre committing suicide? It *is* genuinely shocking. Look, I know no one can get through life without pain, but she seemed so impervious to the usual slings and arrows."

"Please. Stan Giddings dumped her for a younger woman." Nancy lifted her wineglass, held it to light, and looked perturbed. Once she took a sip, she shook her head with weariness and regret, but waved the waiter away. "Didn't he dump his first missus, too, for Deirdre?"

"Yes," I replied. "Her name is Barbara. It was all in your paper. Don't you read it, for God's sake?"

"Not the stories that pander to salivating semiliterates, though I sense that's most of our readership." Several years earlier, Nancy had given up freelance writing to become an associate editor of *Newsday*'s op-ed page. "When I want my trash, I go right to the New York *Post*. They do it right. None of this genteel suburban shit like, 'The medical examiner refused to speculate why Ms. Giddings chose to end her life in a department store after taking an overdose of the prescription drug Nembutal, a common sleep-inducing barbiturate.' " She finished off the wine in her glass and immediately poured herself another.

"Why not stick a straw into the wine bottle and just glug away?" I suggested. "Save all that tedious pouring."

"Why don't you put a cork in it about my drinking?"

With a sigh that I hoped was sufficiently passive-aggressive to induce guilt, I went back to the subject at hand. "A woman like Deirdre doesn't kill herself over a man."

"If she were crazy enough to actually marry that slick, do-nothing piece of work, you don't think she might decide to pack it in when he took a walk?"

"First of all," I said patiently, "he's not slick."

In fact, the couple of times I'd seen Stan Giddings—at the Long Island Heritage Council's annual dinner dance, on line at Let There Be Bagels, I'd found him pleasingly unslick. Tall, broad-shouldered, square-jawed, given to rumpled denim work shirts and tweedy jackets, he looked like an East Coast version of the Marlboro Man. His gray-flecked brown hair was longish, chopped more than cut, and his smile was wide, yet somehow sensual. It let you know he was aware you were woman and he was man—and that he was excited by the difference. A for-real smile, not that lips-together smirk of the ordinary Long Island lothario. A smile from a guy like Stan and you find yourself grinning back, so imbued with your own lusty wench-hood that you momentarily forget you're old enough to be his mother—had you experienced an extremely early menarche. You'd remember that smile, too—for days, or weeks, even though you knew that as soon as he smiled it you were already erased from his consciousness.

"He's not slick," I declared, "just smooth."

"I don't mean slick in the Michael-Douglas-slime-on-his-hair sense. Slick in that his charm has nothing to do with his feelings, assuming he has any." She set down her glass, picked up a bread stick, and snapped it in two. "Inherited money," Nancy observed.

Over the years I've become so used to her non sequiturs that such statements, coming from her, acquire their own logic. "Inherited money has something to do with being emotionally deficient," I articulated for her.

"Obviously."

"Not quite."

"Stan's money comes from socks, for Crissakes!"

"For the U.S. armed forces. From Iwo Jima to the Persian Gulf, and that's a lot of socks, enough to make his family incredibly rich for—what?—three generations. What do socks or being rich have to do with Stan's personality?"

Nancy shook the half bread stick at me the way a teacher

would shake a pointer at a deliberately dense student. "He
never had to earn a living. He never had to *do* anything.
He just had to *be,* and people would vacuum his floors and
groom his horse and admit him to Princeton and treat him
in every respect as if he had done something important."

I tried to come up with a piercingly clever rejoinder to
counter her argument, but I finally said, "You're right."

"Supposedly he runs the company. Except he spends two
months in Vail skiing. And two months up in Maine sailing.
And two months someplace warm golfing, plus everyone
knows that if he actually did run the company the only
place he'd run it is into the ground. He was born to play,
not to think. On the other hand," she added, "he's hung
like King Kong."

"How do you know that?"

"How do you think I know?" In Nancy's mind, Mount
Sinai was the place God had given Moses the Nine Com-
mandments. In her thirty-one years of marriage, at least
fourscore lovers had come—and gone.

"You slept with Stan?" Her head moved slightly: an ac-
knowledgement. "I can't believe you! How come you left
out this one?" I'd sometimes felt as if Nancy was relying
on me to be her official scorekeeper.

"It must have been when you were writing your doctoral
dissertation," Nancy muttered. "You were already over-
stimulated. How could I burden you? Anyhow, everyone in
town knows about his equipment."

"I don't."

"You! You can name every member of Roosevelt's cab-
inets from whenever—"

"From 1933 to 1945."

"—but anything truly interesting always comes as a surprise. 'Golly! You mean Stan Giddings has a foot-long hot
dog? No kidding!' By the way, he knows what to do with
it, too."

All I could say was, "Golly!"

"Of course, there's always the 'but,' " Nancy added.

"What's his?"

"He's an idiot ultraconservative and he can't stop babbling about it. It's like fucking Oliver North, except Stan has decent teeth."

"So if he's that much of a *dummkopf*, his leaving wouldn't have sent Deirdre over the edge."

"I heard something about other reasons," Nancy muttered to her wine.

"Like what?" I probably sounded a tad overeager because she responded with an elegant flaring of her nostrils. I leaned forward, rested my hands on the annoying, chic sheet of butcher paper the restaurant was using instead of a cloth, and demanded, "*What* other reasons?"

"Serious business reverses."

"Where did you hear that?"

She took a slow sip of wine. "I suppose as I wafted past the city room."

"How serious is 'serious'?" Nancy peered into her glass once again. She seemed surprised to find it empty, as though someone had sneaked over and drained it while she was talking. Shrugging, she poured herself another glass. I took my third sip of the night and, for the umpteenth time in the thirty-three years since we'd been in college together, worried about her liver. "Nancy, how bad were Deirdre's business reverses?"

"Why are you so interested?"

"Something's fishy."

"Nothing's fishy."

"I don't buy this suicide story."

She gripped the stem of her glass. "You're not thinking of doing a little detecting, are you, Judith?"

"Please!" I tried to act amused, but the derisive chuckle came out as if I were having some unpleasantness with phlegm. "I only did that once. Twenty years ago. A blip on the radar screen of life. It's just . . ."

"Just what?"

"Hear me out. Suicide makes no sense. Say you want to

kill yourself. But your whole persona is being one cool cookie. So you wouldn't do it violently, like leaping off an overpass into rush-hour traffic on the Northern State, would you? And if you're as meticulous as Deirdre, would you risk breaking a nail hooking up a hose to the exhaust of your car. No. You'd probably do the girl thing, take sleeping pills. Right?"

"Probably," she conceded, although reluctantly.

"And what would happen then? You might just go to sleep forever. But you could also upchuck and choke on your own vomit."

"Must you be so vivid before the first course?"

"And why in God's name would you choose to die in Bloomingdale's?" I continued. "Why would you be looking at shoes in the final moments of your life? Think, Nancy: if you were depressed enough to actively contemplate suicide, would you be worrying about what to wear with your new spring suit?"

"No. Accessorizing is definitely life-affirming."

"Also, if you're one of these controlled types like Deirdre," I went on, "are you going to risk dropping down dead over a display of Ferragamos and losing control of your bowels while you still have your panty hose on?" With that, I waved the waiter over and inquired how much garlic there was in the ribollita.

But after dinner, back home alone, I was still asking questions. So I hauled in the tied-up newspapers I'd put in the garage for recycling and sat in the kitchen. Intermittently, I was distracted by the noise of sleet against the window, like thousands of long-nailed fingers tapping impatiently against a glass tabletop. I read and reread Deirdre's obituary and everything about her death. There wasn't much. She'd been born Deirdre Graubart in Rockville Centre, a town on Long Island. She'd gone to Hofstra College, also on the Island, and after a brief stint (although I never heard of a stint that wasn't brief) working at a gigantic employment agency in the city, she'd founded Panache while still in her twenties. Her clients ranged from Kluckers to a computer software giant, from socialites to professional athletes. By the time she was in her early thirties, she had not only married Stan, but had also gotten him to build her a fifteen-room house on a bluff overlooking Long Island Sound, a place so abounding in Doric columns it was clear she had seen *Gone with the Wind* too many times during preadolescence.

One of the articles had a picture of Deirdre in a coatdress perched on the edge of her Louis the Somethingth desk. She was flanked on the left by a woman in a maid's uniform and a man holding a pipe wrench, and on the right by a man in a three-piece banker's suit and another in a one-piece mechanic's coverall. *Her former husband, Stanley Giddings,* the *Shorehaven Sentinel* reported, *could not be reached for comment, although a spokesman released a statement that said Mr. Giddings was shocked and saddened to learn of Deirdre's suicide.* The shocked and saddened Stan, the paper noted, had, three months earlier, married an artist who went by the name of Ryn, and had moved out of Shorehaven.

The next time I glanced up it was long past eleven o'clock. I'd made a nifty pile of clippings about Deirdre's death, arranged in chronological order, interspersed with older features about her career I found on the Internet. Why had I spent the night doing this when I had twenty-two first drafts of term papers on New Deal agencies to evaluate? Well, Deirdre had called me her friend. On the slim chance she hadn't been full of it, that she was truly so friendless that she considered a near stranger a friend, maybe I owed her something. Or it could have been a gut reaction— suicide is bullshit—and I've learned over the years my gut is right more often than wrong. Who knows? Maybe it was that after dinner with Nancy, on yet one more bleak night alone, a mystery was just what I needed to put a little life in my life.

My husband was gone. True, Bob and I hadn't had a

fairy-tale marriage. Still, even when all that's left is polite
conversation and predictable marital sex, you have to remember (I had told myself all those years) that once upon
a time it had to have been a love story. So I always half
expected the plot would get moving again: some incident
would touch off a great conflict, and lo and behold, not
only would the air finally become clear, but there'd be ro-
mance in it! The two of us would walk hand in hand into
a sunset, happily ever after—or until one of us went gently
into the night in our eighth or ninth decade.

Imagine my surprise when he died before my eyes in
the emergency room of North Shore Hospital. One minute
he squeezed my hand, a reassuring pressure, but I could
see the fear in his eyes. As I squeezed back, he slipped
away. Just like that. Gone, before I could say, "Don't
worry, honey, you'll be fine." Or, "I love you, Bob."

Not only no husband. No prospect of another one. Not
one more blind date, that was for sure, not after the two
Nancy referred to as Old and Older. Periodically, I went to
the movies or the theater with Geoff, a postmodernist from
the English department. I rarely understood what he was
talking about, and his clothes smelled as if he patronized a
discount dry cleaner. No one else was knocking at my door.
My son and daughter were grown, gone from the house.
So who knows? Maybe I was entertaining thoughts about
murder because it was one of those dark and stormy nights,
both without and within, when the notion of suicide—
anybody's—was so terrifying it had to be denied.

I should have felt better the next day. A smiley yellow
sun rose into an azure sky. In the cold air, I sniffed the first
sweetness of impending spring. Actually, I did feel better.
But that was probably because I was sitting across from Dr.
Jennifer Spiros, the number-two pathologist in the Nassau
County Medical Examiner's Office. "I'm not authorized to
give you a copy of the autopsy report," she said, taking her
time with each word. Her long, shiny *Alice in Wonderland*
hair was tied with a dainty blue ribbon with rickrack edges.

That was the good news. The bad was she had a rectangle of a face—along with such a thick neck she looked as if she was the result of her mother's quickie with a Lipizzaner stallion.

"I understand that you can't hand over the actual report," I replied. "But this is for Shorehaven Library's *oral*-history project." We both glanced at the red light on the tape recorder I'd set on her desk between us. Dr. Spiros moistened her lips with her tongue. "It's not a matter of documentation," I explained. "What I'm trying to capture here is the reality of a single death, a view from all perspectives of the passing of one citizen of Shorehaven. From Deirdre Giddings's friends and colleagues to her minister who gave the eulogy to . . . well, to the officials charged with investigating that death." Naturally, I didn't add that if news of this little caper got back to Shorehaven Library's administrator, Snively Sam, I'd be out of a job. I pressed on. "I understand she left a note?"

Dr. Spiros pressed her hands together, prayerlike, and held them demurely under her chin. "I'm not authorized . . ." Her nails, disturbingly long for a pathologist's, were a hideous purplish orangy pink, the color of a plastic flamingo at twilight.

I reached out and switched off the recorder. "On background," I said boldly, crossing my legs, more Rosalind Russell–*His Girl Friday* than historian. Except two seconds later my heart started to race. It demanded what my brain hadn't permitted itself to ask: what the hell was I doing here? Each heartbeat was more powerful than the one before, until my entire chest was filled with what felt like a life-threatening hammering. "I want to get the big picture," I was telling her. Was I nuts? Any minute she'd come to her senses and toss me out on my ear.

"The suicide note said something like 'I can't take it anymore,' " she was saying. " 'It's got to end.' That's about it."

"Was it signed?"

"Yes. Signed 'Deirdre.' On her personal stationery."

"Was it handwritten?" She nodded. "Was she carrying it with her?" I got a blank look. "In her handbag or her coat pocket. When she was at Bloomingdale's."

"No. It was . . ." She glanced at me, a little too suspiciously, but unable to figure out my angle, she continued. "In a manila folder right in her top desk drawer. The drawer was open slightly. The file was marked 'Personal Papers.' Her marriage certificate was in there. Her divorce decree. In a sense, she'd assembled her whole relationship with Stanley Giddings in that file."

I turned on the recorder again. "I'd like to go over what's been released publicly." She nodded, then lifted her hair and let it fall back onto her shoulders. Clearly, and not without reason, she considered it her best feature. "How many pills did she take?" I inquired.

"Our estimate is about thirty."

"Do you actually see them when you do the autopsy?"

"The pills? No. They were dissolved. But we can ascertain from the blood chemistry—"

"How do you know someone didn't just grind up thirty Nembutal and sprinkle them over her Raisin Bran?"

Her patronizing smile was barely more than a puff of air blown past compressed lips. "That's where the police investigation comes in," she explained, too patiently. "They tell us there was a suicide note on her own paper, in her own handwriting—believe me, that was checked out— signed by her. They tell us her friends reported she was depressed over the breakup of her marriage. They find out she was having serious business reverses. And she had a new boyfriend, except she'd broken a series of dates with him."

"What does that mean?"

"It's often a sign of depression," Dr. Spiros said.

"Maybe it's a sign he was a dork and she wanted to lose his number," I replied. She inched forward in her chair. I sensed she was about to lose my number. "If you wanted to end it all," I asked quickly, "would you do it in a public place?"

Empathy did not seem to be Dr. Spiros's strong suit. Instead of looking contemplative, her horse face grew even longer with concern: had she made an egregious bureaucratic boo-boo by agreeing to talk with me? "Lots of people kill themselves in public places," she asserted. "They jump from buildings and bridges, they—"

"In a shoe department, holding a slingback?"

"The effects of the barbiturate aren't immediate. She might have decided to distract herself rather than lying down and just, you know, waiting for it to happen."

"Who from homicide is in charge . . ." Suddenly I had such a lump in my throat I could not complete the sentence.

"Detective Sergeant Andrew Kim," she replied, and gave her hair a definitive flip. Interview over.

I suppose an explanation of my emotional reaction at the mention of the Nassau County Police Department's Homicide Bureau is in order. All right, it's like this. Twenty years earlier, shortly before I passed over to the dark side of thirty-five, at a time when my now lawyer daughter and film-critic son were little more than toddlers, a local periodontist named M. Bruce Fleckstein was murdered. I recall hearing about it on the radio and thinking: Who could have done such a thing? The next thing I knew I was investigating. Before too long I actually was instrumental in determining just who the killer was. But in the course of my detective work, I came into contact with a real detective, Lieutenant Nelson Sharpe of the Nassau County Police Department.

To make a long story short, I had an affair with him. That was it. Six months of faithlessness in a twenty-eight-year marriage. Even for a historian like me, aware of the significance of the past, it should have been ancient history—except I fell in love with Nelson. And he with me. For a time we even discussed leaving our spouses, getting married. We simply couldn't bear being without each other.

Not just for the erotic joy, but for the sheer fun we had
together. But even more than my secret belief that a marriage that rises from the ashes of other marriages is doomed
from the start was our mutual, acknowledged awareness of
what our leaving would do to our children. At the time, my
daughter, Kate, was six, my son, Joey, four. Nelson had
three kids of his own. And so he stayed with his wife, June,
and I remained with Bob Singer. Nelson and I never saw
or spoke to each other. Twenty years.

"If you want my opinion," Nancy Miller began later that
evening.

"No," I said. "I definitely do not."

"Hush," she commanded Southernly. Her telephone
voice was splendid, pure magnolia blossom, the sort that in
her reporting days evoked in an interviewee an overwhelming desire to be indiscreet. "My opinion is that your
going to the medical examiner's offices to interview Dr.
Horse Face was just an excuse."

"Right," I said. "A ploy to get closer to Nassau County
law enforcement so I could somehow contrive to see Nelson Sharpe and rekindle a twenty-year-old flame that still
burns brightly despite the pathetic depletion of the estrogen
that fueled it?" My usual six-thirty, end-of-the-workday
Hour of Fatigue was upon me. Bad enough when you have
a husband for whom you have to prepare the eight thou-
sandth dinner of your marriage. Worse when you don't and
you lack the energy to even dump the egg-drop soup from
its single-serving cardboard container into a bowl before
you microwave it. "Give me a break, Nancy."

"You don't deserve a break on this. Except I'll give you
one. I spoke to the reporter on the Deirdre suicide. He heard
something about her business reverses."

"Doesn't it bother you that the authorities are so quick
to label a high-powered woman's death a suicide?"

"Might I remind you your friend Deirdre left a note?
Might I remind you as well that her beloved Stan, he of
the power pecker, had only recently deserted her for a

younger woman? Might I also add I have information about her business problems that could prove to be the final nail in her coffin as far as your murder theory is concerned? Might you be interested?"

"Go ahead." I held my excitement in check. Pretty calmly, I thought, I stuck the soup in the microwave and cradled the phone against my shoulder while I worked to get the wire handle off the carton of sautéed tofu and broccoli so I could zap that, too.

"Deirdre lost Sveltburgers."

"What in God's name are you talking about?"

"Sveltburgers. *Sveltburgers!*" Nancy repeated. "They're famous."

"Not in my universe."

"They're veggie burgers, you ignoramus. Made around here. In Commack or Center Moriches or Cutchogue or one of those C places I've never been to. Instead of being those flat things that look like a hockey puck, they're thick, so they look like a real hamburger. You never heard of Sveltburgers?" I hate when the person I'm talking to acts stunned by my ignorance, like when my son, Joey, a movie critic for the *très chic*, near-insolvent 'zine called *night* gasped and demanded, "You call yourself a movie lover and you never heard of H. Peter Putzel?"

"I don't know," I muttered. "Sveltburgers? Maybe I have."

"I thought you were a historian. Sveltburgers are a Long Island legend."

"I'm obviously not as good a historian as I think I am."

"This woman, Polly Terranova—how's that for a mixed metaphor?—built Sveltburgers into a multimillion-dollar company from something she started in her kitchen in Levittown." Nancy waited for me to say, "Oh, yeah, right. I've heard of her." I didn't, so she continued. "She signed on with Panache for some kind of package deal—office help, factory workers. Anyway, her story is the accountant Deirdre got for her was a complete incompetent and now she's in trouble with the IRS. Also, she's claiming the factory workers were dropouts from some drug rehab program and kept nodding off when operating the machinery. The FDA health inspectors found pieces of fingers in the Sveltburgers."

"Then they're not vegetarian." The bell dinged and I took the container of soup from the microwave.

"Right. Anyway, Pissed-off Polly told our reporter Deirdre was completely unresponsive to her complaints because she was too busy obsessing over the failure of her marriage."

"If Deirdre was obsessed with the failure of her marriage, then losing the Sveltburger account wouldn't make her OD on Nembutal. And while we're at it, if Power Pecker's leaving her was so devastating, how come she had herself a new boyfriend?"

"I'm only reporting what the reporter told me," Nancy snapped. "According to him, Polly told the cops that when she pulled her business out of Panache, Deirdre was *shattered*."

Shattered? Fine, shattered. For the next few days, having other fish to fry, I gave the cops the benefit of the doubt and let Deirdre rest in whatever peace suicides are permitted. I taught my three classes at St. Elizabeth's, then put on my other hat and recorded an interview with a retired gardener, an eighty-five-year-old man who had come to Shorehaven from Umbria to work in the greenhouses of one of the grand old estates in nearby Manhasset.

But by Saturday night of that week, sometime after watching *Radio Days* for the hundredth time and discovering (and devouring) seven miniature Mounds bars left over from Halloween and reading an article in a history journal on the formation of the Women's Trade Union League in 1903, I decided Deirdre Giddings's demise still needed looking into.

So on Sunday I went into the city, to SoHo and the Acadia-Fensterheim Gallery. GROUP SHOW a banner hang-

ing outside proclaimed. The group in question included two
finger paintings by Ryn, the newest Mrs. Giddings—a tidbit
I'd come up with after going through a half-dozen issues
of *ARTnews* at the library.

I hate when people contemplate a work of art, say an
Abstract Expressionist painting, and then make nincom-
poop remarks like, "My three-year-old kid could do the
same thing." Nevertheless, I spent five minutes in the high-
ceilinged, white-walled gallery studying Ryn's *Purple Opinion* and saw nothing in the swirl of four fingers and one
thumb that Kate or Joey could not have brought home from
Temple Beth Israel Nursery School.

"Like it?" a man's voice inquired. He was in his twenties, with the requisite SoHo shaved head and unshaven
face, so I concluded his question was not a pickup line. He
was either an Açadia-Fensterheim employee or an admirer
of Ryn's *oeuvre*. I nodded with what I hoped was a com-
bination of enthusiasm and reverence. "Are you familiar
with Ryn's work?" he asked.

"No. Is the name some reference to Rembrandt van
Rijn?"

He glanced around: it was only us. "The truth? Her
name's Ka*ryn* with a *Y*. Her last name is—was—Bleiber-
man."

"And now?"

"Now it's"—he lifted his head and pursed his lips to
signify snootiness, although he did it in an appropriately
ironic Gen-X manner—"Giddings."

I gave him an I-get-it nod and inquired, "How much is
the painting?" Apparently, it wasn't *de rigueur* to actually
speak of price, but he was kind enough to hand me a list.
Purple Opinion was going for sixteen thousand. I said: "I
hope this doesn't sound incorrigibly crass, but—"

"Isn't that somewhat high for a painting made with fingers? She's not Chuck Close, right?" He looked to see if
I'd gotten his reference, so I nodded my appreciation. "It's
not high at all, to tell you the truth," he went on. "Ryn

spends an incredible amount of time prepping the canvas to give it the *appearance* of paper."

I offered some vague sound of comprehension, like, "Aaah." We both gazed respectfully at the purple whorls. "Is she from around here?" I asked.

"Well, she has a studio in Williamsburg, but these days . . ." He smiled and shook his head with a clearly unresolved mix of condescension and awe. "She's living out on Long Island. She's married to a rich older guy . . ." He hesitated for an instant, perhaps unsure whether it was chivalrous to say "older" to someone as old as I. "They have a mansion," he confided.

"A mansion?" I repeated, appropriately wowed.

"It has a stable!" he declared. "*And* he gave her a five-carat diamond ring. Like, is that a statement or what? Not that any of those things would make a dent in Ryn's consciousness. You know? I mean, when I spoke to her after she first saw the place, you know the only thing she mentioned? The quality of the light."

"So she works out there?"

"Well, right now she's not working."

"Taking a rest after this?" I inquired, waving my hand toward *Purple Opinion* and *Green Certainty*.

"Getting ready to have a baby. She's due any second. I mean, when we had the opening two weeks ago, we were all praying she wouldn't . . ." He shuddered as if seeing a puddle of amniotic fluid on the gallery's polyurethaned oak floor. I thanked him and, price list neatly folded in my handbag, hurried off to catch the 4:18 back to Shorehaven.

It wasn't until eleven that night, defeated by the lower left-hand corner of the Sunday *Times* crossword puzzle, that it occurred to me that when Stan Giddings married Ryn, she had been close to six months pregnant. A pregnant piece of information, but what did it mean? Having spent twenty-eight years married and only two widowed, I still wasn't used to having some late-night question pop into my head and not be able to ask, "What do you make of this?" Even if the reaction was a mumbled "I dunno" or even an antagonistic "What business is it of yours, Judith?" it was enough of a response for me to begin to either start speculating silently or to think, Beats the hell out of me, and drift off to sleep.

Plainly, Bob would not have taken well to my inquiring into the death of Deirdre Giddings. Like the last time around, twenty years earlier, when I got involved in investigating the Fleckstein murder: At his best, he'd been exceedingly aggravated with me. At his worst, enraged. For him, my business was to be his wife. A historian? Why not? He lived in an era in which powerful men's wives did not churn butter. They held jobs, the more prestigious the better, though not so prestigious as to outshine their husbands.

But even if I couldn't have asked, "Do you think Ryn's six-months-pregnant marriage means anything?" without getting a harsh rejoinder, I still couldn't bear the loss of him. Late Sunday nights hurt the most. I yearned to be a wife, to hear Bob's sleepy voice murmuring "G'night" as he turned over, to sense the warmth of his body across a few inches of bed, to smell the fabric softener on his pajamas. Of course, if I'd have left him and married Nelson, he and I would be riveted, sitting up discussing—*stop!*

Over the years I'd become my own tough cop, policing myself from crossing the line from the occasional loving or lustful memory of Nelson to hurtful fantasy: What is he doing now? Still married? Is he happy? Would it be so terrible to call him and offhandedly say, "You just popped into my head the other day and I was wondering . . ." Stop!

The next morning, on my way to St. Elizabeth's, I dropped by the house of my semifriend Mary Alice Mahoney Hunziger Schlesinger Goldfarb—the woman who talked more than any other in Greater New York and said the least. Annoying? Truly. Vacuous? Definitely. Stupid? Indubitably. However, somehow her pea-brain was opti-

mally structured for the absorption and retention of every
item of Shorehaven gossip that wafted through the air, no
matter how vague. So I asked her, "How come Stan Giddings waited until Ryn was six months pregnant to marry
her?"

"It's a looong story," Mary Alice began. Awaiting the
arrival of her personal trainer, she was decked out in
cornflower-blue spandex shorts and tank top with a matching cornflower-blue terry headband. Clearly, irrationally,
she was proud of her body. Her arms had the approximate
diameter of the cardboard tube inside a roll of toilet tissue.
Her hipbones protruded farther than her breasts. "A *very*
long story."

"I have to get going in ten minutes, Mary Alice. I have
a class."

"My trainer is due then. Tucker? You know him?" She
rolled her eyes to let me know how out of it I was. "I mean,
he's only *the* most well-known trainer on the North Shore.
God, you're an intellectual in an ivory tower! Deirdre used
him, you know." She sighed. Not a mere exhalation of air,
but the drawn-out vocalization a bad actress would make
if she'd read a bracketed *sighing* in a script. "What can I
tell you? Deirdre knew Ryn was"—Mary Alice gazed ceil-
ingward, searching for the right words—"*avec* child, like
the French say, and she wanted to put the pressure on Stan."

"To get a good settlement?"

"Well, *of course,*" she responded, a bit impatiently. Ours
was not a natural friendship. Like cellmates, Mary Alice
and I had come together while doing time—in our case, as
class mothers years earlier. "Naturally," she went on, "Deirdre signed a prenup." Mary Alice, on her fourth marriage,
this one to Lance Goldfarb, urologist to Long Island's best
and brightest, obviously knew from prenuptial agreements.
She took the blue sweater that had been draped over a chair
and arranged it artfully around her skeletal shoulders. "I
mean, someone with Stan's resources isn't going to go into
a marriage without protection, is he?"

"He obviously went into Ryn without protection."

"Can you *believe* that? Well, I can, as a matter of fact. He'd had two kids with his first wife but they weren't working out. Neurotic or dyslexic or something. And Deirdre couldn't have any. Or wouldn't. Whatever. Anyhow, Stan was absolutely dying for a family."

"Isn't that a little risky? I mean, getting your girlfriend pregnant while you're still married to someone else."

Mary Alice blew out an impatient gust of air. "Grow up, Judith."

"What am I being pathetically naive about?"

"About that sooner or later he'd get out of the marriage without fatal damage because he had an airtight prenup. And that if Ryn had the baby before they were married, big damn deal. She's an *artist*. Do you think artists care about having a child being a bastard or a nonbastard?"

"You've got a point," I conceded. "But Stan's not an artist, so he would want the baby to be legitimate. Ergo, Deirdre knew time was on her side."

Mary Alice gave a weary nod which said, "*Finally* she's getting it." It's so annoying to be condescended to by a birdbrain. "Right," she said. "She didn't need her lawyer to tell her it was time to put the squeeze on Stan. Trust me. Deirdre got the picture. And she wound up with the house *and* the pied-á-terre on Central Park West *and* enough cash to choke a horse, except she needed it because she was going to redecorate plus get the works: face-lift, tummy tuck, tush tightening, and lipo, and more lipo. Maybe implants. I can't remember if I heard she wanted them."

"Did she get all that done?" I asked. The last time I'd seen Deirdre, a couple of months before she died, she hadn't looked as if she needed anything tightened or implanted, though for all I know I might have been looking at the results.

"No, no, no. She met someone."

"Who?"

"Do you want some ginger tea?"

"No thanks. Whom did she meet?"

"His name is Tony. Like in Tony Bennett." Mary Alice's white-blond hair was pulled up into a pretty topknot, and she twisted it around her index finger, a gesture that led me to believe Tony was not unattractive.

"What's Tony's last name?"

"Tony Marx."

"As in Karl?"

"What?"

"Never mind. Did you ever meet him?"

"No. I mean, yes. See, she also got the country-club membership as part of the settlement, which I hear just about *killed* Stan because his grandfather had been a founder. Very, very rare for the wife to get the membership, which shows you how much Stan was willing to give to get out of that marriage. He and Ryn are living in the grandfather's house now. Way out in Lloyd's Neck. Practically a château I hear. It's called Giddings House, but it needs *major* fixing up. It'll take *years*. That's why Deirdre didn't want any part of it. Anyhow, I know someone like you with a Ph.D. doesn't take country clubs seriously, Judith, but they mean a lot to people. Anyhow, Lance and I were there as the Shays' guests—" She gave her wedding band, a knuckle-to-knuckle diamond dazzler, a twist. "They don't accept Jews as members." She paused, waiting for a response. I offered none so she explained: "Lance is Jewish."

"I guessed it, Mary Alice. The 'Goldfarb' was a clue."

"That's why we were there as *guests*."

"So you just happened to see this Tony there with Deirdre?"

"Right. Well, we chatted for a few minutes. He was wearing a sports jacket in the teeniest houndstooth. I mean, when you first looked at it, you'd think charcoal gray, not black and white. Cashmere. Stunning detail. You could tell—"

"What does Tony do?"

"He owns a car dealership."

"What kind?"

"Volvo. He kidded around and called it Vulva. Well, I guess not to his customers."

"Is it here on the Island?" She nodded. "How serious was Deirdre about him?"

"How serious?" Mary Alice chewed her thin but well-glossed lower lip, then smoothed over the chewed area with her pinky. "It's serious in that he's very, *very* attractive. But not so serious because he only owns one dealership." I must have looked confused because she exhaled impatiently: "Forget that he's not in Stan Giddings's league money-wise. He wasn't even in *Deirdre's* league. So how serious could she be about a man who couldn't earn as much as she could? No, she'd let the relationship play out, which might take her through the summer. That way, she'd have someone for mixed doubles, then in September she'd just get busy with her business or whatever, then go away after Christmas and come back and get her plastic surgery over with so that by the next summer she could really be a contender. You very well know what I mean, Judith, so don't look like 'Duh?' Contender: be eligible for a really important guy."

"So then why did she kill herself?" I asked.

Mary Alice shrugged. "Maybe what everyone's saying is right. Losing Stan and Sveltburgers just took too much out of her. When all you want is to die of a broken heart and you don't, what do you do?"

"What?"

"Suicide!" she said brightly.

Just as I opened the door to leave, Tucker the trainer ambled in. He was an exceedingly muscular but very short man, not much longer than his gym bag. Yes, he said slowly when I asked him, he had seen Deirdre the morning of her death. Not only had she not been in the zone, she'd actually cut their session short when she glanced out the window of her workout room and spotted a silver Volvo, an S80, pulling into the driveway. When I asked if he'd

seen who was driving the car, Tucker gazed up at me suspiciously. Fortunately, Mary Alice gave him a she's-okay
pat on the deltoid, so he conceded: The boyfriend. Tony?
I asked. Yeah, Tony.

That afternoon I got stuck in a particularly noxious
history-department meeting which ended with Medieval
European shaking his fist at Modern Asian. The day after
that I had a three-week pile of oral-history transcriptions at
the library to contend with, so I didn't get to Volvo Village
until the following morning. I felt I was losing not only
time, but ground. If there was anything fishy about Deirdre's death, the person or persons responsible had had more
than enough time to execute an exquisite cover-up.

I suppose dealing with the American public in the highly
emotional arena of car buying can make someone inured to
surprise, so Tony Marx did not think it at all odd that I
wanted to trade in my 1998 Jeep for a 1999 Volvo or that
I wanted to talk about Deirdre. "I don't know if Deirdre
ever mentioned me—" I said.

"Of course she did," he lied courteously, clearly never
having heard my name.

"I'm so upset," I told him. "I still can't believe it."

"I know." Except for a bit of a paunch, he was a sleek
man in his early forties, with the sort of lifelong, worked-
at tan that turns skin to leather. In Tony's case, it was a
butter-soft pecan-colored leather. "You're looking to
unload the Jeep for a V70 AWD, Judy?" he asked.

"Pardon me?"

"All-wheel drive."

"Right." His dress was conservative—gray suit, white
shirt, maroon rep tie—the getup someone selling safety and
solidity would put on. He himself, though, tall, slender,
graceful, and sloe-eyed, was keeping his inborn flash under
control. He should have been selling Maseratis. "Deirdre
told me you were the man to see about a car." He nodded.
"She seemed to think the world of you," I went on. I expected him to nod again and move on to the turbo charger,

whatever that was, but instead he swallowed hard. "Was she . . ." I began. "I apologize. I shouldn't ask."

"It's okay," he responded. "Depressed? Yeah. But not like, you know, depressed-depressed."

"Not suicidal?" I asked softly.

"No! I mean, when they told me, I thought it was some sick joke. Except I knew it was real because it was a couple of cops who came here and told me. Asked me questions. They had to. Because she died at Bloomie's, not, like, in a hospital."

"Was she depressed about the Sveltburger business?"

His head moved from side to side. "Depressed, angry. Why shouldn't she be angry?" The showroom lights that brought out the gleam of his Volvos made his dark brown hair shine. His eyes appeared moist, too, but I couldn't tell if it was the lighting or tears. "It was so unfair. Like what was Deirdre supposed to do? Run Polly Terranova's business for her?" He answered his own question. "No. Deirdre did her job—got the employees. Polly or whoever Polly picked was supposed to supervise them."

"That was unfair," I agreed. Then, lowering my voice, I said, "Was Deirdre still *that* upset about her divorce?"

"No! At least, not to me she wasn't."

"When was the last time you saw her?" I inquired.

"The night before." Tony touched his paunch gently as if to help him recollect. "We went out to dinner. She'd just put me on a diet. High protein." His eyes grew damper. A tear formed in the corner of his left eye and meandered down his cheek. "She told me I was . . ." He stopped and took a deep breath to compose himself. "Insulin-resistant. That's how come so much protein."

"The explanation about the suicide," I said as gently as possible. "It doesn't feel right to me. Could she have been upset about something else? Some other business thing? Could someone she knew have been giving her a hard time?"

"No," he said firmly. "She would've said something to

me. We had a completely—" He blinked back another potential tear. "We talked all the time."

On the way back to Shorehaven, having vowed to think about the all-wheel drive's viscous coupling, I bought myself a cup of coffee and sat in my Jeep in the parking lot of a Starbucks. Snow began to fall, just enough to frost the windshield, so I gazed ahead into its soothing whiteness. Tony's deal wasn't good enough to tempt me. Neither was Tony. However, I was touched by the tear that trickled down his cheek—although my sentiment was tempered by the fact that he'd lied to me about when he'd last seen Deirdre. On the last morning of Deirdre's life, she had told Tucker the trainer to leave because she'd seen Tony driving up. Tucker himself had seen Tony. Yet Tony had told me the last time he'd seen her was at dinner the night before, when she put him on a diet. Unless Tucker was the one who wasn't telling the truth.

I warmed my hands on the cup and sipped the coffee. Tony seemed genuinely upset by Deirdre's death. Still, I remembered Nelson telling me that if he had a buck for every tear shed by killers he'd be the richest guy on Long Island. But why would Tony want to kill Deirdre? Actually, why would anyone? For once I stopped being my own bad cop and let myself think about Nelson. I asked him: Okay, what was to be gained by her death? He counseled: Approach it by thinking about each person she had a relationship with. I probably did something humiliating, like nodding and smiling at him—good idea!—because I recall how relieved I felt that the window was snowed over.

All right, what about Tony? If he hated Deirdre, he could simply stop going out with her . . . unless, of course, she knew some dark secret about his business or his sexuality and was blackmailing him. If Nelson were really beside me he'd be shaking his head: Farfetched. Keep it on your list, but make it last. Move on.

Polly Terranova? From the bit of research I'd done, it seemed that nothing—not even the doofus accountant and the doped-up assembly-line workers sent out by Panache—could stop the inexorable march of Sveltburgers into America's freezers. Polly might be angry, but she could better get even by taking away her business than by offering Deirdre a Nembutalburger.

Stan Giddings? He might have wanted to get rid of Deirdre in order to marry Ryn, but that had been months earlier. It had probably cost him above and beyond what his prenuptial contract specified. But she hadn't bankrupted him, not by a long shot: he was still loaded enough to give Ryn a five-carat ring and to be refurbishing Giddings House.

Ryn? Again, she might have wished to get rid of the second Mrs. Giddings so she could become the third sooner rather than later. But for once, I thought, Mary Alice was right. It wouldn't matter to someone like Ryn whether a child was born in or out of wedlock. Admittedly, if Deirdre had dug in her heels and tried to sue Stan over the prenup, claiming whatever about-to-be exes usually claim, the baby could be born and Stan might have second thoughts. Sure, he'd support the kid, but support didn't mean a five-carat rock and a house with a name for its mother. So it was in Ryn's interest to marry Stan as quickly as she could. Since she had done that, there was no reason to risk killing Deirdre Giddings.

I turned on the windshield wipers. The snow was fluffy and dry, a benevolent end-of-winter snow sent to remind the impatient yearning for spring how ravishing winter can be. I felt one of those by now familiar waves of sadness crash over me, being alone, with no one to share the beauty. Sure, at the end of the day, I could call one of my children, or Nancy, and describe the fat, silent snowflakes descending on Starbucks, but the "Oh, nice!" that I'd get would be syllables of charity. Well, to tell the truth, Bob would not have been seized by ecstasy either. I put the Jeep into reverse and backed out to go home.

Until I thought of the first Mrs. Giddings. Barbara. Who, according to Bell Atlantic Information—which probably

had only cost me thirty dollars on my cell phone—lived at
37 Bridle Path West in Shorehaven Acres. Shorehaven
Half-Acres would be more exact. And as for the so-called
bridle path, it was, like Cotillion Way and Andover Road
that crossed it, an allusion to a way of life that the residents
themselves had probably never experienced. Still, it was a
pleasant development of neo-Colonials and putative Tu-
dors. The pathetic little saplings planted in the sixties had
grown into fine oaks and august gingkos. It all looked perfectly nice—except for Barbara Giddings's house.

Even the camouflage of snow couldn't hide the neglect.
The driveway had deep gouges; chunks of asphalt lay
around these holes as if the driveway had been strafed. The
house itself was even more forlorn, its white-painted clap-
board peeling. Once it must have been a dark red, because
carmine patches blotched the white facade like some dreadful skin condition.

Barbara Giddings wasn't in such good shape either. At
two in the afternoon, her frizz of bleached hair was flattened on one side. Her eyes had the blinky look of someone
wanting not to be caught napping. Nevertheless, she hadn't
had the energy to pull back her slumping shoulders. Her
blue eyes and small, pouty lips indicated she had probably
once been pretty, although her face was now so puffy it
was impossible to tell if it had been in a Sandra Dee or
Kim Novak way. I felt if I went into my now familiar
vaudeville routine—library, oral history, important contribution—it would wipe her out. So I whipped out a pad and
muttered something about just having a few questions about
Deirdre Giddings.

"I don't think . . . I should call my lawyer," she said.
Surprise. I had expected a voice of the living dead, but she
had the rich, cultivated tones of an announcer on a
classical-music station. So I performed my vaudeville act.
And she invited me inside.

After ten years of wear and a couple of kids, the house
was less neglected than simply run-down. We sat on her

living-room couch covered with one of those beige slip-covers you see in catalogs that are supposed to look fashionably shabby, as if your great-grandparents had old money, but which, sadly, look as though you have a battered couch you can't afford to replace.

"Would you mind if I record . . ." She shook her head so vehemently, I quickly said, "Just for background then," and sat forward, hands in my lap. "Were you surprised by Deirdre's death?"

"No."

"How come?"

Her lips compressed in disapproval until they looked like a pale prune. "She was always a pill-popper."

"Deirdre?"

A quick, dismissive, almost cruel laugh—heh—meant to tell me how uniformed I was. "Yes. Deirdre. You know those long, Monday-to-Sunday pill cases?" she asked. I nodded. "She carried *two* of them in her purse. And that was in the days, let me tell you, that she should have been flying high on her own accord. That was when she was carrying on with Stan—lunch, dinner, no wonder she never had a weight problem. She never ate, just banged her brains out." Barbara's words may have been coarse, but her voice sounded so cultivated. You expected to hear Haydn's Symphony no. 96 in D Major, so what she did say was doubly jarring. But she made me feel so sad, too. With her defeated posture and straw hair, Barbara Giddings had the despondent air of a welfare mother who no longer has the energy to hope. All her aspects didn't add up. It was like a game show and I couldn't figure out which contestant was the real Barbara.

"Do you know what kind of pills?" I asked. "Did she have some illness?"

"Illness?" She laughed. "Diet pills. Amphetamines, I suppose. And downers. And who knows what else. But two pill cases. A blue and a yellow."

"Do you believe it really was suicide?" I tried to sound offhand.

"Do I believe it was suicide?" she demanded irritably. Her pasty cheeks suddenly bloomed scarlet. "Do you think I give a good goddamn?"

"I'm sorry."

"No, no, *I'm* sorry," she quickly apologized, trying to comb her hair behind her ears with her fingers. "What can I tell you? It's one thing to take someone's husband away. Fair and square in the game of love and all that." She managed a small smile, but her combing grew more intense, so she was almost raking her scalp. "I mean, Stan had it all: looks, charm, intelligence. And money." I made myself keep looking at her and not at the graying rug under our feet that had once been some cheerier color. "Money," Barbara Giddings said. "There's a reason they call it the root of all evil."

"That's for sure," I mumbled, just to have something to say.

"She wasn't going to settle for Stan and his wealth and social position. No, Deirdre had to have everything."

"Everything?"

"Everything."

"How did she go about it?" I inquired. I was a little nervous that all of a sudden she'd come to her senses and think, Why in God's name am I talking like this to a stranger? Instead, she seemed relieved I was there, to sit on her couch and be a witness to the outrage that had been perpetrated against her.

"How? She manipulated Stan—trust me, he was a babe in the woods and she knew just how to take him over. She got him to con me into signing a divorce agreement that gave me next to nothing. You couldn't bring up two hamsters, much less kids—one who just happens to have ADD—on what I'm getting. Stan gave me a song and dance about how he wanted to give me the money off the books, you know, like under the table. For tax purposes. What did I know? I was just the ex-maid."

"You'd been working as a—"

"No!" she barked, suddenly showing so much spirit it seemed as though some passionate doppelgänger had supplanted her on the couch. "I was going to Stony Brook! Studying botany. I got a summer job after sophomore year helping out their gardener. Not in a lab, but what the hell, at least it paid. But the story got out that Stan had eloped with the *maid*. I could never shake it."

"How come your lawyer allowed you to go along with the money-under-the-table business?"

"Please. Stan got me my lawyer. A kid from one of the law firms that Atlantic Hosiery used. Atlantic is Stan's family's company. Need I say more?"

I shook my head, but that didn't stop Barbara Giddings's rant. For the next three-quarters of an hour, I heard how Stan's visits to his children dwindled from twice a week to once every month or two—because of pressure from Deirdre. How Deirdre got Stan to hire an architect from Los Angeles to design a new house in Shorehaven Estates. How Deirdre had Stan employ a chauffeur and how the chauffeur would drive in her personal shopper from Manhattan with trunks full of clothes. Prada. Comme des Garçons. Zoran for at-home. Size six. Alligator handbags with gold clasps. A wall of shoes, size seven and a half. How Deirdre was much too much for Stan. How she'd made him over, from the tips of his once-machine-made shoes to the top of his beginning-to-bald head. Italian handmade loafers. Hair plugs. Private wine-tasting lessons. How she'd taken an ordinary rich joe whose greatest joy had been his fifty-yardline box at Giants games and yearly golf weekend at Pebble Beach and transformed him into croquet-playing Social Man who either dined out every night with friends who weren't really friends or who hosted dinner parties in his new waterfront mansion for corporate types who were—

here Barbara stopped to take a breath to propel the words out—Deirdre's clients!

At last I drove off, relieved to be out of a house that smelled like dirty laundry, grateful to get away from Barbara's fixation. Not on her ex-husband, the man she'd presumably loved, the man who'd bamboozled her. But on the Other Woman. It was one thing to be aware of a rival's key asset, a law degree from Harvard or a hand-span waist. Quite another to know she had fourteen size-six suits in her closet.

Two hours later I demanded, "Could Barbara Giddings be gullible enough to believe that a man who's cheated on you with another woman, who's leaving you for her, who's sticking you and your children in a house that probably costs about the same as the Hepplewhite breakfront in your former dining room . . . could she honestly believe he would honor an agreement to pay up under the table?" I was sitting beside Nancy's desk at *Newsday* watching her perform microsurgery on somebody's op-ed essay on government subsidies for the arts. I'd never been to see her at work before and was both dazzled and comforted that the newsroom I'd walked through actually looked like all the newsrooms in movies.

"You know what the answer is," Nancy replied, but gently. She understood I had not dropped by to shoot the breeze. With three clicks of her mouse, she highlighted a paragraph on her computer screen and, with one dismissive tap of a key, deleted it. "Yes. Barbara Giddings could be that gullible," she replied. "If all you're offered is a lie and you're desperate for hope, when you're fucked up the ass you tell yourself you're queen of the May and the thing up your ass is a maypole."

"I know," I conceded. "But is she telling the truth? Could she actually have been given a generous settlement and blown it at the racetrack or on some gigolo or a bad investment? And as far as Deirdre goes . . . Barbara has a dull, lost look, like, 'What do I do now that Deirdre's dead?

Whom can I hate?' What I want to know is if what I saw was an act or the real thing."

"You mean Barbara's really a conniving, murdering bitch?"

"I mean, was she telling me the truth? *Was* Deirdre so into drugs. Could you just ask the reporter who's—"

"Shit on a stick, Judith!" But after glaring at me she picked up the phone. Two minutes later—and some whispered prompting by me—she hung up and declared, "The only drug they found in her system was the Nembutal that killed her. Yes, she did have two pill cases in her handbag. Mostly those big mothers, megavitamins. And a couple of Xanax. The only prescriptions in her name were for the Nembutal, Xanax, and Halcion, you know, the sleeping pill."

"Did they find the Nembutal bottle?" I demanded.

"I didn't ask. I am not going to call him again and have him think Lord knows what—that I'm after his job, or him."

"Then call the cops," I said softly. Nancy shook her head. "I swear to you, Nan, I'm not using this as a devious way to get to Nelson."

"Like hell."

"The police must have a PR person. Just find out if they found the bottle. Also, get the prescription dates and anything else about her drugs."

It's often eye-opening to watch your friend doing what she does for a living: her authority is so startling, you forget the complex and often vulnerable woman and see only the champ. For someone calling cold, Nancy was amazingly adroit. Hi! Nancy Miller from *Newsday* Viewpoints. We're thinking of running a piece on suicide with a mention of the Deirdre Giddings case. Direct, businesslike, but still, she was laying on the Georgia-peach jam so thick I could tell she was talking to a man. When she hung up she reported, "No Nembutal bottle. They surmise she must have thrown it out on her way to Bloomingdale's."

"That's one hell of a surmise."

"The Nembutal prescription was from March ninety-eight. The Halcion is from this January."

"Call him back."

"No."

"Please. Find out where Stan and Tony Marx and Barbara Giddings . . . and Ryn were the day she died."

"In a pig's eye."

Call-Me-Mike, Nancy's new conquest in the Nassau County Police Department's PR office, phoned her back a half hour later, during which time I watched her eviscerate the essay on her screen and call the writer to inform her of having made a couple of minor edits. Call-Me-Mike told her—off the record—that Ryn had gone to her obstetrician in the morning, then had Stan's chauffeur drive her into the city, to the Acadia-Fensterheim Gallery in SoHo, where, presumably, she admired her own work. Tony Marx went from his condo to his Volvo dealership, a fact which did not square with what Tucker the Trainer had told me about seeing Tony's car drive up to the house. Stan was on a plane coming back from Palm Beach, where he had spent the previous day looking at real estate. As for Barbara, well, she had not been interviewed.

"Would you stop it now?" Nancy snapped. Well, not quite snapped, but I could sense she was less than delighted with me. "Deirdre killed herself. Period. *She was not your friend.* You owe her nothing! She was a woman who was losing her husband, losing her big client, probably losing her looks if you got up close enough. Would you want to spend the rest of your life finding jobs for steamfitters and sleeping with a guy who calls his car a Vulva? No, you'd OD and be done with it."

"I would not," I said as I stood. "And even if I were going to, would I take thirty Nembutal in the morning and then go shopping?" I put on my coat. "Or would I take them at a time a person would logically take a sleeping pill—the night before—and just fall asleep and never wake up?"

"Where are you going?" Nancy grilled me, in the manner of a parent sensing her child is about to do something reckless.

I gave her head a comforting pat. "Relax. I'm going to Mineola to look up some records."

"What kind of records?"

"Martha and the Vandellas. Public records, to see what information there is about Stan's divorces. I want to find out if the house Barbara is in now is the one she got stuck with ten years ago when Stan left ... or if she had something better and lost it. Then I'll go back to the library to run a more thorough search on Ryn and Tony."

"Why?"

"Why? Because they seem like the sort of people who could possibly have checkered pasts. And because the alternative is my book group and they're doing *The Golden Notebook*, which I've successfully avoided my entire life."

I drove west on the Long Island Expressway listening to a National Public Radio interview with an expert on lichens. He explained how lichens are formed by a fungus and an alga living together "intimately." The intimacy must have gotten to me because instead of driving to the county clerk's office, I found myself heading for police headquarters. This is nuts, I told myself. What if Nelson sees you? He'll think you've been stalking him for twenty years. Get out. Except I had an idea.

I gripped the wheel. Cool it, I ordered myself as I pulled into the parking lot. It's just a glimmering. Now what was the name of the guy from the police conducting the investigation? I'd only heard it from Dr. Horse Face and come across it a hundred times in the newspaper accounts, but naturally at the moment I wanted it, the particular neuron that had this cop's name on it refused to fire. Well, I could walk right in and ask and they'd say, Oh, it's Detective Sergeant Whatever and I'd go to his office and just say, Hi,

I'm a neighbor of Deirdre Giddings's and what do you think about this? I know it's just a theory but . . . Kim! That was his name! On one hand, maybe Detective Sergeant Kim had enormous intellectual curiosity and would reopen the case. On the other hand, maybe he'd think I was demented. Or I'd go inside headquarters and my heart would be in my throat at the thought that I could possibly see Nelson and so I'd stand before Detective Sergeant Kim and make hideous gurgling noises.

Naturally I was an utter wreck, wanting, not wanting, so I won't even describe my walking in there and finding Detective Sergeant Kim's office, which took maybe four minutes but which felt like four years. It normally would have taken half that time, except I kept my head down just in case Nelson walked by, and I had to wait until I sensed the halls had cleared before I could look up and see the numbers on the doors.

"It's an interesting theory," Detective Sergeant Kim remarked fifteen minutes later. He was a large man in his late thirties who looked as if he'd gained twenty pounds since the time he'd bought his suit. "And I appreciate your sharing it with me, Ms. Singer. Except for one thing."

"No one had any reason to want to kill her," I replied. He smiled, a gracious, be-nice-to-upper-middle-class-citizens smile. "At least no one had any reason at the time she died. On that score you're absolutely right. But what about four or five months before that?"

"What do you mean?" He looked less impatient than perplexed, which I took as a hopeful omen.

"If she wanted to kill herself, why would she take pills from an old prescription? She had a prescription for Halcion, so if she wanted to go to sleep permanently, why not take those?" He waited. He crossed his arms over his chest and tried to lean back, except his chair didn't want to. He gave up and rested his elbows on his desk. "Look," I went on, "say you want to kill Deirdre Giddings. Make it look like a suicide. What do you do? Well, you could slip a compromising letter on her notepaper into a file marked 'personal papers.' 'I can't take it anymore. It's got to end.' With her signature.''

"Doesn't that sound like a suicide note to you?" he asked, still patient. I couldn't tell if he was a naturally easy-going man or a canny cop who used pleasantness as an investigatory technique.

"It could mean *anything* has got to end. It could have been a note to her housekeeper, that she's ironing on too high a heat and burning blouses right and left and it's got to end. To her secretary, that she's calling in sick too often. To her boyfriend, that it's over. Or to her husband, that his philandering or his lying or his late nights have got to end." Kim took a deep breath that looked as if it were meant to propel a sentence, so I talked faster. "To her husband's lover, to end the affair. To her husband's ex-wife—who seemed more than a little preoccupied with Deirdre—to stop snooping around town about what she's doing.''

"So you're saying someone got her note and—if it wasn't the maid with the iron—they sneaked in and stuck it into her folder?" Kim had a sweet face with a pudgy chin and bright, dark eyes, but he raised one eyebrow in the cool, skeptical manner of a film noir antihero.

"No. I'm saying whoever did it did it months ago, when he or she had easier access to Deirdre's things, like her file of personal papers." Kim waited. The smile vanished. On the other hand, it wasn't replaced with a snarl. "It was done before the prescription for Halcion was written, before Deirdre's marriage was over. Was the note on top of the papers in the folder?"

"No," he said cautiously.

"So in the ensuing months, she just stuck other papers in there—like her divorce decree—and never saw the note."

"Okay, then what?" he asked slowly, trying to see where I was going. But there was not enough light for him to make it out.

"Look, if someone dies a suspicious death, what happens? Guys like you look into it. You'll find out what people close to the victim were doing around the time of the death. So if you want to make a murder look like a suicide, the best thing to do is to distance yourself from the place and time of death as much as possible."

"What do you think happened?" Kim asked. It was less a request than a demand to put up or shut up.

"I'm not sure." This did not put the smile back on Kim's face. "Tony Marx lied to me and probably to you about not seeing Deirdre on the day she died." Before he could interject another question I explained: "Deirdre's personal trainer, a guy named Tucker, saw Tony driving up to her house that morning." His mouth opened slightly, that how-do-you-know-that gape. I kept going. "But this murder predates Tony. My guess is he had some trouble in the past and got frightened about being part of any investigation. That's why he lied about when he last saw her." I waited.

Kim finally said, "It's a matter of public record. An arrest for insurance fraud, second degree. Suspended sentence."

"Tony seems to have genuinely loved her." No reaction. "Now, Barbara Giddings didn't love Deirdre, although she's obsessed with her. Knows the precise number of suits in her closet."

"So you're saying she had access?"

"I don't know. Deirdre and Stan lived in a huge, expensive house that must have a sophisticated alarm system. It would be hard to break and enter although I concede Barbara might have been able to con a housekeeper or someone to let her in. But have you met Barbara Giddings?" Kim didn't respond, so I kept going. "She seems too dispirited to be able to pull off a maneuver that would take that kind of guts and inventiveness. My guess is she's got highly sensitive antennae that pick up any snippet of information that was around town about the second Mrs. Giddings."

"And the third Mrs. Giddings, the artist?" Kim inquired.

He was listening, that was for sure. Sitting motionless: no paper-clip bending, no pen chewing.

"Well, for Ryn, a clock was ticking. She was having a baby. Not that she'd be worried about it being born out of wedlock. It wasn't social stigma that concerned her. It was getting Stan to marry her. Once the baby was born, it would be a fact of life. Clearly, Stan would support it. But would he be willing to go through another divorce? Another marriage? There's no way Deirdre would have let him off cheap the way Barbara did. Ryn was running the risk that if a divorce dragged on for too long, Stan would lose interest. She'd wind up with a kid and child support. Sure, that would keep her in finger paints, but it wouldn't buy her a five-carat ring, a family manse, and a husband with the wherewithal to make her career happen."

"Any other suspects?" Kim tried to query lightly, as if amused, but he was too absorbed to pull it off.

I sat forward in the stiff-backed chair and rested my arm on his desk as if we were two colleagues shooting the breeze. "I don't know the other people in Deirdre's life," I told him. "Did anyone strike you as having a motive? Anyone who might have wanted to get Deirdre out of the way?"

Kim caught himself before he answered, but not before he swiveled his head to the right, a prelude to a shake that would have told me, "No, no one." He was so annoyed at this lapse of control that he glanced at his watch, did a damn-I'm-late-for-a-meeting push back from his desk. "I really have to go. Listen, Ms. Singer, what you told me: interesting." He stood and inhaled to close his jacket. "Creative. Believe it or not, there's a lot of creativity in police work. But you have no evidence for your theory that it was a homicide. On the other hand, we have evidence—the note, people saying how depressed she was, the fact that the drug that killed her was one prescribed for her. All our evidence adds up to one thing—"

"The pills in those two cases she carried were mostly vitamins," I cut him off. "Megavitamins. Big capsules, a lot of them. Gelatin, or whatever for the outside, that dissolves in the stomach. Some of them, you can pull the two gelatin halves apart. It wouldn't take a pharmacological genius to grind up thirty Nembutal, stick the grindings into a capsule, and slip it back into her pill case. Then go out of town, or do something to give you a good alibi just in case there was an investigation. But this is the thing. Deirdre didn't take that pill. How come? Maybe she read about some new study that too much Vitamin X leads to liver disease, or dry skin. Or maybe she was beside herself because she knew her husband was cheating on her, or maybe he'd actually asked for a divorce, and she stopped taking care of herself. Meanwhile, the killer is waiting for the kill. Except it doesn't happen. So what does he or she conclude?"

"What?" Kim asked, walking me to the door, but slowly.

"That she took it. That she probably had one of the longest naps on record, but it didn't kill her."

"So how come she finally did take the pill?" The question was tossed off casually enough, but he wasn't going anywhere. In fact, he lounged against the door frame.

"Maybe she read another study that said the earlier study was based on poor methodology. Or maybe she was feeling better and getting back to her old, health-conscious routine. The point is, the killer wasn't going to try again because he or she got what he or she wanted."

"Which was?"

"Deirdre let Stan go." He smiled, a how-amusing smile, like a sophisticate in a Coward comedy. "Tell me, Sergeant Kim, who's your money on?"

"What?" The smile disappeared and he stood straight. Seeing he was about to step out into the hall, I stood in the doorway, blocking his way.

"Is it on Barbara Giddings?" I asked. "She was obsessed with Deirdre. She knew about the two pill cases. But she didn't know there were vitamins in them; she thought they were full of uppers and downers. And then there's the prob-

lem of access. Could Barbara really have gotten into Deirdre's handbag not once, but twice—to get the capsule, then
to return it to the pill case?"

Kim decided to revert to amusement. "The new wife,"
he suggested. He waited, an appreciative expression on his
face, as if he were waiting for a stand-up comic to take
center stage.

"Same problem of access. How could she have done it
without Stan's complicity?"

"Then you're saying . . ." He waited.

The problem wasn't whether Kim was interested. I could
see he was, if only to the extent that, if he were the diligent
type, he'd review the case the minute I left. The problem
was that if he were a shrewd department politician without
a conscience, he wouldn't now holler murder when he'd
already gone public and said suicide.

"Listen," I told him. "I teach history on the college level.
Plus I work in a public library that serves a population of
thirty thousand."

"What?"

"I know from bureaucracy. It might seem to you that
saying it's a homicide now is like announcing, 'I goofed.'
But it doesn't have to be viewed as *your* mistake. More
than likely, it could be sloppy work by the medical examiner's office, or by the first cops on the scene, or something.
And you could be the hero because you had doubts and the
courage of your convictions and went after the truth."

"And what is the truth?" Kim asked.

Before I could answer, a voice from behind me, in the
hall, called out to Kim, "How's it going, Andy?" Oh God.
I knew whose voice that was. I could not bring myself to
turn around and look.

"Not bad. How're you doing?"

"Not bad either," the voice said. The footsteps continued
down the hall for another second or two. Maybe it wasn't
extrasensory perception that made Nelson stop, but a cop's

sensitivity to some infinitesimal motion. For all I know, it could have been my telltale heart.

Nelson looked lousy. He looked wonderful. His salt-and-pepper hair had turned white. His skin had turned the chalky color of a lifelong civil servant. Although I didn't dare give him the once-over, his body still looked fine. His eyes were still beautiful, large and velvety brown. For that instant, they did not leave my face. Naturally, I immediately thought there was some hideous flaw he'd spotted, one of those mortifying imperfections of middle age I couldn't see because my eyesight has gone to hell—a giant hair growing out of my nose, an entire cheek covered by a liver spot. I held my hands tight to my sides so I wouldn't reach up and feel for what was wrong and swallowed hard. And nothing more happened. Nelson gave me a barely perceptible nod and walked on.

Now all I wanted was to get out of police headquarters. But I forced myself to talk to Detective Sergeant Kim: "You and I both know who had access to Deirdre's things a few months back."

"You're talking about Stan Giddings?"

"We know Deirdre was too much for him. Pushing him further than he wanted to go socially. Making him over, from his shoes to hair plugs for a bald spot. He couldn't take that. He was a man used to unquestioning acceptance, a man used to people moving earth and sky for *him*. He wanted someone more than Barbara, but he didn't want a wife who would not just outshine him, but drive him. A man like Stan wants someone with a cute career, not an important one. And he wanted someone who could have a baby, so he could have a do-over the way so many men do when they hit middle age. He wanted to live in Giddings House, be lord of his manor. He wanted to do rich man's things, like winter in Palm Beach. What was he doing the day Deirdre died? Coming home from Florida after looking at real estate. But what was the only thing that kept him from doing what he wanted to do? Deirdre."

"Why couldn't he just wait till the divorce was over? Why push it?"

"Because he is spoiled worse than rotten. He wanted what he wanted when he wanted it. He wanted out of the marriage and he wanted a baby, so he got Ryn pregnant. But Deirdre wouldn't cooperate with him. Somehow she got wind that the baby was coming. Maybe he even told her. But she started holding him up for more than what the prenuptial agreement stipulated. That kind of chutzpah wasn't in his calculations, and he became enraged. He wanted out, and fast, and if Deirdre was going to make it difficult on him, she'd have to go. Why don't you check? I bet there's a period of time when he was out of town. That would be the days or weeks when he expected her 'suicide' to happen. Except it didn't."

Kim stuck his hands in his pockets. Finally he asked: "And how am I supposed to prove this?"

Kim called me that night. The medical examiner's report stated that the stomach contents had included a trace amount of gelatin, enough for a large dissolved capsule.

I waited. In a whodunit, I would have been Kim's partner, leading him (carrying a search warrant) to a dusting of Vitamin X and Nembutal mixture in the pocket of Stan Giddings's cashmere sports jacket. Or I'd be luring Stan into an Edward Hopper diner for a coffee and then snatch the cup and discover—Aha!—the dribblings on the so-called suicide note turned out to be saliva that matched Stan Giddings's DNA from the saliva on the cup. But in life the scales of justice hardly ever achieve the exquisite balance that they do in a whodunit.

To give Detective Sergeant Kim credit, he did his homework, albeit a little late. Two artist friends told him how Ryn had given Stan an ultimatum: a month to finalize his divorce. If he couldn't, she would get an abortion. As to having a child out of wedlock, they laughed. Ryn? No, Ryn knew what she wanted and having a baby was a means of getting it. No "it," no kid.

And yes, Stan had gone to his house in Maine for a month in October with Ryn, around the time he left Deirdre, around the time he was waiting for her to kill herself so he and Ryn could come back and get married. But nothing happened and so Stan's freedom, according to Detective Sergeant Kim, cost him an extra three and a half million dollars.

Finally, the cops did find Stan Giddings's fingerprints on a brown amber bottle of Sunrise Anti-Ox Detox in a bathroom adjacent to Deirdre Giddings's workout room. What does that prove? Stan's lawyer screamed to the district attorney of Nassau County. And the DA conceded meekly: It means maybe he took a vitamin. Thus, Stan's long-standing policy of giving campaign contributions to the local candidates of all parties except blatant commies was vindicated. And, sad to report, Stan Giddings himself was vindicated.

It was too late for true justice, although *Newsday* somehow got wind that the Deirdre Giddings's suicide was once again under investigation, as was her former husband, Stanley Giddings. Suicide . . . or murder? A dandy photograph of Stan and Ryn ran on the front page, along with insets of Giddings House and Deirdre's Tara.

"Good enough for your friend Deirdre?" my friend Nancy Miller demanded that morning. I held the phone away from my ear as she made one of those hideous Southern ya-hoo sounds, half yell, half screech. "None of that 'respected businessman' shit. 'Heir to a footwear fortune' was the best I could do. The powers that be rejected 'playboy' out of hand."

"Nancy, thank you! God bless you!" I held the paper at arm's length and smiled at the photograph of an unhappy Ryn and an outraged Stan leaving church the previous Sunday. They held their baby, wrapped in a pink blanket, awkwardly between them, as if it were a football handoff neither would accept.

"Are you okay on the Nelson front, kiddo?" Nancy quizzed me.

"Fine."

"Being so close to him and not having him even say hello really got to you."

"Yes."

"You're not going to do anything moronic, like call him."

"No," I assured her.

"Or fax him Bob's obit."

"Stop it, Nancy!"

"Hey, aren't I a good friend?" she asked.

"There's none better," I told her.

"No. There's none better than you, Judith. To me and even to that boring clotheshorse Deirdre, poor thing. I just don't want you getting hurt, is all and—"

"Call waiting. Hold on."

I never got back to her that day. It was Nelson Sharpe. He said "Judith," and then—

But that's another story.

TAKING OUT MR. GARBAGE

by Judith Kelman

THE ancient kerosene heater was out of fuel. Leonora Mathis rubbed her ham-sized hands over the last meager puff of heat. "Jan's been on the phone forever. I say we start without her."

"Y-you have my v-vote," Midgie Strickland's teeth clacked like tiny castanets. "The s-sooner we kill off that crummy Casanova, the sooner w-we can get back to civilization."

"What I wouldn't give right now for electricity, running water, central heating," Leonora moaned. "I swear, as soon as I get home, I'm going to run the hottest tub I can stand and soak for a week."

Celeste Lapointe's head bowed in misery. Her blond hair drooped like dying daisy petals. "Please, please forgive me. I didn't know those parasites were going to cut the power to the camp. I told them I'd pay the bills just as soon as I was back on my feet. By the time I got here and found out there wasn't any heat or light, it was too late to reach all of you and change our plans. You can't imagine how terrible I feel about this. You simply can't."

Regina Patterson, dour and Doberman thin, took a generous belt of bourbon from her silver flask. Her raven hair shone like an oil slick in the guttering candlelight. "Quite frankly, I don't give two hoots how you feel, Celeste. Watching you wallow doesn't make it any warmer or more comfortable. I agree with Midgie and Leonora. Let's hurry up and bump off that lousy lothario and get out of here."

Barbie Breslow, reticent to the perilous brink of non-existence, raised her hand halfway like a broken tollgate. "It doesn't seem fair for Jan to miss the murder. That's the best part of our annual reunions. The highlight."

"If she w-wants to participate, she can hang up on whoever she's been g-g-gabbing with on her cell phone for the last half hour and get her butt over here," Midgie said. "I'm not going to h-hang around w-waiting for her until I catch pneumonia. Majority rules. Now who w-wants to get the ball rolling? How about you, Leonora?"

"Let Celeste start. This is her hellhole, after all. She's the hostess."

Tears pooled in Celeste's sludge-brown eyes. Two days of intermittent weeping had puffed the lids and tinged the whites to a soft bunny pink. "It's not mine anymore. As of tomorrow, Camp Pemiquot belongs to the Sackwell Corporation. They bought it from the bank at the foreclosure auction. Next week they're going to bring in the bulldozers and level the place. Those vultures are turning this beautiful property into one of those hideous outlet malls. This camp has been in my family for five generations. Former campers used to come on visiting days to see their grandchildren and great-grandchildren. Now they'll be selling seconds here. Manufacturers' overruns. Last year's goods. It's so tacky, I feel like strangling myself."

"My point exactly," Leonora said. "Remember, Celeste. None of this would have happened if not for that rotten Romeo. If he hadn't swindled you, you wouldn't have needed to take out that giant second mortgage in the first place. If he hadn't dumped you like a load of industrial waste, you wouldn't have suffered that clinical depression, and you wouldn't have lost the camp. So here's your chance to get even. Tell us, girl. How are you going to do that monster in?"

Celeste sighed. "I'm afraid I'm going to disappoint you yet again. For weeks, I've been agonizing over some new interesting way to get rid of that giant rat, but I haven't been able to come up with a thing. Poisons are passé, hanging's ho-hum, strangling is cliché, flaying's plain dumb."

Barbie Breslow tittered into her hand. "You made a poem, Celeste. That's cute."

Despite multiple face-lifts that drew her skin taut as shrink-wrap, Regina scowled. "Cute is not exactly what we're after. Come on, Midgie. You always come up with a devilish plan. What do you have for us this year?"

An impish grin split Midgie's moon face. "Actually, I had some trouble, too. Then last week, I saw this show on the Nature Channel about a very rare cactus that only grows in a jungle in darkest Africa. If you touch it or even get close, the bristles burrow under your skin. There's no way to remove them, and they give off a horrible poison that invades the entire body. Apparently, the pain is so excruciating that most victims go crazy and eventually commit suicide. It occurred to me that if we could get one of those cactuses and get Prince Charming to touch it, he'd get everything he deserves and then some."

Leonora rolled her eyes. "That plan is full of holes, Midgie. For one thing, who would want to handle a plant like that? For another, how would we ever get our hands on one? Dial 1-800 Big Ouch? And anyway, it's cacti, not cactuses."

"It also happens to be ridiculous," said Regina. "You might as well suggest we have him bitten by a rabid unicorn or beaten to a pulp by Mighty Mouse."

"Let's hear you do better, Miss Originality," Midgie challenged.

"It will be my distinct pleasure." Regina's brow arched

in mischief as she took another bracing pop from her flask. "My idea is to tie him down on a gurney with thick leather straps at his wrists and ankles. Next, we rig up a sort of a swinging doohickey with a razor-sharp blade at the end. We suspend it from the ceiling over his head and program it to drop very, very slowly. We hang a mirror above his eyes and tape his eyelids open so he's forced to watch as the blade descends directly toward his private parts." Regina giggled with demonic delight. "Is that fabulous or what?"

"You're suggesting castration *again*? Don't you think that's just a teensy bit redundant?" asked Celeste.

"Redundant is a major understatement. Lop off his privates, vaporize his privates, disable his privates by making them public. It's a yawn, verging on a snore," Midgie observed.

"That's a hot one coming from you, chubby cheeks. All you ever do is parrot some nonsense you got from a television show. You don't have ideas, you have reruns," Regina sniped.

"Reruns, Regina? You mean like your trips to the plastic surgeon? And as far as my so-called chubby cheeks are concerned, if you weren't an anorexic, alcoholic, coin-operated slut, maybe you wouldn't have that prune puss and the disposition to go with it."

"Why, you little—" Regina shot out of her seat and lunged toward Midgie's squat stubby neck, leading with her sixteen-carat, D-flawless, emerald-cut diamond ring.

Leonora caught Regina by her toothpick arms and held her flailing like a hooked fish. "Okay, that's enough. Break it up." As a homicide cop turned defense attorney, Leonora was accustomed to managing testy situations. She looked on sternly until both women settled back in their Adirondack chairs.

"It occurs to me that maybe the reason we're all having such trouble this year is that we're finally over him," Leonora said. "Look at us. Midgie has dropped a lot of weight, and her private counseling practice is flourishing. Celeste may have lost the camp, but she's started a whole new career as a practical nurse. Jan has been promoted to head pharmacist at the Drugs R Us. Barbie's been making a killing renovating houses for resale. Regina's landed a brand-new Mr. Megabucks. My star has risen since I won that murder-one acquittal for Freddie the Fist. The *crème de la* crumbs are lined up to retain me: Vicious Vinnie, Pat the Rat, you name it. More importantly, I haven't placed a single bet since last year's Super Bowl. I've actually deleted my bookie's number from my speed dial. Life is good."

Regina pooched her collagen-plumped lips in thought. "You're absolutely right, Leonora. Who cares about that wretched man? I don't even want to think about him. Lord knows I have far more important things to focus on, like helping Arthur spend all that lovely money of his."

"Hear, hear," said Celeste. "So that creep used us and humiliated us and lied to us and robbed us blind. So he left us with egos like dried peas and tossed us in hideous spirals of self-destruction. That's old news as far as I'm concerned."

"Me, too," Midgie said. "I move that we make this our last fantasy revenge reunion. From now on, when we get together, it can be strictly social."

"Excellent idea. We can have a nice sit-down dinner. Maybe bring dates," said Celeste. "I didn't want to say anything, but I've started seeing a very nice man. We met in bankruptcy court. The two of us were going Chapter Eleven at the same time. Did you ever hear anything more romantic?"

"Once in college my boyfriend and I both had stomach flu," Midgie added.

"We can hold our first soiree at Arthur's summer weekend estate in Bedford Hills," Regina said. "His staff is divine. Clever boy stole the cook from the Four Seasons and the butler from the Sultan of Brunei."

Midgie squealed in delight. "Sounds fabulous. Let's

have champagne. And music. How about that?"

"Definitely. I'll have Arthur ask some of his pals. The three tenors would be nice. And maybe Barbra if she promises not to howl that dreadful 'People who need peeeeple.' "

"Do you think maybe, I mean if it isn't too much trouble, could we have dancing?" ventured Barbie.

"Absolutely. We'll bring in a nice band. Maybe the London Philharmonic."

The door to the social hall burst open, admitting a cruel blast of wind. Jan Schrager stood in the doorway, framed by the black, blustery night.

"Come in, Jan. Wait until you hear what we've decided," Leonora called.

Jan, a slim, striking redhead, stood inert. Her proud-boned face was devoid of expression. The fierce wind lashed her long cinnamon tresses across her cheeks. Clad in nothing but a flimsy cotton blouse and a thin wool skirt, she seemed oblivious to the brutal cold.

"Close that door, for heaven's sake. You're giving us all pneumonia," Midgie whined.

When Jan failed to respond, Regina took matters in her long-taloned hands. She strode to the exit and grasped Jan by the shoulders. "In," she ordered as she shut the warped plank door. "Move! Chop, chop! Now!"

Regina steered Jan into the mess hall and worked her like a bad shopping cart toward the circle of splintered Adirondack chairs.

As Jan entered the wavering pool of candlelight, Midgie's hand flew to her mouth. "What's wrong, Jan? What happened? My Lord, I think she's in shock."

"Sit her down. Give her air. I'll take care of this." With deft, professional moves, Celeste measured Jan's pulse, assessed her color, and stared into her hazy eyes. "No shock, but she's shaken up. That's for sure. Jan, honey? Can you hear me? Are you hurt? Are you sick?"

"It's him. It's my baby. It's a nightmare. God, no!" Jan wailed.

"Shh, sweetheart," soothed Celeste. "I don't understand. You don't have a baby boy. Start at the beginning. Go slow."

Jan shuddered and pulled a breath. "The call I got was from Lydia, my youngest. She's a senior at Lehigh, architecture major. Liddy's always been a great kid, smart, thoughtful, warmhearted. Unfortunately, she's a little shy, so she's never had much in the way of a social life."

"I can relate," Barbie breathed.

"She called to tell me that she met this wonderful guy," Jan went on. "He's older, she said, but he's so wonderful that the age difference doesn't matter. She told me he's an urban-planning visionary, a genius. In fact, she's decided to invest in his company, which Liddy believes will provide the prototype for multiple-unit housing in the new millennium. My ex-mother-in-law died last year and left all three of my girls some money. Foolishly, the old lady didn't put it in trust, so Liddy can do whatever she wants with her share. I'd hoped she would invest, save for a rainy day." Jan recoiled as if she'd been punched. "My God, I must have mentioned it to him. How else would he know?"

"Wait, Jan. You've lost us. You must have mentioned what to whom?" Leonora asked in calm, lawyerly fashion.

"I must have told Carl, or whatever his name is, that Liddy was going to inherit some money when her grandmother died. He must have seen the obituary. You know how he is, that parasite. He can sniff out vulnerable females and financial opportunities like nobody's business."

Regina flushed hot behind her all-weather tan. "Am I hearing you right? Are you saying that that beast, that monster, that rotten, revolting creep has taken up with your daughter?"

Jan started to weep. "I didn't believe it myself at first. But it has to be him. I know it is. Liddy described him to a tee: smooth, charming, eyes the blue of glacial ice."

"Maybe it's not as bad as you think, Jan. How far has

this thing gone? Did she mention the tattoo?" asked Leonora.

"Yes, Lord help me. She's seen it," Jan cried. "Liddy told me that her new boyfriend has a small red scorpion tattoo. Of course she never imagined that I would know exactly where that scorpion is, that I've seen it myself, up close and very, very personally. Poor Liddy. My poor baby. What am I going to do?"

"You didn't *tell* her? You didn't *warn* her?" Regina yelped. "Are you nuts?"

"I tried. I wanted to. But I couldn't bring myself to do that to her. She's so young, so open and trusting. Finding out that she's been victimized by a callous professional like him would break her heart. A thing like that would change Liddy, ruin her, turn her bitter and hard like us. I can't bear that. There has to be another way."

The women lapsed into a brittle silence, reliving the suffering he had put them through. There was no sound but the mournful wailing of the wind, nature's dirge to the loss of Liddy Shrager's innocence.

So many had fallen that way. This man had made a career of preying on susceptible women. He selected his targets with care. Then he stalked and studied them like a cunning cat burglar until he found the surest way to break into their hearts and purses and steal everything of value.

He was a talented chameleon who altered his identity to suit. When Regina met him at a Greenwich gala, he claimed to be Vernon March, a Southern gentleman of means, whose passion was philanthropy. Their striking commonalties had impressed the pampered Regina as few things ever did. She, too, had a firm belief in charity, especially the kind that began at home. Plus, he had the most glorious platinum-streaked hair and eyes like rare blue diamonds. She had imagined those eyes as huge stud earrings and fallen in a hopeless swoon of infatuation.

To Barbie Breslow, he had appeared as a devoted dad and a widower, on hand to root for the neighborhood children at a field-hockey match. He introduced himself as David Steinberg, an accountant from nearby Westport. He confessed that he was something of an introvert, which had made it terribly hard for him to meet people since his precious Marilyn passed away a decade ago. Marilyn had lost a valiant battle with heart disease, he said, the same thing that killed Barbie's beloved husband, Sam. Blushing fiercely, he'd admitted that what he loved to do above all was dance. By astonishing coincidence, Barbie had a long-standing passion for Argentine tango, salsa, and swing. She collected tapes of Fred Astaire movies in the uncolored originals and haunted the local thrift shop for Ginger-quality ball gowns.

Midgie had met him an Overeaters Anonymous meeting. Afterward, over cheesecake at the Bull's Head Diner, he had told her that his full name was Charlie Baumwaller. By amazing coincidence, his family came from the same small town in Germany where Midgie's ancestors had lived. He confessed that he'd always wanted to slim down, but his ex-wife had ridiculed that as she had all of his aspirations. Naturally, the divorce had been painful, as Midgie knew from hard personal experience. Three years earlier, her husband of nineteen years had run off with a terminally perky personal trainer named Pammy. Charlie's ex-wife had left him for the handsome young organic-produce manager at the Food Emporium. Midgie and her new man shared an additional dessert, a slice of apple pie *à la mode*, to blunt the pain.

To Celeste, he appeared as Jean-Paul La Croix, a cardiologist from Geneva who believed that sleep-away camps were more critical than hospitals to family welfare. Leonora had met him at a sports bar, where both of them sat until closing time one bleak December morning watching instant replays and commiserating over their strikingly similar losses. That time, he'd claimed his name was Ricky Moran.

Jan had fallen for him instantly when he rescued her from an abusive customer at the downtown Stamford drugstore where she worked as an associate pharmacist. The man had demanded Viagra. When she explained that she could only dispense the anti-impotence drug by prescription, he had grabbed her by the lab-coat collar and squeezed. "There's your prescription," he growled. "Now give."

She was about to pass out from fear and lack of oxygen when the handsome blue-eyed onlooker knocked her assailant unconscious with a box of extra-large, overnight Depends.

Jan's rescuer had identified himself as Carl Simmons. After ascertaining that she was unhurt, he'd expressed his outrage in no uncertain terms. A dedicated, talented scientist such as Jan should be revered, thanked, and treated with proper respect, he railed. She had peered in gratitude into those opalescent eyes and the rest was history.

The rest had been history for them all. The slime, by any name, had taken them all for a horrible ride. He had broken their hearts, emptied their wallets, dashed their hopes, taken a wrecking ball to their spirits and their lives.

After he dumped her, Barbie had spent most of a year in her kitchen baking tray after tray of brownies and tollhouse cookies like a windup Martha Stewart doll. Midgie's weight had soared to a record-breaking two sixty-two. Celeste had taken to bed for six months, during which time the director of her fiercest competitor, Camp Watasconset, wooed away many of her prized campers. Jan had suffered intractable insomnia, nervous tics, and rashes and had needed to medicate herself heavily to find even momentary relief. Leonora's bookie was able to afford the Porsche Boxster he'd had his eye on for years. Regina's entire household staff had resigned, and given her reduced financial circumstances and fearsome reputation in the domestic-service community, she'd been unable to replace any of them save the upstairs maid and the resident masseuse. Naturally, she sank into a stew of utter despair.

Things might have remained in that sorry state, but fate

intervened. Barbie's youngest daughter's second-best friend
from school came down with the flu and Barbie went to
the child's house to deliver six dozen cookies and a tray of
brownies. The mother of the ailing child turned out to be
Celeste, who slogged out of her room to answer the door.
Barbie, who always found a good word for everyone, com-
plimented Celeste on her house and her hair, which after
six months in bed resembled a pressed-daisy corsage. She
gushed about Celeste's lovely daughter and mentioned what
wonderful things she'd heard about Camp Pemiquot. In return, Celeste praised Barbie's daughter and her baked goods
and her reputation as an accomplished ballroom dancer.

The two women became fast friends and, after a time,
trusting confidantes. Painfully, slowly, each confessed that
a man had victimized her. They compared notes and
reached the stunning conclusion that Celeste's ex-beau,
Jean-Paul, the Swiss cardiologist, was the same traitorous
lout who had wooed Barbie in the guise of David Steinberg,
the introverted accountant.

Buoyed by their shared travail, they decided to create a
support group. They placed an ad in the local paper, seeking other women that had been scorned in similar fashion.
To their amazement, four of the seven attendees at the kick-
off meeting reported that a man with glacial blue eyes and
a scorpion tattoo had broken their hearts.

Five years had passed since that first fateful meeting and
the six victims had completed an arduous recovery process.
But their healing was fragile and Jan's horrific news sent
all of them staggering back down Memory Lane. Stunned
by the news, they forgot about the darkness and the bone-
piercing cold. They were heedless to the storm raging like
a Regina-quality tantrum outside. Every mind in that dreary
mess hall seethed with murderous rage.

Celeste was the first to give it a voice. "There's only
one way to handle this, Jan. And we all know what that
is."

Leonora nodded gravely. "If garbage is stinking up your place, you take it out."

"If *Mister* Garbage is stinking up your life, you take *him* out," Midgie pronounced.

"Exactly," said Regina. "We take out Mr. Garbage, and that will be the end of it."

"But what about Liddy?" Jan said.

Regina sniffed in dismissal. "You can make up a story. Tell your daughter that Mr. Garbage couldn't reach her at school, so he found your number in the book and left a message with you. Say that he was called away on a family emergency to some remote South Sea island. A couple of days later, you say that one of his relatives called to tell you that a sudden storm came up, and the boat he was taking over to the island disappeared. Missing and presumed drowned. Is that romantic, or what?"

Jan shivered. "Liddy thinks she's in love with that rat. She'll be devastated."

"She's young. She'll get over it," Barbie assured.

"Plus, she'll be a wonderfully tragic figure, which is bound to boost her sagging love life," Regina predicted. "Consider it sort of a social Wonderbra. She'll have a new boyfriend in no time."

"I suppose there's no choice." Jan sighed.

"The only choice we have is how and when." Leonora rummaged in her briefcase for a legal pad and the solid gold Montblanc she'd gotten as an acquittal present from Freddie the Fist. The inlay on the stem was reputed to be genuine femur of stool pigeon. "Okay, people, let's brainstorm. I'll take notes."

Celeste's finger popped up like a turkey timer. "I've got it. We can fix the brakes in his car so he loses control. A fatal accident would be just the thing for that rotten excuse for a man."

"No good. We can't be sure that he wouldn't take some innocent people with him," Leonora said.

"Why don't I send him a tin of poisoned brownies? You

know how he loves sweets. I'll make the ones with hazel-nuts and Reese's Pieces. Even if he gets them anony-mously, he won't be able to resist," Barbie suggested.

Leonora shook her head. "Same problem. Somebody else might eat one by mistake."

"Why don't we just hire your friend Freddie the Fist? Whatever it costs, I'm sure Arthur will be delighted to foot the bill," Regina offered. "After all, what's money for?"

"Freddie's retired. But even if he weren't, I don't believe in mixing business with pleasure. This is our garbage, and we need to take it out ourselves."

"You're right. Why should someone else have all the fun? I have an idea. Why don't we go through the hit pa-rade of murder ideas we've had at these reunions? One of them is bound to be perfect," Midgie said.

"Excellent suggestion," Leonora said. "Who remembers the winner from our first retreat five years ago?"

Regina dipped in a regal bow. "That was mine. I pro-posed that we arrange for him to fall into a vat of boiling chocolate syrup at the Hershey plant in Pennsylvania. Talk about sweet revenge."

"Amusing, but not exactly what I'd call practical," Ce-leste said.

"The next year, I won," said Midgie. "He told me that he's always wanted to learn skydiving but it was too ex-pensive, so my plan was to inform him that he'd won a free lesson in a random drawing. When he pulled the rip cord, instead of the chute opening, a sign would pop up that said, 'April Fool.' Pretty diabolical, if I do say so my-self."

"Unfortunately, none of us knows how to fly a plane," Leonora lamented.

"Barbie won the next year, but now that I think about it, the venomous-snake thing might not work all that well," said Jan. "Given who we're dealing with, he and the snake would probably hit it off and become great friends."

"Last year, the winner was Midgie again, but even if

that plan were to work, we'd have to wait for the opening day of next year's deer-hunting season and find the pelts and the antlers and some way to glue them on so he couldn't rip them off. Plus, what's to stop him from standing up and making it clear that he's really a two-legged animal and not a sweet, four-legged Bambi type at all?" Regina said.

Leonora tapped her walrus teeth with the pen. "Think, people. We need to come up with a fresh, ingenious, foolproof plan."

"How about setting fire to his house? We nail the doors and windows shut from the outside, so he's trapped. As far as I'm concerned, burning is an excellent way to deal with rotten garbage like him."

"Brilliant scheme, Regina. There's only one tiny thing wrong with it," Midgie said.

"What?"

"He doesn't *have* a house. You know how he lives. He's forever moving around, woman to woman, thing to thing, town to town. He stays on the go so he doesn't get caught or sued or arrested or shot. I don't even know how we'd go about finding him."

"You can always reach him on his cell phone," Barbie said meekly. "He's kept the same number right along."

"How would you know that?" Celeste challenged. "Don't tell me you're still calling him. I thought you had that under control."

Barbie buried her face in her hands. "I do, mostly. It's only once or twice a month now, never more than once a week, and I hang up the second I hear his voice."

"Pathetic," Regina said.

"Don't you think I know that?" Barbie swiped a tear. "The hold he has on me is a living hell. I want him gone as much as anyone does. Maybe more, because of the obsessive behavior. In fact, I have this recurring dream where I'm pouring new footings for a house I'm working on, and he's lying unconscious in the wet cement. I keep pouring and pouring until he disappears. Then I pull up a chair, a really comfortable Barcalounger, and watch while it sets. I wake up laughing so hard my stomach hurts."

"That's it! Barbie, you're a genius." Leonora pulled her timid friend up from the Adirondack chair and danced her in a dizzy circle.

"Excuse me. What am I missing here?" Regina asked.

"Beats me," Midgie said. "What are you talking about, Leonora? Calm down and speak English."

Leonora planted the gasping Barbie back in her seat. She settled in her own Adirondack chair and leaned forward. "Here's the plan. We get Mr. Garbage to come to here later this week. We do him in and hide the body under a pile of junk. Then, when the construction crews show up, they excavate, bury the debris, and pour the foundation for the parking structure and the mall stores. Our handful becomes landfill. Talk about poetic justice."

"I love it, Leonora. The only thing wrong is that I didn't think of it myself," Regina said.

"Wait. That's not the only thing wrong." Celeste nibbled her lower lip. "You're proposing an actual murder, Leonora. Talking about it is one thing. When push comes to shove, I don't believe that any of us is actually capable of killing a person."

"Since when is *he* a *person*?" Regina's flask was empty. She bent down to fill it from the fifth of Jack Daniel's that lay at her feet like a faithful dog.

Midgie frowned. "I'm afraid Celeste is right. Admit it, Regina, you may be a raging bitch and a blatant gold digger, but I don't see even you taking an actual life."

"I suppose it would be messy," Regina admitted. "I could break a nail."

"Liddy means the world to me, and I'd do most anything for her, but I honestly don't think I could kill anyone in cold blood," said Jan.

"Well, his blood is ice-cold. You, Barbie?" Celeste challenged.

"I could watch him die. I honestly believe I would enjoy that, but I don't think any of us could actually make it happen."

"It's true," Midgie said. "In my psychology studies, I learned that committing a homicide requires serious pathology. The killer must either be a sociopath, which none of us is, or a normal person terrified or enraged enough to put normal conscience and morality aside. We're obviously all far too healthy to do such a thing."

"*Way* too healthy. Plus who wants to risk a jail term?" said Jan.

"Not me," Barbie said. "Who'd look after my children?"

"And mine," said Jan.

"Who'd look after my patients?" Midgie mused.

"Who'd look after my clients?" Leonora pondered.

"Who'd look after my hair?" said Regina.

"Wait a second. Back up. I think Barbie's hit the nail on the head again," Leonora exulted. "We don't need to murder the creep. All we need to do is set it up, sit back, and enjoy."

"You've lost me again, Leonora." Regina groused.

"It's dead simple. Let me explain."

As Leonora laid out the plan, the women listened raptly. To dispose of garbage effectively, you needed to promote rot and breakdown until the putrid debris was reduced to base, harmless elements.

In this case, they had everything they needed to ensure a clean, thorough waste-removal process. "Here's what we know," said Leonora. "He has a family history of sudden heart attack, which is how he knew enough to fake that business with Barbie about losing his wife. In fact, his father and his older brother died at forty-three, which he happens to turn this year."

"I remember him mentioning that years ago. He's really spooked about it," Barbie said.

"Plus, he's a major hypochondriac. Always popping

pills, forever obsessing about some symptom or the other," said Jan.

"True, and he told me that his doctor has warned that he has a monstrous bad cholesterol level. He claimed he was really worried about it, but he never did anything at all to help the situation," said Celeste. "His diet is atrocious, and he never gets a lick of exercise. He drinks too much, and smokes those hideous cigars."

"Exactly. He's a setup to join his relatives at Fairfield Memorial Park. All we need to do is give him a tiny, little push," said Leonora. "Here's what I'm thinking." Leonora laid out the plan in great gory detail. The women giggled in anticipatory delight. The creep was a goner.

Regina frowned. "No fair, Leonora. Everyone has a part but me. What can I do to help?"

"Just be yourself, dear," said Leonora. "That's bound to push him over the edge."

"Excellent," said Regina. "Count me in."

• • •

THE appointed day got off to a perfect start. Jan, who sounded exactly like her daughter Lydia, called Romeo on his cell phone and lured him to a street corner near Liddy's college dorm. There, Leonora and Midgie pounced and wrestled him into the trunk of Regina's waiting Mercedes. Barbie bound his feet and mouth with electrical tape from her construction business and Leonora slapped on handcuffs that were a souvenir of her days on the Stamford force.

The women's luck continued on the trip. The ride to the camp took half an hour less than expected, smooth roads, clear skies, no traffic. They all pretended to ignore the bumps and muffled protests from the rear.

In the week since their last visit, the property had been transformed. The rutted access road was peppered with warnings. CONSTRUCTION AREA, KEEP OUT. AUTHORIZED PERSONNEL ONLY. HARD HATS REQUIRED. Huge interlocking dollar signs, logo of the Sackwell Corporation, obscured the splintered Camp Pemiquot sign. Bulldozers, backhoes, and cement mixers littered the grounds.

As they pulled up beside the mess hall, Celeste raced out to greet them. "Thank heavens you're here. The construction crew came in with all their equipment earlier today. They already dug a test pit and filled it with cement to test the setup rate under these soil and weather conditions. I told the foreman I was here to pick up some stuff I'd forgotten, and he said I'd better hurry and get out. Apparently, the mall developer has offered a bonus if the project comes in ahead of schedule. Starting first thing tomorrow, they'll be here in force, working around the clock to level the buildings, dig the foundations, and excavate for the parking lot. We've got eighteen hours, tops."

Leonora peered at Casanova, cowering in the rear seat. His opalescent eyes bulged with fear. His chest heaved and his skin had taken on a sickly blue cast. "Piece of cake. I'll be amazed if he lasts half that long," she said.

They ferried him into the mess hall and set him down, still bound and gagged, in an Adirondack chair. Celeste looped a pressure cuff around his upper arm. "Terrible color, clammy skin. Looks like a nice, serious case of shock is setting in. Lovely." She pumped the bulb. "His pressure is normal. How odd."

Mr. Garbage struggled to speak. He chafed against his bonds and wriggled like a hooked flounder.

"That'll change. I'd tried to relax if I were you, Vernon honey," Regina said. "You're a major heart attack waiting to happen. Doesn't he look dreadful, girls?"

"Absolutely," said Jan. "I think this poor, pathetic creature needs medical help. Take the tape off dear Carl's mouth, Leonora. I have just the thing."

Leonora peeled back the duct tape, spread his jaws, and tipped his head back. "Open up, Ricky boy. Say 'ah.' "

Jan poured in a mixture of over-the-counter medications guaranteed to throw his system in total chaos: Ex-Lax, Imodium, No-Doz, Sleep-ez, on and on. Regina followed with a stream of Jack Daniel's from her flask. "Down the hatch, sweetie. Yum, yum."

He was sputtering and coughing when they slapped on the tape again. "Oh my. His pressure is still normal," declared Celeste. "We'd better try harder. We need to bring on a stroke or a heart attack, and fast."

"I'll lay you three to one it's a heart attack," said Leonora.

"I thought you weren't betting anymore," Midgie chided. She walked to the picnic table, dipped into the candy bowl, and filled her mouth with peanut M&M's.

"And I thought you were on a strict maintenance diet," Leonora shot back.

"Everyone knows that what you eat standing up doesn't count."

Jan scratched her neck. "Oh no. Don't tell me that hideous rash is coming back." She rummaged through the pillboxes in her purse, desperately seeking relief.

Regina's flask was empty. She picked up the bottle and drained it in one long, determined pull. "Don't anyone dare say a thing to Arthur. I promised I wouldn't drink anymore."

"Well, you're certainly not drinking any less," Leonora observed.

"Who asked you, horse face?"

"Ladies, please. There's no need for anyone to get angry or upset," said Barbie. "I know. Why don't I build a fire and whip up a nice batch of tollhouse cookies?"

"No baking, Barbie. You swore off, remember?" Jan scratched like a flea-ridden dog.

Celeste dropped her stethoscope and pressure cuff. "I'm so tired all of a sudden. If nobody minds, I think I'll go lie down."

Barbie's hand flew to her mouth. "My Lord. What's happening to us? How come everyone's falling apart?"

Leonora signaled for a time-out. "Hold your horses. No

one is doing anything of the kind. He's the only one falling apart. In fact I'll bet a C-note he doesn't make it past midnight. Who's in? You, Jan? Regina?"

No one responded. Each of the women had sunk into a cold private hell. Midgie kept shoveling in the candy. Jan scratched herself raw. Celeste was a waxen puddle of despair. Barbie went off in search of cookie ingredients while Regina dashed out to fetch the spare fifth of bourbon from the trunk of her Mercedes. Leonora kept begging for someone, anyone, to cover her action. "Come on, Celeste. Don't be chicken. How about you, Jan? I'll give you three-to-one odds on midnight and two-to-one on eleven P.M."

Jan raked at her left arm, then moved on to her flaming right knee. She scratched her ankle with her toes and tortured her ear across her shoulder. "Leave me alone, Leonora. Can't you see I've got my hands full?"

As soon as Regina staggered in from the car with the fresh bottle of Jack Daniel's, Leonora pounced. "Okay, Miss Megabucks. It's up to you. Show us what you're made of, baby. Mama needs a new pair of shoes."

"Go to Bloomingdale's or Saks, then. They have adorable Ferragamos all the way up to a size thirteen," Regina slurred. "Try the blue crocodile. Very chic."

"I'm talking about a wager, Regina. A little betsky wetsky."

"I only bet on men, Leonora. Rich ones."

"Nobody will cover? What's wrong with you people? — Where's your spirit of adventure?" Leonora's pleas resounded in the chill, dark hall. "Won't somebody take my action? Anybody? How about a measly fifty, then? Twenty? Two bits?"

She fell silent, waiting. All the women went mum, shocked mute by their own appalling regression. The mess hall was still except for one odd sound. It was a low, repeating tick like the noise of a reluctant motor. They all cast around for its source.

"Look." Midgie stuffed her mouth with potato chips,

then leveled a pudgy finger at their prisoner. "He's laughing."

"The nerve!" railed Regina in drunken outrage.

"You stop that right this minute," Jan demanded as she scratched.

Mr. Garbage laughed harder, doubling over in the chair. The color seeped back in his cheeks and his pale eyes flashed with defiance.

"He's enjoying himself. Having a great old time. I can't believe it." Celeste dragged up from her chair and took his blood pressure. "Still one-ten over seventy. This can't be."

"Maybe there's something wrong with the gauge," Jan suggested. "Here, check mine." The arm she presented was a patchwork of flaming welts.

"Yours is through the roof, Jan. Let me try yours, Midgie."

Celeste tested each of the women in turn. Everyone had dangerously elevated pressure, ragged pulses, and other symptoms of life-threatening stress. "Nobody panic. We all need to sit down, calm down, and get a grip."

The women endeavored to follow her prescription, but as they settled in the ring of Adirondack chairs, Casanova continued to laugh. He was tickled by Jan's scratching and Midgie's gorging and Regina's tippling and the others, who twitched with compulsion and need. Tears of mirth flowed from his ice-blue eyes. His bound body shook with unbounded delight.

"Somebody stop him," demanded Jan.

"I can't stand it." Midgie clutched her ears and howled.

"Cut it out, right now, or I'll fix it so you never laugh again." Regina wielded the bourbon bottle like a club, which only added to Romeo's amusement.

"Okay. You asked for it, you get it." Leonora butted his seat like a dyspeptic bull, toppling it on its side. A puff of surprise escaped Mr. Garbage as he spilled from the chair and sprawled on the hardwood floor. His laughter ceased.

"That's better," Midgie declared. "Now, you want to see

something really funny? Watch." She lifted herself heavily from her chair, flopped on Casanova's abdomen, and bounced.

"Tsk, tsk, Midgie. That's terrible. You're knocking the air out of him," Leonora said. As his face slackened with relief, she went on. "It would be much better if you stood. Get more leverage. Maybe crack a couple of bones. Move aside and allow me to demonstrate."

Leonora stomped Casanova as if he were on fire. Next, Barbie demonstrated a fancy break step in the Argentine tango on his chest.

"Great work, girls. He's not looking so all-fired terrific anymore," said Celeste. She knelt beside him and took his pulse. "Damn," she frowned. "He takes a licking and keeps on ticking. It's as if he's not human."

"That's because he isn't," Jan observed.

"Stop right there," said Leonora. "Jan hit the nail on the head. We've been looking at this all wrong. In fact, if we bump him off, we're not really killing anyone. Legally speaking, taking out garbage isn't a crime, it's good citizenship."

"I couldn't agree more," Midgie said. "But how should we do it?"

"I've got the answer," said Celeste. "We're sitting in it. This mess hall is highly flammable split-log construction. Dry as dust. We can lock him in, light the match, and poof."

"Excellent idea. Nothing like a nice big bonfire. Anyone have marshmallows?" Jan asked.

"As long as all the *people* are safely outside, no harm would be done," Leonora observed.

"Definitely. We'll make sure all the *human beings* are out before we torch the joint. Come, girls, let's go. Out Midgie, out Leonora, out Barbie, out Jan. Out with you, Regina. Chop, chop," said Celeste.

The women filed out, chattering happily amongst themselves. They paid no attention to Mr. Garbage, who struggled against his restraints and emitted muffled terror noises.

Celeste exited last and fastened the lock behind her. Midgie and Jan raced around the rickety structure, latching the storm shutters. "There's some kerosene in the equipment shed. I'll get it," Celeste said.

She returned in moments with a five-gallon can of the flammable fuel and splashed it liberally across the front of the mess hall. Regina produced a gold lighter. "I'll do the honors."

"Can't I, please?" Barbie said.

"No way. He went after my daughter. I'm all over this." Jan tried to wrest the lighter from Regina, who bared her bonded teeth and growled.

"I said, I'll do it. Now back off!"

Celeste entered the fray. "It's my mess hall and I get to burn it down."

"No, me," screeched Midgie.

"It was my idea," Barbie intoned with rare conviction. "Now give!" She grabbed for the lighter, but Regina held fast.

"Ouch! Now look what you did. You chipped my polish, damn you," Regina yelped. "Now everyone, all you cows, back off!"

"Wait. Cut it out. Cool down." Leonora stepped between the feuding friends. "Now, shut up and listen. I just realized something. This is not going to work."

"Why not?" asked Midgie.

"If we burn down this building, the construction people are bound to get suspicious. They might ask questions, bring in the fire marshal to investigate. Who knows? It's too risky."

Jan sighed. "She's right."

"What do you propose then, Leonora?" asked Celeste.

"I don't know. We have to be creative. Let's try to think about this as if we're trying to come up with the best-ever revenge fantasy winner."

Slumped in defeat, they filed back into the mess hall. At

the sight of them, Mr. Garbage started laughing again. His body shook and his cold eyes flashed with sadistic merriment.

Leonora pulled the tape off his mouth. "What's so damned funny, you lying, thieving, two-timing creep?"

He roared with hilarity. "You are, that's what's funny. You dumpy frumps can't get anything right. If you want the truth, I've always thought of you as a bunch of cartoon characters." His head tipped toward Midgie, Celeste, and Regina. "There's Betty Boop and Blondie Bumstead and Morticia Addams, and of course you, dear Leonora, sort of a King Kong in drag." He turned to Barbie. "Of course, I'm not forgetting you, Minnie Mouse, or you, Jan baby, the Little Orphan Annie of pill-pushers. Did any of you really believe that a man like me would give any of you a genuine tumble? Can you really be that dumb?"

"It seems we could," Celeste rasped behind clenched teeth.

"Yes. But we've wised up. Haven't we, girls?" said Jan.

"Definitely," said Midgie.

"Yeah sure. Now, I've given you hags more than enough of my valuable time and attention. Untie me, Leonora. It's been amusing, but I have far better things to do."

"No you don't, Carl. We're going to see to it that you don't do any more *things* ever again," Jan said tightly.

He chuckled. "I must say that daughter of yours is a tasty morsel. But she's not exactly the killer type and neither are you. Fact is, I'm going to do exactly what and *whom* I please, and all you're going to do about it is scratch."

"The nerve of you!" shrieked Midgie. "I'll remind you that you're in no position to insult anybody, you disgusting pig."

"Takes one to know one, Porky."

Midgie's lip quavered. "You'd better shut up, or we'll shut you up."

"Sure, sure. You'll do nothing but stuff your face as usual."

"Leave her alone, you rude, horrid man. She's doing the best she can. We all are," said Barbie.

"All you ever do, Betty Crocker, is bake someone crappy."

"You take that back," Barbie demanded in her tapioca voice. "I haven't baked a thing in months."

"You broads are so predictable, it's pathetic."

"You'd better quit while you're ahead, Ricky boy," Leonora said. A feral growl rumbled deep in her chest.

"Or what?"

"Or we'll teach you some manners—the hard way."

He snickered. "Fat chance. All you're going to do is feel sorry for yourselves. Blondie will cower under the covers, and Olive Oyl will drown herself in booze."

"I'm telling you to stop!" Leonora barked. "I'm warning you."

"Give it a rest, Godzilla. I bet all you're going to do is call your bookie and drop everything on some long-shot dog."

Leonora rose like a tidal wave. "I'll take that action, Ricky boy. The only dog I'm going to drop everything on is you."

He chuckled harder. "Whoa, lookee. I'm shaking in my boots. Tell you what, Mighty Joe. I'll call you and raise you one."

"And I'll see *that* and raise *you* one." Leonora hefted her Adirondack chair overhead. With a simian roar, she brought it down on Casanova's cranium. A startled look replaced the arrogant glint in his eyes. Then he went blank and still.

Celeste knelt and checked his pulse. "My Lord, Leonora. You've killed him."

Leonora shrugged. "He asked for it."

"This is terrible," Jan cried. "He didn't suffer nearly enough."

"Ah well. Good riddance to bad garbage." Midgie frowned. "Now, anyone have a good idea about how to get rid of it?"

"Construction always involves disposing of a lot of trash. Leave it to me," said Barbie. She climbed in the cab of a giant backhoe, maneuvered to the filled test pit, and started scooping out the fresh cement. In minutes, the hole gaped wide enough to accommodate a major pile of trash.

Leonora, Midgie, Jan and Celeste dragged Mr. Garbage from the mess hall and deposited him in the crypt. Regina tossed in every one of her bourbon bottles and Midgie threw in the remaining candies and chips. Barbie ripped up her top-secret brownie recipe and scattered the scraps over all. Leonora followed with the little black book that contained her bookie's numbers and a cheat sheet for calculating odds. Celeste contributed her antidepressive medications and Jan tossed in the dozen pill bottles from her purse. They would not need any of those pitiful crutches anymore.

Barbie worked the giant mixer and frosted everything in a smooth, even layer of cement. Then each of the women carried out an Adirondack chair and settled down to watch until it set. Except for the occasional peel of merriment, they savored the moment in silence.

The first light of dawn crept over the horizon. A crisp, fresh breeze stirred the air. It was going to be a lovely, lovely day.

COLLABORATION

by Warren Murphy

"NICE. Who's your decorator? I might get him to redo my pigeon coop. The toilet without a seat is particularly *eleganza*."

"Well, well, well, if it isn't Detective Slivovitz, the half-wit's answer to Sherlock Holmes. I was expecting the priest. You know, the part where he comes to save my soul before I go shuffling off to Buffalo or wherever hell is these days."

"I save dimes in a jar on my dresser."

"You would. What's the point?"

"Apart from that, Dalton, I'm not much of a saver. You want to save your soul or anything else, the priest'll be along later. That fit in with your busy schedule? Should I check with your appointments secretary?"

"Nasty to the end, Slivovitz. I don't know what I did to earn such hatred."

"Breathe."

"Well . . ." The one called Dalton looked at his wrist-watch. "In just ninety-two minutes, you won't have to worry about that anymore, will you? You can go back to tracking down criminal masterminds who've double-parked . . . more challenges for Super Sleuth. Unless, of course, something happens. A power failure, I escape."

"Dream on, Dalton. You'll never escape. The lights go out, I will find you in the dark and personally beat you to death."

"They'll know you did it. They're not all as dumb as you, you know."

"Nobody will know I did it because nobody will give a rat's ass. We're talking about *you*, Dalton. They'll just make sure you're dead, we'll all pee on your corpse, call it suicide by drowning, and then go across the street and get drunk to celebrate. Remember: You're the totally expendable subhuman."

• • •

THE man who had been addressed as Dalton frowned.

"I don't know about that, Freddy," he said in a hesitant voice. "Maybe too harsh?"

"Harsh? You're a killer. You murdered your boss. When I came after you, you stalked my wife and tried to rape her. So I send you up and now I've come to death row to watch you be sautéed. We hate each other. What harsh? And besides, you started it. I come in, you call me stupid right away. You bet I'm harsh. And you do a lot of calling me stupid."

"Hey, these are only characters, hah? Slivovitz is here to get something out of Dalton. Would he do that by insulting him?"

"He'd never believe it if Slivovitz was trying to be nice. Look, have we got to argue this every time? After all these years? Do what I tell you, okay? You're doing all right. You're making a lot of money, which is what you really care about. So you do your guy, I'll do my guy."

"All right, if you say so," the one called Dalton said. "Good touch with saving the dimes."

"Let's just move along, huh?"

"Christ, you're in some mood. Where were we?"

"I beat you to death, pee on your body, we all go get drunk, bibbity, bobbity, boo."

"Okay."

• • •

"I think I'd just as soon have you leave, Slivovitz. Spending my last minutes with you isn't exactly my idea of a bon voyage party."

"Make believe you're on the *Titanic*."

"Just leave."

"You know you don't want me to."

"Oh? Tell me about this great insight, Slivovitz."

"Because there's nobody after me. Nobody's waiting outside to talk to you. I'm all there is. Everybody else has forgotten about you, so you need me if you want to explain yourself before you go to that great short circuit in the sky."

The one called Dalton laughed derisively and the other said, "Share the joke. If it's real good, I'll send it in to *Reader's Digest*. Humor in Prison Garb."

"I just realized why you're really here. You still aren't sure what happened and you're waiting for me to tell you. What is it? After all these years, you finally afraid you got the wrong man? You having trouble sleeping at night, Slivovitz?"

"I sleep just fine."

Dalton ignored his answer. "It's the money, isn't it? You're sure I did the killing alone but you're still wondering how I got that ten thousand dollars in my bank account."

"I couldn't care less."

"All right. Then get out of here."

"But if you want to tell me where the money came from, I'll keep you company while you're reminiscing."

"I thought you might," Dalton said.

"Look, if you weren't alone, tell somebody. Who knows what happens next? In the meantime, you're still alive."

"I don't know if you want to go there, Slivovitz."

"Try me."

"How's the wife?" The one called Dalton smiled.

• • •

IN an adjoining room, Nora Baines and Mimi Florell sat, sipping wine, in what had quickly turned into an awkward failed attempt at their first real get-acquainted meeting.

Ordinarily, with guests, Nora was gracious and easygoing, but since Mimi Florell had arrived, she had found herself fidgeting, running back and forth out of the room, to get ice cubes, napkins, tissues—tangible signs of unease—and it was all a little tiring.

Mimi had been trying hard to show how excited she was at having become the wife of the great television writer Freddy Florell, who was half of the even-greater television partnership of Freddy Florell and Ted Baines, and now she was saying that she thought it was "cute" that the two writers still collaborated on a script the same way they had when they started writing together twenty years earlier—by locking themselves in a room and acting out the story.

Nora found it hard to concentrate on what Mimi was saying. In fact, she was finding it difficult not to simply regard the young, pretty woman sitting across from her as just the ordinary, attractive imbecile hired for marriage by an ordinary aging man who had more money than was good for him. But there was something about the new Mrs. Florell that made Nora uneasy.

It wasn't only that Nora was older; these days it seemed to her that everyone was younger than she. But Nora had been close with Jane Florell before her tragic death and now she knew she was never going to be close with Mimi in that same way. She and Jane had gone through the hard times together and had been friends for years. Nora just didn't have that many years left to spend on making friends with Mimi.

Making friends wasn't something you did over a week-

end. It took a lifetime and the results were supposed to last
a lifetime. People weren't supposed to go die on you. And
Jane had done that. And then Freddy, who should have had
more sense, had gone off and married this woman who was
not much more than a girl. Nora and Ted, Freddy, they
were all pushing sixty. And this Mimi had miles to go before she even saw thirty.

*God save the aging widower from the jackals in the
secretarial pool,* Nora thought.

She looked at the young smiling woman, a megawatt
testimonial to dental hygiene and happy thoughts, and tried
to concentrate on what she might have been saying. It
wasn't fair to think she was from the secretarial pool. She
had been something else at the offices with Ted and
Freddy's production company. What was it?

A reader. She had been a reader, which in a way was
curious, because being a reader of unsolicited proposals for
unnecessary television shows was just a way-station job.
Nobody held it for more than a couple of months, but Nora
seemed to remember that Mimi had been working for the
Florell and Baines production company for a couple of
years. She came right out of college and she had a small
office right outside Ted's. Ted had said she was a good
reader.

Mimi was staring at her and Nora nodded, not quite sure
of what she was agreeing with. Something about how tragic
Jane Florell's death had been. Mimi had been with her. She
had gone to Jane's midtown apartment to deliver some
mail, and found poor Jane dead on the sofa. She had suf-
focated, apparently choked to death, because there were
pieces of cashew in her mouth.

Mimi had called Ted, who had gone over to the Florells'
and then handled all the awful business of calling the police
and breaking the news to Freddy. It must have been awful
on the young girl, Nora thought, although in truth the look
on Mimi's face as she babbled on about the events seemed
more excited than dismayed.

It was all very depressing, Nora thought. People her age and Ted's age and Freddy's age should not have to deal with sudden awful deaths like Jane's. Their only meeting with death should be in the upstairs bed at the end of a long placid illness. Mimi would not understand; she was just too damned young.

She hoped Freddy and Ted would finish working on their script soon so that Mimi would go home. She did not like death, thinking about it or talking about it. And suddenly she had a great resentment for Mimi, who seemed to be enjoying the recounting of Jane's death. *Almost as if were an accomplishment of hers.*

• • •

"YOUR trouble, Slivovitz, is that you're not a creative thinker."

"Oh, I'm really hurt, being criticized by a genius like you. That's always been your problem, thinking you're smarter and better than everybody else and that you're able to get over on anybody about anything."

• • •

"WHAT's that got to do with the story, Freddy?" Ted Baines asked.

"Forget it," Florell snapped. *"Let's just keep going. I'll do it again."*

• • •

"OH, I'm really hurt, being criticized by a death-row genius like you," Slivovitz said.

"You just couldn't shake that idea that I killed Watson because he found out my accounting firm had stolen all this money from his law practice. That's what you peddled to the district attorney."

"Something like that."

"But there was always that sudden deposit of ten thousand in my bank account just before . . . just before it happened. You never figured that out, do you?"

"I didn't have to," Slivovitz said. "I just had to show you were there and it was your gun and you had a motive, and that was that, that was my job, nothing more. I was just doing my job."

"Yeah, sure. The Nazi defense. 'I vass chust doing my chob.' But deep down, you're wondering, Was someone else in on this? Did someone else get away with it?"

"And you think the ten thousand proves that? That somebody hired you to hit Watson? You? A contract killer? You were a lousy accountant. I wouldn't hire you to hang wallpaper. Get outta here."

"You say it easily. But you're not sure, are you, Slivovitz?"

There was no answer.

"Somebody could have trusted me to do it," Dalton said, and grinned. "I don't know if I should tell you anything. Maybe I should just let you stew about it, for the rest of your life, thinking you blew this case."

"Whatever you say."

"Does your wife know you're here, Slivovitz?"

"Look, I told you before, let's just leave my wife out of it, huh? Or you won't make it for the next ninety minutes."

"You still got that rape thing in your mind, don't you?"

"Rape's not something you forget. I show up at your place to question you and I hear screaming and I find her in your bedroom. Yeah, that's something I don't want to make into a Kodak moment. I'm just glad I got there in time to save her and nail you."

"Well, look at the bright side. You were the big hero and she winds up marrying you out of gratitude. You don't think you had a chance with her otherwise, do you? She's a hotshot lawyer. She is Watson's favorite. He's going to make her a partner. You think she was going to marry you because she wants to eat at Taco Bell for the rest of her life? She's beautiful and smart and young, and you, on your best day, look like old dog food that was left out in the rain."

"So I'm supposed to thank you?"

"Someday, maybe not today, but someday, you'll remember this conversation and then you *will* thank me."

"Yeah, well, forget that. We were talking about your fantasy that somebody hired you to whack old Watson."

The one called Dalton shook his head sadly. "What do you think we *are* talking about? Man, you are dumb, Slivovitz."

• • •

SHE had started out very politely, addressing Nora as "Mrs. Baines" and referring to Ted as "Mr. Baines," but Mimi Florell had become awfully familiar in a hurry, Nora thought.

It was probably the generational gap between them. Young people were like that. And, of course, Mimi was now Freddy's wife. She was the new fourth wheel on the old wagon. But, still, wouldn't simple manners suggest that she move gently into this relationship with her new husband's longtime friends and partners?

"Well, just naturally, I thought of calling Ted. Because, you know, being around the office with him and all, you see what a take-charge kind of guy he is, and so, well, when there was trouble, of course, Ted's the one I'd call right away." Mimi was talking, talking, talking . . . talking as if by compulsion, talking as if she wanted to establish, for all time, a permanent record of her actions, and Nora wished she would shut up. She forced a smile as Mimi chattered on.

"I've always respected Ted and he's taught me so much about the television theater form. That's what I want to do in the future, write my own television dramas." Mimi smiled engagingly at Mrs. Baines, who was delighted to see that the young woman had a piece of bright yellow cheddar cheese stuck between her teeth. "You were never interested in writing yourself, were you?" Mimi asked.

"Why do you assume that?" Nora responded, but there was a small ache growing in the pit of her stomach. Perhaps she should pay a little more attention to what this dimbulb was talking about.

"I . . . er . . . I mean, I never saw any script with your name on it or anything," Mimi stammered. She nodded, as if to encourage herself in a lie. "Yes, that's it, I always expected to see one of your scripts but I never did, so I just figured you weren't interested in the artistic end of the business."

"Jane, Freddy's late wife, and I were very alike," Nora said crisply. "She wasn't interested in being a writer either."

Mimi smiled happily. "That's what Ted said. Very alike."

The pain in the pit of Mrs. Baines's stomach seemed to spread.

• • •

"YEAH, but who besides you had any reason to kill Watson?"

"You expect me to do all your work for you, Slivovitz? You pretend to have a brain. Try to use it, as unfamiliar an action as that may be."

"You know, I'm only seconds away from slapping you silly."

"In my own jail cell? Committing assault? Please."

"I can leave."

"And you'll never have your answers," Dalton said.

"I don't think there are any answers left," the one called Slivovitz said. "I think your boss at the law firm caught you stealing. He was going to have your ass arrested and you killed him. When I got on your tail, you thought to freak me out, maybe get me off the track, by raping my girlfriend. You dragged her over to your place, but just by good luck, I got there in time, before you could do anything, and then I found your murder gun and the state sent you here. I don't have any questions."

• • •

"Now here, Slivovitz heads for the door of the cell and somehow you've got to stop him," Florell said.

"Suppose I just tell him the truth, that his wife's a murderous tramp?" Ted Baines answered.

"You're really convinced that's where to go with this?"

"Of course. She's the one behind the whole thing. She was the thief; she was the one who seduced Dalton into killing the boss. The rape was a crock. She hollered rape just so she wouldn't get nailed, too, and Dalton didn't see any reason to hand her up. Except now. Maybe he wants to cleanse his immortal soul. He ought to tell Slivovitz the truth, that his wife's a bimbo. It's his way of getting even with the guy who sent him to death row."

"Why did I know you were going to dump all over the only woman in the story?" Florell asked.

"Because women are the root of all evil."

"And it's a cliché, the unfaithful wife, blah blah blah."

"Most clichés are true," Baines said.

"Why not something different? Maybe Dalton blames it on Slivovitz's wife, but she's really innocent and Slivovitz figures it out?"

"Too complicated," Baines said. "How would we ever show that?"

"Hey, you're the big genius," Florell said. "I read about it while I was on my honeymoon. 'Ted Baines, the driving force, the genius, behind the string of hit TV shows from Florell and Baines.' Maybe we should change it to Baines and Florell. Anyway, a little thing like this shouldn't cause you any trouble, big genius that you are. I read all about how you were 'carrying on' for the partnership. Just keep carrying on."

"All right," Baines snapped. "You want it your way, you'll have it your way."

• • •

"SEE you," Slivovitz said. "Have a nice life—for eighty minutes or so."

"Sure. *Sí, sí, sí, sí, sí*. What's the look for, Detective? *Sí*. That means yes in Spanish."

"Don't get wise with me."

"And *Sí, sí, sí* means yes, yes, yes. I bet some women even shout out things like that when they're making love. I wonder how many do the same thing when they're being raped."

When the one called Slivovitz just stared at him, Dalton said, "Sound like something you've heard?"

"You're a liar."

"You're worried so much about the ten thousand dollars that got into my account. Did you ever look at your wife's savings account? Did you ever see that ten thousand came out of it? Was that part of your investigation? Or were you so busy being goo-goo-eyed over the sexy lawyer lady who came on to you that you forgot to check?"

"I don't believe you," Slivovitz said.

"Of course you don't. You can't believe that your wife was the one who looted Watson's firm. That when he found out, it was her idea to get rid of him and she talked me into doing it and paid me, too. That I was in her bed collecting my regular bonus when you showed up that night and she pretended rape so you wouldn't suspect."

For long moments Slivovitz did not speak.

• • •

MIMI Florell could not hold her liquor well, so it had been an easy matter to convince her that drinking Grand Marnier was not any different from sipping a glass of wine, and soon the young woman was sleepy-eyed and thick-lipped.

But she was still talking. Apparently, nothing less than total coma could shut that young mouth, Nora thought.

"All my friends say that Freddy's too old for me but I

don't think so. Besides, he needs me. Even before his wife died, he was real nice to me in the office. Ted even said Freddy liked me a lot, and so when what's-her-name died, like choked on those cashew nuts, I was just there for Freddy. And he's not too old at all. I'll say. *Sí, sí, sí.* Not too old at all."

She winked lewdly and waved her glass at Nora, who refilled it from the squat brown bottle on the coffee table. Mimi held the drink tenaciously with two hands and sipped.

"It makes you realize how precious life is," she said, but her speech had become muddy and she could not quite get her tongue around the word "precious." She tried to say it again and seemed to lose her train of thought halfway through. "It makes you realize . . ."

"What does?"

"Oh, how easy she died," Mimi said, sipping, smiling, her eyes glinting over the top rim of the snifter.

"It couldn't have been easy," Nora said.

"It was easy. One minute she was breathing, the next she wasn't. And she was so small. So weak." She smiled again. "We're going to be such good friends. I want to spend time with you," Mimi said. "I think Ted would like that." She paused and added, as if in an afterthought, "Freddy, too."

Nora nodded and could feel her rapid heartbeat resonating in her throat. Curiously, she remembered some old lines of joke dialogue from when she was a kid.

One kid would say, "See ya," and the other would respond, "Not if I see you first."

She looked at Mimi. *Not if I see you first,* she thought, and then she wondered if Jane ever knew, if she had known she was going to die before it happened to her. Suddenly, she was very angry. There was just no one in the world you could trust. No one. No one.

• • •

"I'M out of here. You're delusional," Slivovitz said, "and I'm not just going to stay around so you can pull my chain."

"Go ahead, go. You found out what you came for. What you really expected to find out, too."

• • •

"I just don't feel right about that," Florell said. "There's something that plain sticks in my craw about Slivovitz's wife being a killer."

"Hey," Baines said, with a smile. "She's a woman. They're all defective. You can't trust any of them."

"Maybe you've been hanging out with the wrong kind of women. Or maybe too many of them. Maybe that's why you're pulling more and more money out of the partnership," Florell said.

Baines looked toward the door, beyond which he knew his wife was sitting with Mimi Florell. "So that's what this is about," he said. "Well, don't you worry about my women," he snapped, in a sharp low voice. "I don't need any lectures from you. Let's just finish this, huh?"

"And I don't care what you do, as long as it doesn't interfere with the work and the profits."

"And now I'm interfering?" Baines demanded.

"Yeah. You're drawing out every cent you can get your hands on. Plus, this rotten view you have of everybody, it's just seeping into our stories. Everything's a bummer."

"Life's a bummer," Baines insisted.

Florell sighed and Baines asked, "So what'll be the end of the scene?"

"We'll think of something. Let's just finish and get out of here. I'm getting a headache."

"All right. So Slivovitz is going to the door to be let out by the guard and Dalton stops him," Baines said.

• • •

"You know those dimes you collect on your dresser?"

Slivovitz grunted.

"You know why the dumb jar never gets full?"

"I'm sure you'll tell me."

"The jar never gets full 'cause your wife is stealing the dimes. She steals the change. She takes money out of your wallet. She's got total contempt for you. Everything you think you own, you worked for, she's got in her name. What you got, Slivovitz, is spit. She's got everything else. And you know what she does with it? She gives it to her boyfriends. Friends, Slivovitz, not friend. She's got a lot of them, besides me. I saw it when I was with her. And you ought to wise up. Just think of everybody who's always just leaving the house when you come home from work. The grocery boy, the guy from the gas station, the parcel-post guy, your partners at the precinct, everybody. They're all there. They're all always there, with your wife, and they're all laughing at you behind your back, you the big detective, and you, you damned fool, you keep sticking your little dimes in your little peanut-butter jar and—"

"What?"

"You heard me . . . your little peanut-butter jar and you ought to go take a dime if she left you one and call a suicide hotline, then blow your brains out. Choke on it, Slivovitz. What! What? What are you—"

"I'm gonna rip your throat out, you son of a bitch."

"Come on, Slivovitz, stop it."

"It's too late for that. You've taken everything from me. Now my turn."

• • •

"STOP it, Freddy. Enough's enough. Let go."

"Never," Florell said. "You said peanut butter. How did you know I use a peanut-butter jar? You and Mimi. The two of you. Die, you son of a bitch. Die, die, die, die, die."

• • •

FREDDY Florell stared at the body of Ted Baines, arranged so neatly in a reclining chair that it looked as if the man were sleeping. He waited until his hands stopped shaking, then left the study, almost bumping into Nora, who was waiting outside the door.

"Nora, I . . . I killed him . . . he . . . Mimi . . . they were . . ."

"Worse than that," Nora said. "They killed Jane. I think you and I were supposed to be next."

He stared at her for a moment. "Where's Mimi?"

Nora pointed behind her and now Florell could see his young, pretty wife lying on the floor, her eyes open, her face turned toward the ceiling.

"What happened?" Florell asked.

"I arranged for her to choke on a cashew," Nora said.

Florell sank back and sat on the floor. "Oh, my."

He sighed and Nora said brightly, "I'll make us some tea. And then we'll sit down and work out a story together."

When he looked up, she was smiling and he felt a small ache growing in the pit of his stomach.

THE HUNGRY SKY

by Justin Scott

T HE cat had no friends. At least none he could remember. Not when he found himself miles from his home farm with a dog suddenly bearing down on him roaring murder as he trotted past the dog's house on his way to visit a certain lady cat across the four-lane interstate.

Of course, memory was not one of his long suits, or he would have remembered the human mother—a kindly friend whose smell made his heart race and his knees grow weak; or even Old Roger—a large, demented standard poodle, retired from the navy SEALS, who followed the cat around the house like a trained seal. But Roger and the human mother were miles away. And the cat's lady friends—like the one he was visiting tonight—weren't the kind of friends you brought to a dogfight.

There was little subtlety in this dog's attack, and less art. The murderer had already abdicated any pretensions to ambush with a long, loud growl that rattled as it ran. A boxer lurked somewhere in its motley lineage, the cat noticed as he inventoried his immediate surroundings for a way out of this mess. It had some bulldog blood, too, which

accounted for the snuffling and snorting from its flat nose.
A bobbed tail left it somewhat rudderless; the entire rear
end swayed, and the cat concluded that this dog had as
much chance of suddenly changing course as a pumpkin
rolling downhill.

Which presented all sorts of wonderful opportunities.

The cat picked up a little speed. And the dog, predictably
as thunder trailed lightning, loosed a frenzied howl. Fine
with the cat; the more noise it made, the greater the strain
on its already overworked thinking apparatus.

The cat himself was not a thinker by nature—prolonged
exercise of brain power drove him to sleep—but he was
extremely capable of distinguishing execution from desire:
it didn't take a thinker to figure out that if you wanted to
catch something you didn't start by alerting it, Here I come.

He weighed his options. There was a deep ditch on the
other side of the road, gurgling with autumn runoff. A well-
timed sidestep—a little shuffle-and-hop—and the dog
could be reasonably expected to plunge headlong into a
snoutful of cold mud and, with a little bit of luck, a broken
leg. Tempting, too, was a multiflora rose hedge with a
slightly smaller than dog-size tunnel through the thorns.
The hedge fairly glistened with thorns; but on the down-
side, whoever had burrowed that considerably larger than
cat-size tunnel might be disinclined to share it.

He settled on a strategy that combined the best of both
options: the sidestep accompanied by a claw in the nose. It
was an admittedly risky maneuver—as the dog was five
times his weight and had teeth like a sawmill—but the cat
was rewarded by a startled snort, a pained howl, an angry
splash, and a muddy whimper.

Sadly, no broken leg. He took off like a shot, ran flat
out until his heart was hammering. Up a tree for a look
back. The dog was heading home with an unconvincing
swagger that looked more like a slink. The cat dropped to
the ground and headed on toward the lady's farm at a miles-
eating trot.

He could hear the four-lane interstate miles before he saw it. First a murmur like the wind, then a growl like a flooded creek, soon a roar like a millrace, and suddenly a violent thudding, pounding, crashing racket that numbed his senses just when he needed them most.

Crossing this misery was nasty work in the best of times, but late fall afternoon, with cars and trucks thundering into a blinding sunset, could not be considered by any stretch of the cat's limited imagination to be the best of times. Best to curl up for a snooze in a thornbush and wait for the traffic to die down. Except that he was particularly fond of the lady on the other side, and when something in the air urged a visit, "wait" was a word no longer in his lexicon.

Besides, he was an old hand at this highway-crossing business. Though it slipped his mind, as he hunkered down in the gravel and broken glass on the shoulder to judge the speed of the cars and trucks, that when it came to cats and interstate highways, he knew old cats and he knew bold cats, but he knew no bold, old cats.

Four concrete lanes yawned before him, divided by a narrow strip of grass into two sets of two lanes, rimmed by black asphalt shoulders. Speed was more important than the size of the vehicles hurtling by: the dumb possum decorating the fast lane could have been flattened just as flat by a motorcycle as an eighteen-wheeler. Predictability was the key. The more predictable the vehicle, the steadier its course and speed, the safer. He watched carefully for deadly nose dips.

Most cars were no sweat, though the boxy Suburban Assault Vehicles—like the bobtail overweight dog he had just eluded—lurched and swayed unpredictably. As for trucks, the bigger the truck the more dependable its speed and course. (Pickup trucks could be a real problem because they threw off the cat's fragile concentration: the human father at his farm drove a pickup and the cat enjoyed sleeping on its warm front tire beside the engine, which ticked as it cooled, like a mother's heartbeat.)

The killers were the dip noses. They were not predictable.

Cars, trucks, vans, and pickups roared. The cat flattened lower in the gravel, getting with their rhythm, gathering his muscles for his move. He edged to the concrete. A killer saw him and dipped its nose. He edged back. It passed, and he crept forward, every juice and sinew focused on the dash.

A bird landed in the bush beside him. A blue jay, fat with fall berries, exhausted from long days of burying acorns.

"Hey, how you doing?" asked the cat.

It was amazing how often this simple ploy worked, how often the feathered fool, delighted to be noticed, would settle down to preen and chat about clouds and sky and dragonflies, upon which the cat could discourse with genuine pleasure long enough to get close enough.

"My name is—" He couldn't remember his name.

Someone was always trying to name him. A freshman English major came home to call him Grimalkin, a sound the cat enjoyed but would not answer to. Old grandmother called him Tom, which left him cold, as did Kitty (all visiting children), Big Guy (the human father), That Damned Cat (ditto), and Damned Fool Cat (ditto, again). Only the human mother knew his name, and when she called, his knees went weak.

So after an uncomfortable moment, which gave the bird time to think, he made up a name a bird would trust. This one didn't. It gave a startled squawk, nearly fell off its perch, then clawed skyward, jagged as burning straw.

"Good move." The cat shrugged, thinking that he'd get plenty to eat at his lady's farm, and stepped into the road.

Instinct got him through most days, but this evening his finely honed highway-crossing instincts had run afoul of his bird-eating instincts and his visiting-ladies instincts. He should have nailed that bird, and he should not have stepped into the path of a killer dip nose.

His blood ran cold when he saw the car slow violently. It squealed. It was in the passing lane, passing a heavily laden tanker truck and closely followed by a flatbed running light. He didn't know which way to turn. There was no predicting its course, no way to guess its intention. The cat might as well try to guess the movements of an oak tree struck by lightning, or the route of a boulder bouncing down a rugged slope.

He tried to reverse. As soon as he started to turn a shriek of rubber seared his ears. It dipped its nose deeper and began to waffle to the right. The cat jinked left. It went left. The cat pirouetted right. The dip nose lurched right and flashed its headlights. Bright beams drove twin spikes of indecision through the cat's brain. Flat-footed, he waited for the end.

The car swerved in front of the tanker, so close that it clipped its rear on the big truck's bumper and began to spin, rotating on its axis as it hurtled at the cat. White smoke gushed from the tanker's brakes. The nose dip skidded back into the passing lane, smack in front of the flatbed, which bucked and roared and jackknifed and slammed sideways into the tanker.

Both trucks and the car turned over and came rolling, banging, screeching at the cat, who stood frozen to the road, watching the tangled trio thunder at him. It was as if powerful claws had emerged from the concrete to lock onto each and every one of his toenails. He could not move. Suddenly, at the last minute, a deep blast of a tractor-trailer air horn shook his hair loose and him back to his senses. He stepped aside.

Burning fiercely, the trucks tumbled to a stop in a heap of twisted steel, blocking all four lanes of the highway.

A heavyset human climbed down from the wreckage. He picked up the rear bumper that had fallen off the nose-dip car—to which was affixed a bumper sticker. Waving it at the driver, he yelled, " 'I Brake for Animals'? Well I'm an animal and you didn't brake for me!"

With that he swatted aside deflated air bags, unbuckled seat belts, and yanked the driver out by his shirtfront. A second, even-heavier-set human crawled out from under the wreckage, calling, "When you're done, I'd like a word with him."

The cat sat down in the middle of the road to smooth his coat by the firelight. Taking inventory of limbs and tail, he thanked the moon that no damage had been done.

Then he trotted on to his lady's farm, surprised to smell snow mingling with her perfume on the wind. The air was getting cold, and heavy with moisture. It felt like a good night to spend inside.

Her newest-born little kitten was frisking by the barn door, shaking its head to ring a bell that was fastened around his neck with a broad red leather collar.

"What in the moon is that?" the cat asked the kitten.

"A collar with a bell. The human child gave it to me. It's a present."

"Caught any birds lately?"

"No."

"Any idea why?"

"I think they hear me coming. I'm going to gnaw it off."

"Lotsa luck, kid. Stuff's like shoe leather. Here's what you do at the bird feeder: hunch your chin down like this, muffle the bell . . . Keep trying, you'll get the knack of it. Your mom around?"

"She's taking a nap in the hayloft."

"Say, why don't you amble down to the pond, practice that chin thing on the ducks—but hurry back when the snow starts."

"What's snow?" asked the kitten.

"You'll know it when you see it."

Up the ladder into the hayloft, he found her sprawled luxuriously in the hay. Sleeping off chicken livers, it appeared. He couldn't help but notice she'd left half in the bowl. They went right to his head. Polishing them off, he, too, sank sleepily into the hay. Just a nap, then a proper visit.

• • •

WHEN she woke him, hours later, to report that her most recent firstborn had been lost in the sudden blizzard that swept her farm, the cat licked her ear reassuringly and fell back to sleep.

She shook off the sweet hayseeds that speckled them like wrong-colored leopards and began pacing the loft.

The cat opened one eye. "He's fine. Curled up in a snowdrift, warm as toast."

She bounded to the windowsill and peered through the ice-glazed glass. "He's never seen snow. He was born last summer, you may recall."

The cat, who had trouble recalling the previous afternoon, opened his other eye. Things had turned serious in the way they usually did with her—suddenly. The instincts that kept him ahead of dogs and out from under trucks suggested, "Of course I recall."

And as she seemed to consider him partly responsible for last summer's kitten, it seemed appropriate to add that he would be glad to go hunting for the kit as soon as the snow stopped. In the meantime, while they waited in the warmth of her sweet-smelling hay barn, why not put some thought to next summer's kittens?

"I'm going out," she said.

"I'll do it. Soon as the snow stops."

"It could snow all night."

"Be done in an hour."

"How do you know?"

"I know."

In an hour, the snow had stopped and a half-moon was lighting the icy window.

"Well?"

A clear sky after a blizzard brought fierce cold. But when he tried to explain this, she threatened again to go looking herself. He stood up, stretched. She was a nester, no wanderer. She'd freeze to death or get eaten. Or she'd get lucky and find the kitten herself, and he would not be invited back. He padded down the ladder to the barn floor.

"Where are you going?" whispered the horses.

"Kitten's lost."

"Which one?"

"The dumb one."

He slipped through a crack in the door, face first into a snowdrift. Mood darkening, he followed a narrow path the wind had carved on the lee side of the barn, but soon had to plunge into deep stuff to cross the barnyard.

Suddenly he stopped, caught in the open. A weasel was slithering his way—a long, sinewy, swift, strong, bloodthirsty coil of muscle fringed with teeth. The cat froze his silhouette into the shape of a broken rake leaning on a chopping block, and prayed to the moon that the killer didn't spot him. It came snakelike through the snow, eyes active, snout twitching.

Had the kitten stumbled into it? If so, the little guy was a goner. But no, the weasel's face fur looked flat on one jowl, like it had just woken up. It veered his way. The cat thought his rake act had failed; running juices surged through his legs. But it was a whiff of chicken on the wind that had set the weasel salivating. It headed for the henhouse, eyes suddenly red with desire, and passed the cat without noticing him.

When it had disappeared beyond the barn, the cat bounded through the deep snow and climbed the pig fence to get a view.

The pig's bright little eyes gleamed from the door of his house. "What's happening?"

"Kitten's lost. You didn't happen to see him tonight? Little guy with a red collar?"

"Nope."

"The human kid put it on him. Has a little bell."

"Didn't hear a bell."

The cat cast the pig a sharp look. Both knew that the pig was not above snacking on kitten, given half a chance.

But even the kit wasn't dumb enough to give a pig half a chance. "You sure about that, pig?"

The pig reconsidered. "As a matter of fact, now that you mention it, he might have gone skittering past here before the snow. I was half-asleep, but it was something about his size. Something woke me. Could have been a bell."

"Truth?" asked the cat.

"Truth," said the pig, who was not malicious.

"I gotta find him before his mother goes nuts."

"Make sure you don't get eaten in the process," the pig warned. "I thought I smelled weasel."

"You did."

"Wouldn't want to be a chicken tonight."

The cat surveyed the moonlit snow. A broad meadow stretched down to a distant pond beside a grove of pine trees. The snow gleamed because the cold and the wind were crusting the surface.

"All sorts of things get hungry after it snows," the pig rattled on. "Not just weasel. Raccoon. Coyote. Fox. Owl. Hawk. Pine marten. Crow."

The cat scanned the frozen meadow for movement, searching in vain for a tiny hairball struggling home. He cocked his ear for a plaintive whimper. Or the little bell on his collar.

"Could have happened to the kitten," ventured the pig. "Eaten."

"Probably headed for the pond," the cat mused. "Thought he'd find the ducks sleeping."

"Ducks'll peck his eyes out."

The cat jumped to the snow and started breaking trail down the long sloping meadow. It was heavy going, the surface only partially frozen, so every few steps he broke through the crust and rammed his chest into crackly cold.

What the kit thought he would do with a sleeping duck was beyond the cat's comprehension, but the kit was a kit and kits would be kits: when the snow had started falling, he'd have fluffed his nose in it, batted it with his paws, chased his tail, rolled over. Ending up with wet fur and ice clots between his toes, he'd have limped into the shelter of the pines and curled up in the needles, forgetting that only a damned fool or a porcupine slept on the ground where things that eat, ate.

The cat stopped. The pine grove loomed blue in moon and starlight. Still as stone, he cocked his ears to listen. Wind skating the snow. Water rummaging under the ice. No kitten.

His mind, never firmly anchored, began to drift. He tried to remember what he was doing out here in the cold, footpads stinging on the icy crust, out in the open on slippery ground. But as his mind floated away like a dandelion puffball, his instincts focused on the essentials. There was risk in the open and his body bore him swift and low to the shelter of the trees, where he slid down the edge of the snow and landed on a heap of dry nee-dles, ears alive.

Deep breathing from the far side of the grove. Too big for the kit. Stank like a sleeping raccoon. The cat ventured deeper into the trees, closer to the raccoon, testing the air.

No blood. Large-and-Hairy was not sleeping off a kitten snack. Probably eaten his fill from the farmer's garbage cans.

He heard a fox bark. But miles away. Coyote howls even farther. Slowly, warily, he circled the soft floor of the pine grove, listening for the kit. He checked all the trees and the snow rim. And there, near the point he had entered, he found the kit's tracks.

His worst nightmare. The baby prints were deep, which meant the little bastard had started home before the crust froze. Slim chance of beating him back. His lady friend would waste what was left of the night fussing over the kit, and the cat hadn't a hope in the moon of any reward for this cold misery.

In a thoroughly unpleasant frame of mind, the cat headed back up the frozen meadow, which, as the wind blew colder, seemed to stretch to the sky. The kit was probably mewing in his mother's embrace already. Grumping, muttering, he followed the little footprints, and pondered upon revenge: coax the kit onto the barn roof next time it rained and leave him there . . . Better, there was a dog on a nearby farm that pretended to be sleeping when it wasn't; the kit would have an opportunity to experience the phenomenon . . . In fact, he recalled darkly, there was a road where enormous trucks—

The little footprints stopped abruptly.

In the middle of the meadow, far from both the pine grove and the barn, where the ground was flattest and the sky most broad, the baby prints just stopped.

He looked back. They dotted along in the moonlight, beside his, from the distant grove to where the cat stood gaping, and simply disappeared.

The cat looked for a hole in the snow. No hole. The little guy hadn't fallen through the crust. He felt the snow in front of the last print, wondering had it crusted so hard that the kit could walk on top without a trace. But no, the crust was thin. It might have carried him a few steps, but he'd have broken through eventually. The cat bounded ahead to test it and, sure enough, crashed through the crust.

Returning to the kit's last print, he sat on his haunches and gazed at the sky. It was as if a star had reached down and scooped the kit up. But the cat was not of a mystical bent. Though he might complain to the moon, pray to it, or even thank it on occasion, the world he mastered nightly with eyes, ears, and nose demanded real answers.

What was he going to tell the kit's mother?

His haunches got cold as he sat puzzling. The moon, lowering in the west, threw a long shadow, pouring away from him like dark water running downhill. He studied his shadow, and began to forget why he was sitting in a snowy, moonlit meadow.

Then his gaze fell on another shadow, a narrow shadow of the sort a snake would cast if snakes went out in winter. But this was cast by a low ridge of snow about as long as the cat and half as wide. Something had swept across the snow, before it had crusted, two or three steps from where the kit's paw prints disappeared.

The hairs on the cat's back rose like a wire brush.

He flattened his chest and belly to the snow and looked over his shoulder at the starlit sky. He knew what had happened to the kit, and every nerve end in his body screamed that it was going to happen to him next.

Somewhere up in the stars, a hungry owl swooped silently on six-foot wings. The owl could see in the dark, could spot the twitch of a mouse whisker five hundred feet below, could dive quiet as a bat and faster than the wind, and when it picked you up in its claws, it severed your neckbones with one slash of its powerful beak.

Its wing had brushed the snow, piled the low ridge as it wheeled down to take the kitten.

The cat ran. One kitten did not make dinner for an owl with six-foot wings.

He poured over the snow, running full speed long before he realized what he was doing, his paws barely touching the thin crust, his ears flat against his skull, his heart pumping fast and smooth, his lungs alive with cold air, his tail a streak behind him. His brain had shut down to the essentials. Something was interfering with the moon. It caused the light to change. A shadow plunged.

The cat jinked left, fell through the snow crust, found his feet, and got moving again all in the time that the shadow merged with the owl that clawed the snow where the cat had been. He didn't see the owl. But its shadow was real enough to make him a believer, and gaping while running was never a good idea.

His back hairs prickled.

The cat did not ask why. He stopped dead. Slid on his face. He felt a surge of air as the monster flew over him.

On his feet and running again. The moon had moved. He put it back where it belonged, over his right shoulder, before the owl spooked him into running in circles.

His tail prickled. The owl was floating from behind again. This time he jinked right and was rewarded with a crunching noise as the owl clawed empty snow.

"Up yours, Owl," he screamed in triumph.

"Wait," hissed the owl, regaining the sky with an effortless sweep.

Running over crusted snow was not effortless. His heart pump was ragged now and the bitter air burned his lungs. The meadow stretched forever. All he could see was flat snow. The moon had moved again. He changed course. Somewhere ahead was the crest and beyond it the pig's house and the barn.

He neither saw nor heard the owl until it was diving at his face. Like something from the dark side of the moon, it attacked with widespread claws, talons scything the snow in case the cat was thinking of ducking low.

Fortunately for the cat, he was not thinking at all.

Instinct said, Jump, and the owl was not the only one surprised when the cat soared over the bird and crashed behind him, breaking crust, scrambling out, and running blindly. Close behind him the great wings blotted out the stars as the owl wheeled into the air for another shot.

"Over here," called the pig.

He'd almost made it to the barnyard. But so had the owl, perched silent as death on the pig's fence. The cat felt the spirit drain out of him, felt an overwhelming desire to just sink down in the snow and let the owl eat him.

The owl sensed despair. And it asked in a mocking hiss, "Sleepy?"

The cat staggered a few steps closer. Then, as if fatally confused, he veered out into the open, toward the barn. The owl spread wings, talons, and beak simultaneously and launched itself down from the fence like a falling tree.

"Stupid?" asked the cat when the owl was irrevocably committed in that direction, and bolted toward the pig fence.

"Here," cried the pig. "There's a hole right here. Come on in."

"In your eye," said the cat, who hadn't escaped owl claws in order to polish pig teeth with his bones. He wedged his back into a solid corner of fence and sty and watched the owl, who circled, hissing disappointment. Finally, like smoke in the trees, it drifted toward the top of a lightning-blasted oak that stood alone between two fields.

"Close call," said the pig. "I thought you were a goner."

"Never laid a glove on me," said the cat. Which wasn't quite true because something was burning his back, and when he investigated he found sticky blood in his fur.

"Did he get the kit?"

"Looks that way."

"I warn everybody about that owl. Look out for that owl, I tell 'em. It's up there just waiting. Yup, you're right. That kit's a goner."

The cat checked the sky before he crossed the ice crust to the barn. Then he padded, slowly, reluctantly toward the ladder to the loft.

"Did you find him?" whispered the horses. "Is he all right? What happened?"

"Owl got him."

"No! You're kidding. How do you know?"

"His footprints disappeared in the middle of the meadow."

"Maybe he . . . Or . . . Well, it's possi—"

"Maybe not," said the cat.

"What are you going to tell his mother? Oh, you can't tell his mother. Go out and look some more."

"Good idea," said the cat. Anything was better than climbing those rungs to tell the kit's mother that her most recent born was owl bait. He went out, checked the sky very carefully, and darted across the open ground to the dairy.

"Hey, Cat," said the bull, wide-awake despite the hour. "What's happening?"

"Misery."

"Sit down. Tell me about it."

The cat sat on his haunches, and talked toward the mountainlike dark shadow that was the bull. "Long story."

"I got all night."

"Owl got the kitten."

"It happens."

"Yeah, but why did it have to happen tonight?"

"Tonight was the night?"

"It was supposed to be," said the cat. "I haven't seen her in a month."

The bull rumbled good-humoredly, "Best-laid plans, my friend. Best-laid plans."

"What a night. Almost get nailed by a dog. Then nearly run down on the highway. And now that stupid kitten, if I get ahold of him I'm going to—"

"You got my sympathy, pal. You got my sympathy."

"And on top of it, the kitten was so little, the damned owl's still hungry. Took my life in my hands just coming over to say hello."

"I appreciate the gesture."

"Yeah, well," said the cat. "What are friends for?"

"I got an idea," said the bull. "You know that collar he was wearing?"

"Yeah?"

"Go find it."

"What for?"

"Bring it to his mother."

"Why?"

"Show her you really care."

Not a bad idea. The cat stepped out of the dairy, scanned the sky, and hurried back to the pigpen to get his bearings and figure out where the owl might have the dropped the collar when he was done eating the kitten.

"You back?" the pig called sleepily.

"Go to sleep."

High in the blasted oak across the fields, a breath of movement hardened into the owl spreading its wings again. It began wheeling around the tree, circling repeatedly, swooping around it like a human that had dropped its truck keys. Odd, thought the cat. What's it lost? Puzzlement had wrinkled his psyche like a walnut when suddenly the night was shattered by a *boom* of shotgun fire.

A long, red tongue of muzzle flash blinded the cat.

Boom! Shattered his ears.

Again. And again.

"Farmer's shooting at Weasel!" yelled the pig. "Fat chance he'll hit him."

The cat's ears were ringing. "Huh?"

"End up shooting his own chickens," the pig chortled. "If Weasel left him any."

The cat blinked, trying to remember what had led him to the pigpen. There, in the northeast, a big bird wheeled across the Milky Way. The owl, startled by the shotgun.

"I warn everybody to look out for that owl . . . No one listens. Strut around like—"

"Shhh!"

The cat had heard a faint, faint tinkling like a bell. Musical ringing in the wind. Icicles? Shotgun echoes in his ears?

Again!

"Does the owl live in that tree?"

The cat's home farm was many miles from this particular lady friend's, and what with other obligations around the county he didn't get by here regularly enough to keep track of every nuisance in the neighborhood.

"It lives in the sky," intoned the pig.

The cat looked at him.

"But it maintains quarters up there if that's what you mean."

"That's what I mean."

"Disgusting nest, I'm told," the pig confided. "Old feathers, bones, and fur—hey, where you going?"

The cat streaked across the open barnyard and along a stone wall, hugging its moonshadow. Unless he'd heard wrong—and no one had ears like his—the ringing came from the blasted oak where the owl roosted.

Just before he reached the place where its broad and gnarly roots had jumbled the wall, he smelled blood. Chicken blood. He stopped dead.

A shadow in the shadows.

Weasel drifted out of the snow, lurched drunkenly toward him, stumbled right by, and started climbing up the tree. Up and up until thirty feet off the ground it disappeared into a hole. The cat gave it time to worm its way in deeper, then started up the oak, an easy climber with jagged bark. He passed the weasel hole and kept going.

He was seventy feet above the ground when a bell rang in his ear. The kitten, cowering inside a woodpecker hole. Its head was bowed and the cat could see the deep gash the owl's beak had gouged in the thick leather collar that had saved the kit's life.

"Hey, you!"

The kit looked up in disbelief.

"You going to sit in that hole all night or are you coming home?"

"Where'd you come from, Cat?"

"The moon. Let's go."

"The owl thought I was dead. So I pretended I was, like a possum."

"It's called 'playing possum,'" said the cat. "An excellent trick. Just don't try it on the road. Let's go."

"Then I ran when it put me down."

"Good move. Let's go."

"But I had to hide because every time I move the bell rings."

The cat saw that the bell was going to be a problem. He could chew the leather until his teeth fell out, but there was no way he'd get the damned collar off. "What are we going to do?" the kit whimpered.

"Let me think."

He had fallen asleep when the bell woke him.

The kit was trying to gnaw the ice clots out of his toes.

"Stop ringing that bell or I'll feed you to the owl." The cat emphasized his sincere threat with flashing teeth and all claws spread—a sight that combined the worst elements of a power rake and a chain saw.

"But it rings and the owl will hear it."

"Tuck your chin over it, like I showed you how to stake out the bird feeder. Okay? We're outta here—don't look down."

That his warning was too late was apparent by the fact that the kit had frozen with height fear and was now as stiff as a dead fox terrier. Under ordinary circumstances, he'd leave it to the humans to call the fire department to rescue the little bastard; down-climbing was rarely a pleasure, and never when carrying a whimpering deadweight. But the owl would be back.

"Moon, moon, moon." The cat sank his teeth into the scruff of the little bastard's neck and started sliding down the tree. "Tuck your chin," he mumbled through fur.

Halfway to the ground, his knees were shaking with the effort, but he was beginning to feel hope.

"Going somewhere, boys?"

The owl darkened the stars.

The cat, who'd been keeping track of holes in the oak, dragged the kitten into the nearest one. The owl circled, 'round and 'round the tree, caressing the air with easy twitches of the feather tips of its wings. "I can wait," it hissed. "I have all night. All day. All tomorrow night."

"What are we going to do?" mewed the kit.

"Go to sleep."

"But what are *you* going to do?"

The cat was already probing deeper recesses of the oak, which like other lightning-struck trees of his acquaintance was honeycombed with connecting tunnels that led to separate hollows. "I'm going to find something to feed it."

"Me?"

"No, no, no."

"But you said—"

"You're not big enough to make him a full meal," the cat said comfortingly. "Besides, your mother would never forgive me."

He squeezed down through a tunnel about his diameter, paying close attention to his whiskers. When he came to a tunnel twice his diameter he kept going, having no desire to blunder into the winter den of anything twice his diameter. The next tunnel he poked his head into set off whisker alarms. Too narrow.

The third was about half again his size—weasel size— and smelled like death. He entered boldly. The tunnel curved up into a fair-sized den, wherein the weasel, drenched in blood and feathers, was sleeping off its chicken dinner.

Up close, it looked strong and surprisingly unscarred for a middle-aged killer, which meant it won all the fights it got into.

The cat poked it hard. "You are the ugliest weasel I ever saw in my life. I don't like weasels. They kill cats. But you're too fat and stupid to kill me, so wake up *now*!" This last, screeched in the weasel's ear, got the intended result and it rolled over, blinking.

"You I'm talkin' to!"

It was drunk on chicken blood, but not so confused that it didn't get a cold mean look in its merciless eye. "What?"

"Wake up."

"Cat?" The weasel looked around its den in disbelief. "A cat? I'll kill you."

The cat turned tail and ran down the weasel's tunnel to the main tunnel. He looked over his shoulder to make sure the weasel was following. It was. Very closely.

"I will feast on your brains," screeched the weasel, with what even the cat had to admit displayed a dismal ignorance of cat anatomy. Gaining fast, it slithered after him with murder in its eyes.

"Gang way," he warned the kit as he barreled past. "Trouble behind."

He leaped out the hole, got a good grip on the knobbly oak bark, and howled, "Owl!"

"Right here," hissed the owl, plummeting out of the sky like a rock with claws.

"Weasel," the cat called back into the hole, "what's taking you so long?"

The weasel emerged from the tree teeth first and pounced at the cat, who'd have been in serious trouble if the owl hadn't slammed into the weasel and wrenched him skyward in his claws.

Showing no sign of disappointment to have caught a fat weasel instead of a lean cat, the owl slashed its beak down in a killing blow.

But the old weasel had seen that trick before, and the last the cat observed as he and the kit tumbled out of the tree and raced for the barn, the predators were headed swiftly toward the ground locked in a deadly embrace.

• • •

THE cat's lady friend mewed with joy as he herded the kit up the ladder and sank into the warm hay for a much-needed rest and his hard-won reward.

"You're bleeding!" she cried.

"It's nothing," said the cat. "Just a scratch."

But she was addressing her kitten, madly licking him with her long and graceful tongue.

"He's not hurt," said the cat. "That's *my* blood."

"Poor baby. You must be so frightened. Here, sweetheart, curl up with Mother and have a nice, long sleep. I'll just kiss you all over."

"What about me?"

"Shhhh! The poor little thing's had a terrible night."

THE GEEZERS

by Peter Straub

"CLYDE was a hell of a shock," Ray Constantine said to Gus Trayham, the man on the next bike.

"Shock to us all," Gus said. "You weren't shocked, you wouldn't be breathing."

"I mean, besides that," Ray said. "The whole thing reminds me of Paolo. It brings it all back." Nine years earlier, Paolo Constantine, a student at the Rhode Island School of Design, had died of a drug overdose. Ray's wife, Fabiana, whom he had met during his fellowship at the American Academy in Rome, had eventually packed up everything she chose to salvage from their marriage of twenty-five years and returned to Italy.

"Don't you think it brought Linc back to me? All that misery when he went upstate? Linc passed three years ago, this April."

"*I* remember," Ray said. Neither he nor the other two men who met every weekday to exercise in Dodge gymnasium at Columbia University and lunch together afterward had known Lincoln Trayham, Gus's elder brother, but it was an article of faith with them that although Linc may have done some bad things and made some bad choices, as Gus put it, he had been falsely convicted of second-degree murder and railroaded into a life sentence.

For a time, they continued pedaling furiously, though perhaps a touch less so than the three teenage sylphs beside them. One of the sylphs wore a Philips Exeter T-shirt and spandex shorts and, Ray noted, had not once lifted her stunning little face from a hypnotic perusal of the book propped on the console before her, *Killer Diller* by Grant Upward, a onetime friend who by dint of writing the same book over and over had entirely eclipsed Ray's own, less frequent fictions. "Maybe we shouldn't have come today," he said.

"Do us good," Gus said. "Sweat out some pain before we talk to the Man."

Dismounting more gracefully than Ray, Gus strode past the sylphs and ejected a panting, long-haired beanpole from the biceps curl machine by the simple mechanism of standing before him, lowering his head, and glowering. After the boy muttered an apology and slipped away, Gus adjusted the weights from fifty to one hundred and fifty pounds, positioned his upper arms on the pad, settled into the seat, wrapped his fists around the handles, and began smoothly raising and lowering the stack of weights. Gus Trayham's father had coached football and swimming at Fisk, and despite the distinguished appearance given him by the bald head, grizzled white beard, and spreading waistline he had assumed as he approached sixty, Gus was the strongest and most athletic of the four friends.

Ray walked over to the lat pull machine located next to the stationary rower, where blond, still nearly boyish Tommy Whittle was going through his reps while answering the bemused smile of a dark-haired girl moving toward the water fountain. Tommy's acting career was recovering from the layoff imposed by a three-year-old mugging that had put him in the hospital for a month, but people who had watched a good deal of television during the late eighties and early-to-mid-nineties often imagined him to be an acquaintance whose name they had temporarily misplaced. Tommy referred to this sense of baffled recognition on the part of strangers as his "infamy." Now he watched Ray lower the seat of the lat pull and said, "How do you think they'll handle it? One-on-one, or all at the same time?"

"One-on-one," Ray said. "That captain—what's his name?"

"Brannigan," Tommy said. "Like the John Wayne movie."

"What John Wayne movie?"

"Brannigan," Tommy said. "He played a Chicago cop who goes to London to bring back a suspect. Mid-seventies. Not bad, not bad at all. But I'm a freak for the Duke."

"Tell me about it," Ray said. He set the pin for one hundred and seventy-five pounds and straightened up to grasp the long bar attached to the weights.

"One-on-one, huh?"

Ray let the bar ascend, carrying his arms with it. "Brannigan is going to park us in a room somewhere and call us out individually. We'll tell him whatever we know. Are you nervous, Tommy?"

"Sure I am. Clyde, that was a hell of a blow. Will you take a look at Leo? There's a guy who is really *upset*."

Ray agreed with Tommy Whittle's assessment. Leo Gozzi was executing halfhearted abdominal crunches with long pauses between each one. His olive face had a gray tinge, and purple bags drooped beneath his eyes. After Leo's report of dubious financial practices on the part of his employer, a computer company, had been leaked to the press, first his job, then his marriage had disappeared, and he had moved twenty blocks north into an apartment on West 107th Street, only a block from Pepper's two rooms on West End Avenue. It was Leo who had introduced Clyde into their group.

When Ray finished his reps, he moved across the aisle and slid into the back press, the machine next to Leo's. He had adjusted the weights and begun to push backward before Leo glanced over his shoulder.

"Hey, Ray," Leo said.

"I hate to say it," Ray said, "but you look like shit."

"This thing with Clyde has me tied up in knots. I got about ten minutes' sleep last night. I just lay there, feeling my muscles getting tighter and tighter. It's amazing I can stand up straight."

"Do your laps, and we'll relax over lunch. Everything will be fine."

Leo performed another desultory crunch. "Does Sally know what happened?"

For a little more than a year, Ray had been on-again off-again with an attractive, deeply messed-up editor at Ballantine named Sally Frohman. Currently they were on again, though indications such as the frequent usage of the word "relationship" had led Ray to anticipate a period of sexual drought within a matter of weeks, perhaps even days. "Why?"

"I guess I was wondering what you said, and what she thought about it, how she reacted, that's all."

"Is that right?" Ray asked.

"Well, you know," Leo said.

"Okay, Leo. Sally was pissed off about something. She was sitting on the sofa, staring at the floor with her hands pushed into her hair, and I was at the kitchen table, doing revisions. The phone rang. That detective, Brannigan, told me about Clyde, probably the exact same way he told you. When I hung up, Sally said, 'Am I allowed to know who you're meeting tomorrow afternoon?' 'Yes, Sally,' I said. 'I have to talk to a detective at the Twenty-sixth Precinct. About two hours ago, one of my friends from the gym, Clyde Pepper, was found in Riverside Park with his throat cut and his head bashed in. You never met him, but Clyde was a nice guy, and for some reason I'm having trouble believing he was murdered while you and I were sitting here ignoring each other.' 'Oh, honey,' she said, 'I'm so sorry.' She started to cry. I made a drink for her and a drink for me. Then Gus and Tommy called. Sally and I went to bed, and for some reason we had the best sex we've had in months. Afterward, I began to tell her a few things about Clyde, and I choked up. Pretty soon, we were both crying."

"I called Tommy and Gus," Leo said. "I would have called you, but I figured Sally was spending the night at your place."

"Your tact is greatly appreciated," Ray said.

The four of them proceeded through their rounds of the exercise machines and returned to the locker room to change into bathing trunks. Four flights below, a utilitarian passage led to a scarred gray door and the labyrinth containing the swimming team's lockers and two small, green-tiled chambers lined with showerheads. After brief, obligatory showers, they padded up a cement ramp and two by two, goggles swinging from their hands, went down a narrow corridor and through a metal door into an echoing underground vault.

Eight lanes wide, the Columbia University pool was open to the general student population, faculty, staff, and alumni every weekday afternoon from noon to two P.M. Red plastic cones and wall plaques claimed the central lanes for "fast" swimmers, the two at their left for the "medium," and the first two and the eighth, long ago dubbed the "geezer lanes" by Gus Trayham, for slowpokes. Within each lane, a blue stripe at the bottom of the pool divided inbound left from outbound right, and its occupants swam in circles. In the past, unless the presence of too many other swimmers forced them to alter the pattern, Leo and Clyde Pepper had taken lane 1, Tommy Whittle lane 2, and Ray and Gus wider, deeper lane 8.

Composed more of faculty, alums, and staff than students, the fifteen to twenty swimmers who shared the pool with them separated out into the unobjectionable (those who did their laps in a steady, businesslike manner), the tolerable (who swam too slowly but were reasonable about it), and the offensive (people who barely moved at all, strayed out of their lanes, kicked up geysers of spray while mooching along, charged into people instead of detouring around them, and those whose ugly, ungainly strokes made them appear to be crippled). In the latter category were "the Monitor," whose floundering crawl suggested that one of his arms had been amputated; "Cruella," an elderly woman with a permanent sneer who did not actually look too bad until she followed a deliberate blow from a passing foot with a death ray delivered through her radioactive blue goggles; and "Creeping Jesus," a mournful character thought to be a professor of biblical history given to crouching in silent prayer by the end of the pool for fifteen minutes before crawling into the pool and thrashing, apparently in utter panic, from one end to the other.

Ray noticed the Monitor and Cruella making life miserable for the two Japanese girls also in lane 1, so he was not surprised when Leo announced that he would take the far lane today, although he secretly thought that Leo would have done the same had only the Japanese girls, ordinarily a great attraction, occupied the first lane. Tommy slipped into the water and joined two sturdy middle-aged women who were churning back and forth like horses. Ray, Gus, and Leo wandered past the diving boards to the far end, where a crop-headed blond lifeguard whose piglike face always reminded Ray of a dissolute peasant in a Dutch tavern painting looked up from his perch and said, "The big guys!" He glanced at Leo Gozzi, then back at Ray. "What happened to your buddy?"

Leo came to an abrupt halt and recoiled, as if he had bounced off a wall.

"He dropped out," Ray said.

"Suddenly called away," said Gus.

"Sorry to hear it," said the boy. "For an older guy, he had major pecs. Hey, you're all in great shape. I hope I look the same at your age."

"Be enough to get to our age," Gus said. "What with putting your life on the line three days a week."

"Hah," the boy said.

One by one, they lowered themselves into the pool and breaststroked toward the far end, Gus in the lead, then Ray, Leo behind him, each of the latter two waiting until the man ahead reached the middle of the pool before pushing off. For the first four laps, Gus was rolling into his return just as Leo ducked underwater and started back up to the far end. According to the same custom by which Gus invariably led off, thereby setting the pace, they did not break rhythm to stop and rest until after the tenth lap, but after Ray dipped into the turn for the back half of his sixth, he saw Leo floating down at the other end, one arm over the rope lane divider, the other propped on the splash ledge. Gus plowed through the water and executed his turn without saying anything to Leo. When Ray came to the end of the pool, he looked at Leo, who waved him on. Ray spun under and kicked off.

His shoulder muscles stretched to meet the resistance of the water, seeming nearly to take in breath. There was always that moment when you and the resistance locked together and you felt your relationship with the water change from unconscious acceptance into a working partnership in which the resistance became a springy, yielding support. The difference had to do with consciousness, with being awake to your context. This moment of contextual awareness, Ray thought, resembled those periods when, immersing himself for the fiftieth time in a new book's early scenes, he finally noticed how greatly his conception of certain characters diverged from the selves announced by the actual words they spoke. Supposedly sympathetic characters said things like, "Roger acts like he's cynical and coldhearted, but down deep he's a real monster." While writing his seventh novel, Ray had learned at last how to listen to his characters; a decade later, consciousness of this other context had come to him only after months of reporting to Columbia's pool. You had to pay attention to the medium through which you moved: if you did not, you were blind and flailing.

Leo was still clinging to the rope when Ray swam back. He said, "Keep dragging your ass, you might as well get in with Cruella and the Monitor."

"I needed a rest," Leo said.

Ray set off again for the top of the pool. Halfway there, he looked back and was relieved to see Leo swimming toward him.

After Ray and Gus's tenth lap and Leo's eighth, they took a breather, bobbing in the water and holding on to the ledge. "Leo," Gus said, "I gather you had a rough night."

"You didn't?" Leo asked.

"Well," Gus said, "Thursday is Ruth's night. We had dinner at Jezebel and went back to my place. I stood on Junior. After Lieutenant Brannigan woke me up, *you* talked to me for half an hour. Then Tommy called. I sent Ruth home and talked to Ray. I kept thinking about how you brought Clyde in, how we all hooked up with him. I was trying to get my head around what happened. Took me hours to get to sleep, all the crazy shit that was going though my mind. We all had a rough night, and now we got to carry on, hear what I'm saying?"

"I know, I know," Leo said. "But I was closer to him than the rest of you."

"Then you got to deal with that," Gus said, and swam away.

• • •

CARRIE, their waiter (or "waitress," as the geezers would have put it) at The Heights, said, "What happened to your buddy?"

The pig-faced boy who guarded the watery realm of Cruella and the Monitor three days a week had used the same words, and although the question had not been addressed to him, Ray answered as before. "He dropped out."

"The man took a hike," said Gus, putting a more active spin on the concept that Clyde had been called away.

Leo turned his head to the long second-floor window looking down on Broadway and muttered, "You could put it that way."

Carrie awaited further clarification. She was a slender, small-boned young woman, and her waiting had an open, expectant quality. A couple of seconds passed while the four men at the table examined the silverware, the chalkboard listing the day's specials, the mixture of Columbia students and neighborhood funk milling on the sidewalk. "*Ohh*-kay," Carrie said. "Four spinach salads and two Cokes, coming up."

They had the same lunch every day, and their regular waiters, Carrie, Troy the Boy, and Melissa, had been trained to add extra bacon and blue cheese to the salads. Ray suspected that they just went into the kitchen and said, "They're here."

"Leo," Gus said, "I'm a little concerned about you."

"Don't be," Leo said. "I'm not supposed to open my mouth?"

"Open it all you like," Gus said. "But don't put your business on the street. Say, Carrie reads about this business in the paper. Say, she sees his picture on the news. Until that happens, and I don't think it will, because I never heard Carrie indicate she gives a damn about the news unless some movie star gets his tit caught in a wringer, but until it does she's better off thinking Clyde moved out of town. Why spoil her day?"

"I get it, I get it," Leo said.

"All of us have to deal with what happened to Clyde, but we don't have to drag other people into the process."

"Gus," Leo said, "please stop lecturing me."

"You'd learn what a lecture was, I ever gave you one," Gus said. "This here is friendly advice."

"Try keeping the friendly advice to yourself for once," Leo said.

Gus held up his hands, palms out, and smiled at Leo.

Carrie set their plates before them and went through the routine with the pepper grinder. Ray and Tommy Whittle got the Cokes. All four men ran their knives through the salads half a dozen times, cutting the spinach leaves into smaller and smaller sections, and began eating.

When the silence became unendurable, Gus said, "Who saw Clyde last? I guess it must have been you, Leo."

"As far as I know," Leo said. "After the three of you got into a cab, Clyde and I went down Broadway to 107th. He dropped me at my building and kept walking toward West End. That was the last time I saw him."

"Anybody call him that evening?" Gus asked.

"Not me," Leo said. "Did you?"

Gus widened his eyes. "I don't think I called Clyde but twice in the past two years. Once when you had to spend all day tinkering with some movie star's computer, and once when I had an extra Knicks ticket and couldn't get any of you to go with me. He turned me down, too, so I wound up taking Louise, my Tuesday regular." Gus Trayham had long ago evolved a complicated system which allocated certain days of the week to the inner core of his sexual partners, most of them married women operating on tight schedules. "Did you two talk to Clyde last night?"

"No," Ray said. "Outside of this, I never saw Clyde that much. We had dinner a couple of times last year. One day when the gym was closed for Christmas break, we went to a movie together. And about two weeks ago, he called up around nine, ten at night to say he was down the block from my place, and I invited him over. We had a few beers."

"The same thing happened with me," Tommy said. "Last Friday, the phone rang. It was Clyde. He said he was out for a walk, noticed he was in my neighborhood, and wondered what I was doing. I told him to come up. We shot the breeze, and he started looking though my videotape collection. 'I guess you do like John Wayne,' he said.

'Have you got *She Wore a Yellow Ribbon*?' 'You bet,' I said, and we watched the whole thing. Great movie."

"That's interesting," Gus said, "but you didn't say if you talked to him last night."

Tommy's head snapped forward. "Last night I didn't talk to anyone until Brannigan gave me the bad news. He said he got our names from Clyde's address book. Right away, I called Leo, but I guess he was talking to you, because I tried you next, and both lines were busy."

"Clyde should have wandered back to our neighborhood instead of getting stupid and going to Riverside Park," Gus said. "Time to settle up and pay a visit to the Man."

• • •

A bored uniform glanced through a pane of bulletproof glass that looked as though someone had once tried to shatter it with a brick. He listened to Gus's explanation of why they were there. He asked him to repeat it, then he looked wearily at Ray.

"Lieutenant Brannigan asked us to come here at three in connection with the death of Clyde Pepper," Ray said.

Although he was wearing a watch, the uniform consulted the wall clock and observed that the time was two fifty-eight. He shook his head and loafed to the door to request, very slowly, that another officer conduct these gentlemen to Lieutenant Brannigan's office. Without saying a word, the second officer got to his feet and began slouching down the corridor.

At the back of the station, the officer led them into a squad room where prematurely jaded men and women in their early thirties sat at desks crowded with papers and cups of coffee. He flapped a hand at a wooden bench and a row of plastic chairs. Ray and Gus took the bench, and Leo and Tommy dropped into the chairs. The officer knocked once at a wooden door, slouched inside, and returned a moment later, followed by a tall, balding ex-fullback wearing a handsome Italian suit, a sparkling white shirt, and a lustrous silk necktie. His eyes were the color of wet cement, and his lipless mouth had all the warmth of a mail slot.

The geezers stood up as the ex-fullback strode toward them and introduced himself as Lieutenant Brannigan. The mail slot lengthened into a deathly smile as Brannigan shook their hands. His mushroom-colored teeth seemed too numerous and surprisingly small.

"This is what we're going to do," Brannigan said. "You were Clyde Pepper's only friends in the world, looks like. I want to pick your brains, see what you might be able to tell me. Chances are, his assailant was a mugger, and we're doing everything we can on that front, but the degree of violence here exceeds ninety percent of muggings, including those that result in homicide. So we have to keep our minds open. We have to consider other options. I want to find out a few things about you, hear whatever comes into your mind about the deceased. You never know what might give us a lead, no matter how insignificant it seems to you. The procedure shouldn't take much more than an hour. Are we in agreement?"

Each in his own way, the four men assented.

"Thank you for your cooperation. Let's begin with you, Mr. Constantine."

• • •

BRANNIGAN pointed Ray to a chair, sat behind his desk, and opened a notebook. For a moment, the wet-cement eyes bored into Ray's. "Are you comfortable about having this conversation, Mr. Constantine?"

"Absolutely," Ray said. "I guess I was assuming that a mugger must have killed Clyde, so I wasn't sure how we could help you. I'm happy to tell you everything I can, though."

"I appreciate that. Were you aware that before taking retirement your friend was a homicide detective assigned to this precinct?"

"All I knew was that Clyde was a retired police officer."
Ray paused, but Brannigan simply sat behind his desk,
watching him. "Did he work here a long time?"

"Twelve years," Brannigan said. "Most of that time, Detective Pepper lived out on the Island. After his divorce, he
moved into a high-rise in Riverdale. Right after he retired,
he came into the city and took the place on West End."

"He must have missed his old neighborhood," Ray said.

Brannigan displayed another deathly smile. "What kind
of work do you do, Mr. Constantine? Most people can't
take two, three hours off in the middle of the day to work
out in a gym."

"I'm a writer."

Brannigan tilted back his head and raised his eyebrows.
"That so? What do you write?"

"Fiction. Novels."

"What kind of novels? Anything I might have heard of?"

"Thrillers," Ray said, steering around the words "crime"
and "detective." He named his last three books.

Gentle Death, The Iceman, and *Dying Fall* seemed to
have flown beneath or above Brannigan's radar. The lieutenant said, "Do you know Grant Upward? I like his stuff,
but he writes books so fast I can't keep up with the guy.
Two of my detectives out there, they read Grant Upward's
books as soon as they come out."

"Actually," Ray said, "Grant and I are old friends."

"I'm impressed. Now, tell me about this group of yours.
How you met, what the other men do, your connections to
Columbia, things like that."

"We're all neighbors," Ray said. "I met Gus Trayham
in 1980, '81, something like that, when we used to go to
the same bar on Columbus Avenue. He works as a grip for
companies that film commercials. Gus took some classes at
Columbia in the late sixties, I think, and he started using
the gym before the rest of us. I got an MA at Columbia in
1966, so one day I went with him and signed up. That was
in the spring of 1990.

"Around that time, my computer started going haywire, and a writer friend of mine, in fact it was Grant Upward, said I should talk to a guy named Leo Gozzi, who helped writers with their computers, setting them up, doing upgrades, hand-holding, whatever they needed. I called Leo. He came to my place and straightened everything out. He was great. After that I called him every time I needed advice. Leo and I spent so much time together and became friends, which was a good thing, because half the writers in the New York area wound up hearing about him. Later on, through Tommy, he began getting calls from actors, too. If he didn't already know you or like your work, you were out of luck. Turns out, Leo graduated from Columbia. When he said he wanted to start exercising, I thought, Why not?, and introduced him to Gus. That's how he got in."

"What about Mr. Whittle?"

"Tommy's an actor who lives on my block. He grew up in our neighborhood, and Tommy and Gus are old friends. After I started going to the gym, Gus and I told Tommy all he had to do was say he was an alum, and they'd let him buy a card, because they never check."

"Do you work out five days a week?"

"If we can. I might have to meet a deadline, and Gus sometimes has a string of twelve-hour workdays. Leo gets stuck in Westchester or New Jersey with a client who's flipping out because his system just crashed. The actors Tommy put him in touch with introduced him to some famous actors, and those people are like babies, they want everything right now. Tommy goes to a lot of auditions, so he can't make it every day, either. Clyde was pretty regular, though."

"How did Clyde Pepper come into your group?"

"He and Leo lived about a block away from each other. After they started hanging out, Leo arranged for us to meet Clyde for dinner one night, and he fit right in. For one thing, Clyde looked like he'd been working out all his life.

He certainly wasn't going to be an embarrassment or slow things down. Besides that, he was an interesting guy. In some ways, Clyde fit in better than Leo."

"Oh?" said Brannigan.

"Well, Leo's a friend of mine, and if you need someone to hook you up with an Internet provider or lead you through the ins and outs of a software program, he's your guy. And by working out with us all these years, he managed to get himself in good condition, but that's not really where he's coming from. Leo went to Bronx Science."

"I'm not sure I follow you."

"I'm talking about an involvement in athletics. Do they even have sports at Bronx Science? Computers are Leo's whole life. Right out of college, he was hired by one of those outfits where everybody wears jeans and works twelve hours a day. A few years later, the company took off, and Leo did very well until he discovered the owners were screwing their suppliers. When he spoke up, they dumped him. He went freelance because he couldn't get another job, and then he came into our group. But he didn't have the same background."

"An athletic background?"

"Yes," Ray said. "It makes a difference."

"Did Clyde Pepper have an athletic background?"

"Clyde grew up in Inwood, and he played basketball and ran the half mile in high school."

"What about the rest of you?"

"Gus played football and basketball at Fisk. Tommy was an all-conference guard his senior year at New Trier, in Illinois, and he made the football team his first year at Carleton, before he got interested in theater. I did varsity football, basketball, and track all though high school. The point is, Clyde had worked under coaches, he'd been through a sports program. He knew about discipline. He set goals for himself."

"His death must have come as a shock to you."

"It still is a shock," Ray said. "If he had to take a walk, I wish he'd come down to our neighborhood, called one of us up, stopped in for a beer or something. Clyde did that, sometimes. Who goes into Riverside Park late at night?"

"That's an interesting question," Brannigan said. "Was it a habit of his, do you know?"

"You got me," Ray said. "But you'd think a guy who used to be a homicide detective would know better."

"When was the last time you saw him?"

"About an hour after we left the gym. We always have lunch at a place down on Broadway. When we're done, Gus and Tommy and I get into a cab, and Leo and Clyde walk home. The last time I saw Clyde, we were hailing our cab."

"Did you talk to him yesterday evening?"

Ray shook his head. "Last night, I was with my girl-friend, Sally Frohman. Around midnight, whenever it was, you called and gave me the news. I talked to my friends for about an hour. We could hardly believe what happened. You don't expect a friend of yours to get killed."

"You were with your girlfriend all night?"

"Depends what you mean by all night," Ray said. "Sally rang my buzzer about eleven, maybe a little later. She was worried about something. Well, she was pissed off at me and wanted to make sure I knew it. Hold on." He smiled at Brannigan. "Are you checking to see if I have an alibi for the time Clyde was murdered?"

"I'm asking you what you did last night."

"What time *was* Clyde murdered?"

"According to the medical examiner, sometime between ten and twelve."

"Then I have half an alibi," Ray said. "But I didn't do it, if you had any doubts about that. I was fond of Clyde, I liked him a lot. After Sally and I finally got to bed, I cried. I really did, I cried like a baby."

"Murderers cry all the time, Mr. Constantine. Don't take

this the wrong way, but I've seen dozens of people who committed murder break down and weep. Some of them were sitting right in that chair. They cry because they almost always killed a friend, a spouse, or a child of theirs. You should put it in one of your books."

Remembering a scene near the end of *Dying Fall,* Ray said, "Now that you mention it, I already did. Funny, isn't it? Sometimes you write things you weren't aware of knowing. Grant Upward and I used to talk about that. He said it was one of the reasons he wrote—to discover what he knew."

"You get the same thing in police work now and then," Brannigan said. "If we could bring Clyde Pepper back to life, I think he'd agree with me. The man had one of the best records in this precinct, maybe *the* best. Not a man who gave up easily. Did he ever talk about his work?"

"Not that I remember," Ray said.

"He never mentioned a boy named Charles White? Charlie White?"

Ray looked up and brought the tips of his fingers together. "If he did, I've forgotten all about it."

"Three years ago, the case attracted a lot of attention in the press. It wasn't as big as Robert Chambers and Jennifer Levin, but it was almost in that league. I'm surprised you don't remember it, being in your line of work."

"This was something Clyde was working on?" Ray asked.

"It was one of his last cases. Around three one morning, a Barnard student and her boyfriend saw a kid lying on the ground inside the gate to the Columbia campus on 116th Street. He was curled up behind his backpack in the dark, off to one side. If his white polo shirt hadn't caught her eye, the girl would never have spotted him. They thought he was drunk, and they went in to see if they could help him. After they got a good look, the boyfriend called 911 on his cell phone. The kid had been beaten to death. That was Charlie White. He was in his last year of premed at Columbia, and he lived in a fraternity house on the other side of 116th Street, a couple of doors down. Ring any bells?"

"Maybe," Ray said.

"In one of his pockets, our premed frat boy was carrying five grams of cocaine in individual packets. The backpack was even better. A rock the size of a walnut wrapped up in a plastic bag was rammed down next to his books. Turned out, Charlie White had a reputation for dealing coke to his fraternity brothers. Plus other interested parties."

"Oh, yeah, Charlie White," Ray said. "Sure. He was from a well-off family in the Midwest, wasn't he? His father had a big job in the Carter Administration."

"Missouri," Brannigan said. "His father was undersecretary of the treasury during Reagan's first term."

"He must have been killed over a drug deal," Ray said.

"Your friend Clyde didn't buy that theory. I've been looking through his records, and I wouldn't be surprised if he was right. In the end, Pepper came up empty-handed. Must have been frustrating for a guy like that."

"Well, yeah," Ray said. "But what makes you think he was right?"

"A couple of things. To beat someone to death, you have to keep coming at him, keep putting in the effort. Drug-related murders are like executions. Turning a guy's face into mush takes anger, it takes passion. It's personal."

"Maybe the kid burned one of his customers," Ray said.

"Could be. But I suppose it would be the first time in history that a guy killed his dealer and didn't rip off his stash."

"Uh-huh. That makes sense."

"Do you see what I'm thinking, Mr. Constantine? Clyde didn't want to give up that case. Who knows, maybe he moved out of Riverdale to keep working on it. So I was interested if he ever talked about this to any of you. Anything he might have said could be useful to us."

"No, he never did," Ray said. "Not to me, at least."

"Well, I had to ask," Brannigan said. "Thank you for your cooperation. Would you send in Mr. Gozzi, please?"

Ray left the office, closed the door behind him, and went over the side of the room. "Your turn in the barrel," he said to Leo, and when Leo stood up, Ray said, "Did any of you ever hear Clyde mention an unsolved case he was still working on?" None of them had. "Too bad," Ray said. "We might have been able to give them some help."

Ray watched Leo Gozzi enter Brannigan's office, then sat down beside Gus to wait until the last man came out.

• • •

"I'm sorry, but I think we're at a dead end," said Sally Frohman. "I really wish I didn't, because I like you a lot, Ray, and I thought we had a relationship that was going somewhere. You're a good writer, too—I never had any doubts about that. When I got my first job, some of the women told me never to get involved with writers, and it didn't take me long to learn why, but I always thought it could be different if you respected the guy's work. I guess I was wrong. Or there might be some other problem, one that has nothing to do with your being a writer, I don't know, at this point everything seems connected to everything else, but what I do know is, this thing isn't working, and I think it would be better if we stopped seeing each other."

She had left two messages on Ray's machine, arrived at his door toting a manuscript-laden briefcase, shared take-out Thai food and a bottle of Beaulieu Vineyards Chardonnay at the kitchen table, adventurously and with a hint of desperation observable only to an experienced Sally Frohman watcher strewed her clothes here and there on both floors of his brownstone apartment and concluded her farewell performance in a bravura trifecta, most of which, Ray hoped, had been genuine. Presently, which is to say at 10:35 P.M., they lay recumbent between daisy-printed sheets. The fragrantly chromatic harmonies of Fauré's Second Quartet for Piano and strings drifted about them, courtesy WNYC.

"Gee," Ray said, "you respect my work?"

Sally gave him a dark, deeply reproving look. Her hair frizzed out electrically around her head, and the distance between her eyes seemed an inch wider than usual. "Is that your final comment?"

"No, sorry. Just an ill-advised attempt at levity. You never told me anything like that before."

"*Didn't* I?" For a moment, she seemed stricken. "Well, maybe not in so many words. But you're changing the subject. Tonight was lovely, and I'm going to miss you, but we're not going anywhere, are we? This is as much as there's ever going to be, and it isn't enough."

"Sally," he said, "your timing is incredibly bad. One of my closest friends was killed yesterday. Clyde didn't have a heart attack, he wasn't wasting away from some disease, he was *knifed*. Some creep cut his *throat*. The guy smashed in Clyde's *skull*. I don't see how you can . . . Aaah, hell." He flattened his palms over his eyes, then dropped his hands at his sides. "If you want to know the truth, Sally, in a way—and take this however you like—it's like my son died all over again. This is not the moment to start whining about our relationship, all right?"

"No," Sally said. "It isn't all right. I'll overlook the part about whining, because I know none of this is easy for you. Ray, I am very, very sorry about your friend." She sat up straight and wrapped the sheet around her. "Do you know why I came here tonight? I wanted to do whatever I could for you—I wanted to help you get through this. I thought you might *need* me, Ray."

"I'm glad," he said.

"But did you talk to me about your friend? Did you let me know what you were feeling? Ray, you completely shut me out. Before dinner, I asked you about what happened at the police station, and you said it was nothing. During dinner, you said that your friend Leo looked distressed at the gym today, and I gathered you were concerned about him, but when I asked, you clammed up. You wouldn't have said anything if I hadn't forced the issue. You're like this glassy, frozen surface—you never open up. In the entire time we have been together, you never told me any more about your son than that his name was Paolo and he died of an overdose. I don't know how old he was, or where he was when it happened."

"He was twenty," Ray said. "It happened, as you put it, in his apartment, during his third year at RISDE. RISDE is an acronym for the Rhode Island School of Design, located in Providence, Rhode Island. Is that what you wanted to hear? Do you feel more informed?"

"You're never going to let anyone in," Sally said. "I feel sorry for you. Even more than that, you make me sad. You have nothing but those guys at the gym and your work."

"You'd be surprised at what I have," Ray said.

The telephone rang. Sally did not take her gaze from him, and the telephone kept ringing.

"What happened to your answering machine?"

"I turned it off," he said, and leaned sideways and picked up the receiver. After a short time, he said, "No, I haven't heard from him." Ray listened to his caller some more and said, "Okay, yeah. I'll be right there." He hung up.

"Don't take this personally, but I have to leave. That was Gus Trayham. He's been trying to talk to Leo all night, but Leo isn't answering, and Gus is worried. He and Tommy are up on 107th Street, trying to convince the super to let them into Leo's apartment. I should be there when they get in."

"Why? What do you think is wrong?"

"I don't even want to say." Ray got out of bed and began hunting for his clothes. "Talk about lousy timing. What do you want to do, stay here?"

"I'll wait for you to get back," Sally said. "Unless you want me to come with you."

"No, no," Ray said. "With luck, I won't be gone more than half an hour. If it's going to be later, I'll call."

A few minutes after midnight, Ray let himself back into his apartment. Fully dressed, Sally was seated on his sofa, dividing her attention between the stack of pages on her lap and Channel One, the 24-hour local news station.

"Well?" she said.

Ray shook his head and walked into the kitchen. He took a glass from a shelf, dropped in ice cubes from a bowl in the freezer, and half filled the glass with whiskey. When he turned around, Sally was leaning against the counter just inside the entrance, part of the manuscript still in her hands.

"I see you need a drink," she said.

"That's nice," Ray said. "I appreciate your support." He sat at his table and swallowed whiskey without taking his eyes from her.

Sally took a step toward him, then stopped moving and tucked the pages under one arm. "I assume you got into Leo's apartment."

"Yes," Ray said. "That we did. It took a little heavy-duty persuasion, but the super finally opened the door to Leo's disgusting pigpen. The results were unsatisfying. They lacked a certain resolution. The pigpen was empty. In the sense of its tenant being nowhere in sight. Looked at another way, the place wasn't empty at all, since garbage was piled up everywhere you looked. We waited around until we were about to pass out from the stench, and then we gave up."

"Do you think he killed himself? Is that what you were worried about?"

Ray leaned back in his chair and gazed at a spot on the wall five or six feet to her right, pretending to consider her words. He appeared to be mildly amused. "I would say . . . I would say that your question is too narrowly framed. Our anxieties are free-floating and essentially undefined. They are of an inclusive nature."

"That's not—"

He interrupted her, still contemplating the spot on the wall. "I will say this, however. If I had to live in that filthy dump, thoughts of suicide would never be far from my mind. Seeing his apartment puts Leo in an entirely different light. I had no understanding, none whatsoever, of the way he lived."

She looked at him in silence for a suspended moment. "Have you had any new thoughts about us?"

"Now?" Ray took another swallow of whiskey. After a few seconds, he shifted his gaze to Sally. "Do you know how ridiculous that question is? That doesn't mean you can't spend the night here, by the way."

"Here's another ridiculous question," she said. "How would you describe the way you're feeling at this moment? Or, if you are uncertain about your feelings, what are you thinking?"

"Oh, I'm completely clear about my emotional condition," Ray said. "It's as though a huge explosion just went off a yard or so away from me. Chunks of metal and parts of bodies are flying all over the place. People have begun to scream, and the screaming is going to continue for a long time. I'm still on my feet, but as yet I don't know if I have been injured. I almost have to be injured, but I'm afraid to look. That's how I feel."

Sally quivered.

Ray tilted the last of the whiskey into his mouth and thumped the glass on the table. "And what I'm thinking is this. Betrayal is the ugliest, most repulsive thing I can imagine. I hate being betrayed."

Sally wavered backward. "We have nothing more to say to each other. Stay there, don't walk me to the door." She spun around and left the kitchen.

"For God's sake, Sally," Ray said. "I wasn't talking

about you." He stood up and poured more whiskey into his glass. From the living room came the rustle of papers being stuffed into a briefcase. "Sally?" The next sound he heard was the closing of the door.

SHOW US THE WAY

by Whitley Strieber

TWELVE years is a long time to be alive. Mikey had thought this actually since he was a little towheaded eight-year-old. Life was a long hall that you never stopped going down. At least he had Jake with him. Friends, yeah. Livin' rich in these rich houses. Mikey was never gonna make bread like his dad did. Who wants that office crap?

Jake was fourteen. He had burned the Burtons' hound for Mikey, after it barked and got him caught goin' in their damn house, see if he could locate a little drugs're sumpin.

"I have another mission for you," Mikey said over the phone. Jake grunted. It was after ten. They'd both been drinking in their separate rumpus rooms half the night and calling each other if some guy got offed on TV in a really cool way. Mikey's folks had just bought a digital TV, so he was watching even more. Because it was really cool, no matter what you watched. He watched *Mister Rogers* every afternoon—upstairs in his room with the door locked and the volume of the little portable color set real low so his sister wouldn't hear.

Mikey felt the floating of being drunk and knew that he

had to hang on to it just here with sips or he would go really high and wake up on a school morning hung.

"Whaddaya think about Sarah, Debbie, and Mira?"

"What?"

"I mean, which one is, like, you'd like to collect her panties?"

"What's it to you?"

"I just want to know, 'cause they screwin' up my brain, go on."

"You wanna get into those broads? *Those* broads? Man. That is *so* poor."

"What if I said I needed something different."

A short silence. Then, "What different?"

"If some sister jivin' on your reputation, she need killin,' man."

The silence was longer this time. Mikey used it to light a Camel. He took a deep drag, held the smoke, waited until it got working. Then he took another little tiny sip from the Blue Label in the Teachers bottle that he had exchanged. But who's gonna gag on Teachers when there's two-hundred-dollar-a-fifth Blue Label right there in dear Daddy's bar? Let Daddy drink the Teachers.

What was going on with Jake, anyway? "Hey, man, you whippin' it're somethin'?"

"You the one whips weenie, you little pervert. What I'm thinkin' is, I don't wanna get in no newspaper, man."

"Come on, man!"

"So you do it, man!"

He sucked the Camel, sucked the bottle. Screw school, he had to go way, way down tonight because he was gonna have to waste his eyes on those bitches in the morning.

"I can't do it. I'm not a good enough shot."

"Oh, yeah, I gotta go up to Hofford for *years* 'cause you're a bad shot? I don't think so, man."

"You know who you talk like? You talk like DiCaprio trying to sound tough."

"You callin' the wrong cracker a fag, man. Fuck you!"

"Fuck you!"

"You wanna off them bitches, you do it. I'm pushin' The Age, man. I got a birthday next week."

"That's eternity, man. I want this done at recess tomorrow."

"All three of 'em?" His voice had gone little boy. Little bitty boy, Mikey thought, and thought Jake is so damn dumb, like this is real. This guy was, like, seizured. Like, why would he do what some kid like Mikey said? Go *on.*

Somewhere off in the house, Dad's voice yelled, "I smell cigarettes and in one minute I am coming looking!" Yeah, okay, you do that. "Look, I'll come back to you, brother. I got damage on me."

He slid the Teachers bottle full of Blue Label in under the sofa cushions and thought for the millionth time: "If I could get a way to off that old turd, I'd be worth, like, millions at age twelve." He went up the gracious front staircase that dumb magazines always wanted to take pictures of and entered Becky's boudoir. She was deep asleep. "Hey, Monica," he said to Monica the Poodle, who slept on the foot of his sister's bed. He'd had a damn fox terrier that he'd rolled over on and killed just when he was getting to like it. And he still has these dreams where he is choking it to death. Hard on, man.

He got her ashtray out from under her bed, then walked around the room puffing the Camel and blowing smoke rings. They glowed in the moonlight that was slanting softly in the east windows. From outside, there came a scent of magnolias, rich and sweet, a scent he associated with being awake in the sweaty night and thinking about putting bitches down down down.

Crushing out the Camel, he went to his own bedroom, turned on his desk light, then went into his bathroom and gargled with Scope until he thought maybe he oughta just drink that, it was so much better than lousy whiskey. Why didn't they make, like, Pepsi-flavored vodka? Or Jolt Cola with gin in it? Stupid jerks.

Voices. Daddy bum pie comin' up the stairs. Then he goes into Becky's room. Goody, this is good. They yell, yeah that's on along. On along. Oh, shit, he gonna do a smoker on her butt! She cries out, she is just begging, and then—well, hoo? Why the silence? Why not the *thwack thwack* of her pretty bottom getting palm-burned?

Man. He comes across the hall, what the hell? Mikey hits his bathroom, frantically gargles Scope. Just as he gets back to his desk, Dad comes in. "Yes, Dad?"

"What's that you're studying, son?"

"Modern history. I've got a test tomorrow."

He holds out his claw. "Give me your hand, son."

Wha' dis? Obediently, he holds out his hand. His father looks down at it in the light. He parts the fingers. Fucker is lookin' for *stains,* man! This is *way down,* man! "Is anything the matter, Daddy?"

"You're very deceptive, son." He goes over to the bed, sits on it. "You blew smoke in her room."

"Did not!"

"Then who did? The devil? *You* crushed out that cigarette in that ashtray."

He thought fast. This was almost over and he was on his back flat. Perfect comeback: "She has an ashtray?"

He stared at Mikey, looking at him in a funny way, a kind of scary way. He wasn't like Mom, Mom would just blast you. She'd beat you in the head with a shoe, she wanted to do the physical thing. Dad was, like, careful. He did it like Jesus wanted, or so *he* said. Mikey's personal opinion was that Jesus was as dead as anybody and didn't give a rat's behind what some guy like Beauford Harlan did to his kid.

His phone rang. Jake. "I ain't gonna do the bitches. I mean, that other one was a *dog.* I'll tell you what, I'll do their dogs. Okay?"

He hung up. "Sorry, Dad."

"Sorry for what?"

He jerked his chin toward the phone. "The interruption."

"Son, you put that ashtray in there. You blew smoke in that room. You constructed a deceit. So there are two crimes here: smoking and lying. Do you understand how what you did was a lie? How an action can be a lie just like words?"

Whippin' comin' down. Sheet!

Becky appeared in the door, her pink nightie fluttering with the breeze. Dad took off his belt, nodded toward the bed. Across the foot Mikey went.

He shut down inside, closing his inner doors behind him as he went into the middle of the middle of himself. There he said, "You ain't gonna feel nothin', 'cause you already dead."

Twelve long years: the spattering sound the belt made when it came out of the pants. Becky watching, her eyes moist with what looked like pity but he knew was just pure pleasure.

Mom's voice: "Not too hard, Beau."

Whip one. Don't make no sound. Whip two. Goes up and down your legs, hurts a lot. Whip three. Shit, man! Four. Five. *Six!* Fuck, this is insane. *Seven,* he is totally insane! *Eight!* Daddy! NINE! Oh, Daddy, please! And then he is lost in his agony, screaming and crying wildly, his abnegation making his sister's heart beat hard and his mother slide her lips back from her teeth as if her flesh, also, was being seared.

There is this kid hurting somewhere in the world, just this kid screaming his guts out somewhere in the world "o help."

It stops. He sits up, gobbling and bawling—then he stops, stifling it by a massive effort of will. Flicking the tears from his eyes, he asks, "You done?" He sounds tired, old. His voice is cracking in its attempt to stifle his sobs. Becky stuffs laughter back in her throat because of that cracking.

"Honey," Mom says, "come kneel down and pray with

me." She glances up at her husband. "What was this for, Beau?"

"Cigarettes," he says, "lying." His voice is indifferent now. Chore's done, that's it. Dad and Becky go off into her room, where they will pray together on their own. He goes to his knees beside Mom.

"O Lord, we thank you for our husband and father, and for the good work of your discipline that he does in our family."

"I thank you, Lord, for my dad's wisdom and the love he showed by helping me tonight."

"Oh, Michael, that is *so good*! That—Beau, did you hear that?" No sound from the dark. "Oh, well, they're praying together, too." She clears her throat. Hu-hum! "Dear Jesus, we are feeling our love and our gratitude right now," she says. "O dear Jesus, we love you so much that we are just *all* love!"

Mikey says, "Whosoever shall offend one of these little ones that believe in me, it is better for him that a millstone were hanged about his neck . . ."

Mom nods, her hairdo bobbing. She's fat, no two ways about that. She has little eyes that are made littler by the fat. She looks to Mikey like something that oughta be butchered up into chops and sold in a store. "Hon," she says, "I don't think you quite understand. Some of the things that Jesus said were meant for gentler times. Remember 'He that spareth the rod hateth his son'? What does that mean to you?"

His butt was killing him. "Daddy whips me like Jesus would. He whips me God hard."

Mom got up and kissed him on the top of his goddamn head and went through her goodnight-love-Jesus drill.

"Good night, baby. God bless you and keep you."

Good fuckin' night, bitch. "Good night, Mommy."

He bought X-tasy at school when Gene Hobbes had it, which was pretty much all the time now. I mean, the *English* teacher. But Christ, with three babies and a wife at home, he had to have a second income.

Mikey phoned Jake. "You put the bitches down at recess and that is a fuckin' order, man!"

"Now, I ax you, why should I take orders from some punk kid got a hard-on for to off some bitch wouldn't let him stick it in her fuckin' ear? Why should I do that?"

Mikey hated to remind him. But he had to, he saw that. He spoke in a whisper. " 'Cause of . . . you know."

Jake went into yet another of his long-silence routines. Jake was the kind of person who needed time to think. "Why do I get you to do it, Mikey? Am I gay?"

As he always did when Jake asked this nervous question, he replied, "Nah." But why *did* he like it? They were just these two kids where one of them wanted this and the other did it to him. Twelve years is so damn long. "You pop the bitches, cuntface."

"Man, I'm goin' down, I do that!"

"Look. You take that ought-six, that one with that sweet scope. You go down Montmorency, way back to where the woods start. Shoot outta there, then you go around to Governor and Spearman and you home, man. You just put the piece back in the rack and make yourself a sandwich. Pop. Pop. Pop."

"Mikey, Jesus!"

"*Do it!*" He put the telephone back in the cradle and went into the bathroom.

A moment later, he rushed out and called Jake again. "I'm comin' over there right now! I'm gonna do you right now!"

"Shut up, man, just *shut up!*"

He hung up. Downstairs there was that ancient dickhead music, Frank the Fuck Sinatra. He lay back listening to it. Jake was probably over there right now gettin' hisself ready. Now, this was a guy, was a *real* asshole. What Jake didn't know was that there was no way out of this house after the slopes put on their dumb alarm system. They didn't, like, exactly give out their code, man. Nine at night and Harlan House became Harlan Prison.

He wished he dared go downstairs and at least get his bottle. Suck all night. Suck forever. Suck and watch the sky turn night to day, night to day. Suck and wait for the do. I mean, they never did nothing to nobody, they just bitches talkin' about one guy and another. He just thought they needed killin,' and that was what was goin' down.

He longed for something—another cigarette, a huge drink, sucking on the old bottle like it was Mommy's tit. Or doing some of mom's Zoloft. But they were pill-counters, and he didn't think he could stand the bottom heating he'd get for stealing their many drugs.

Oh, man, could that old scum whip. He wished he was a big kid like Tucker Gains what lit into his dad and whipped *him*. You looked at Tucker Gains with that sunken chin of his and those drooly eyes always glued to the girls, you thought total greenskin. But you had to say, "This is one kid whipped back." He got *respek* at Memorial Middle School, go on.

He went back into his bright yellow bathroom. When he was little, he used to shit the floor just so he could listen to them say, "Now, Mikey, you *missed*. Uh-oh, uh-oh." Soc. I experiment: you pop your slopes, write a paper: "Life Without Parents." He wanted his bottle, he wanted his ciggies, he wanted a whole bunch of caps, man, X-tasy and uppers and downers.

Dad gets out some magazine, says, "X-tasy causes permanent brain damage. Now, I'm sure you don't use any of these drugs, but just be aware that this one is particularly dangerous." And you are thinking, Permanent brain damage—so *gooooood*!

You got that girl, that cock pumper Wendy Willerson, she takes these uppers, man, these real *upper* uppers *and* she takes these downers, man! These real downer downers, man. And she is like, totally schitzed. She pisses in a booth at McD. Later, at the club, she asks this, like, adult woman, I mean—can I *eat* you? I mean, she actually *does* this! At the bar. At the country club. The woman was Mrs. Roma, the lady wife of Jack Roma Pontiac.

He got his pants and shirt off, hissing as he pulled his underpants away from his tenderized butt. I mean, they're, like, mashed into my damn *skin*, man! Ouch, shit. He oughta whip some little kid. Whip some little first-year, take him out behind the gym and whip his tender first-year butt. "What'd I do, man?" "Man, you fuckin' *drew breath*, man!" That movie. That was from that movie.

He lay down. Almost at once, the clamor of his thought faded.

He slept in air-conditioned isolation, and so never knew the seductive peace of the spring breeze outside, nor smelled the sweet of the Georgia night. Outside, the breeze was awakening an ancient and very different world. The magnolia offered its flowers to the shadows, the bullfrog boomed by the lakeside. Bass rushed in the black waters, reeds hummed in the breeze. Coons and possums and skunks moved in the shadowy edges of the garden that surrounded the house, and snakes climbed in the dark old oaks, sniffing for the eggs earlier laid by fluttering dove hens and oriole hens and, mixed in the cunning interiors of low shrubs, sparrow hens and chickadee hens. A thin memory of the moon slipped westward; the stars of Orion settled low.

Mikey sighed in his sleep. His sister stole into his room very late, and sat beside his bed quietly weeping. She laid her hand in his and drew it against her cheek, and in the glittering eyes of her doll's face, there appeared infinite pain. After a time, she went away. Outside, the compressor snapped on, causing two deer at the edge of the garden to briefly raise their heads. Somewhat later, there was a cry deep in the house—a brief, astonished shout. Not the children, the voice was too mature. So it must have been Christine or their servant out in the wing behind the kitchen, Idella.

What nightmare rode the disturbed party? Becky, who

began sometime last year to suffer from the syndrome known as Guarded Sleep, awoke with a start. She sighed, got up, and peed. She drank some water, considered doing an Ambien, but it was too close to morning. Back in bed, Monica stretched out beside her. Girl and dog dreamed then, across the deeps of the night.

By and by, morning began to skulk toward the ancient plantation house and the ancient lake, the untilled acres that once had been crowded at this planting season by creeping slaves. No more, but if the chief financial officer of a burgeoning HMO had wanted people in his fields, there would have been people there.

Now the eastern sky began to become more defined as dawn's earliest twilight evolved. The horizon acquired a green as deep and soft as memory.

To look upon Tolson's Mills, with its cluster of wealthy homes along Siper and Woodley and Carew—streets named for captains and colonels and generals of the Lost Cause—would be to see dark buildings and deepest silence, the profound silence that encloses peaceful spirits at their rest. Farther out, hugging the misty river, were the seven old plantations, the Pemmody, the Gates, Summerwell where Mikey now slept the sleep of childhood, Gaithers, Mill Run, Cinnamon Hill, and Oak Lane. All were antebellum, all elegantly designed to conceal the harder realities of the world that had built them.

None of the present owners were related to the builders. In fact, Mikey's family had come to Atlanta with General Medical in 1990. They were, like the Coxeys in Mill Run and the Gainses in Pemmody traveling the velvet highway of the corporate vagabond.

Not only was the world of the mansion builders gone, so was the one that had replaced it, which had taken the position of the black man in society as its central issue. This world had been kindly and cruel, maddening mature human beings with unneeded paternalism, while at the same time trapping them in a poverty so brute it appeared as if they did need the hypocritical "help" of their oppressors.

These worlds were gone, all remaining of them being a few very old men in the tatters of past prosperity, faded linen suits, and dusty Cadillacs.

The next America, the one that had come beating down from the north on the drum of civil rights, that hopeful, compassionate America that had identified itself so loyally with its ideal of dignity, was also gone. All those dreams had slipped into forgetfulness.

What concerns us presently are the sorrows of a richly alive and beautiful child who is trapped in the cruelest of all the worlds that have inhabited this place. His world is unmoored from the intellectual content not only of old America, but also from old Europe. In fact, it doesn't have any intellectual content. To replace the culture of compassion that raised this country's voice to singing, has come a savage culture of blame.

And Mikey is angry because he's a mean little cuss who's life is cursed by a discipline that worked for the redoubtable author of the Book of Proverbs, a biblical treatise directed at a culture of semiliterate shepherds.

He has never been moved by an idea. He has never tasted beauty. If he is amazed, he says, "Fuckin' A, man, go on." He is amazed by monster trucks. He is amazed by tales of sexual conquest. Mandy went down on Jo-Jo went down on Priss went down on Kev. Fuckin' A, man, go on.

It is the creak of the wheel of his life, fuckin' A, man, go on.

We will intrude on his privacy, but ever so discreetly, without waking him up before the hour appointed for the radio to begin blasting the voice of the Grateful Dead into his vibrating skull.

Mikey is four feet and seven inches long. He is pale of skin, with hair that would be called russet blond. His lips, lying partly open now, seem to speak a little, perhaps reflecting a boy's nascent dreams of white skin and curvy places, or running in some soccer field. Around his eyes there is the freshness nature grants young things.

Having never known the matter of the old world, Mikey is a pioneer on the far edge of this latest America. At age twelve, he has never heard of O. Henry or Mark Twain, much less Beethoven or even Chuck Berry. His America is like a bright ship without a crew, its whole management dependent upon the party-mad passengers. It has come un- moored, its destiny committed to the ocean. Seeing that it moves only slowly away from the dock, the passengers laugh. For the while. Franz Kafka called the destination to which it is committed Away From Here. But Mikey has never heard of Franz Kafka and he never will, not in any lecture hall or classroom, and certainly not at home. Nor Willa Cather and *Death Comes for the Archbishop* or Kath- erine Anne Porter and *Pale Horse, Pale Rider*, nor Tolstoy nor Spenser, still less Molière or Rimbaud or Bellow. The first thing an unmoored ship loses is its past.

The sun's first rays rise, setting the mist afire, gleaming in the dewy trees and along the drops of dew that crowd neat white fence lines and the edges of porches. In those drops there come to be reflected moving automobiles. First is the Stacy family Lincoln Navigator, a sumptuous room on wheels filled with a shambles of Stacys, among them Mira, twelve three weeks ago and herself as soft as the dew. She sits against the left rear door, her eyes closed, catching a last doze before being plunged into the savagery of Me- morial Middle School.

In another car closer to the school, Debbie Burns drinks milk. Debbie is hale, her face red, and she is overweight. There are Cocoa Puffs and Toaster Strudel on the breakfast table and nothing else. Her mother kisses her on the top of her brown head and tells her to hurry up. Debbie's entire thought is concentrated on one thing: Jonathan Shultz Looked at Me. Jonathan Shultz is just the richest and most popular kid at Memorial. Jonathan Shultz is, like, the *cutest* boy at Memorial. And when his eyes met hers, she offered herself in longing, lascivious response. She cannot believe that he did not even see her, innocent that she is. She does not yet know that she is plain, and has not discovered just how much this will circumscribe her enjoyment of life in the world to come. If her life is not to end today, of course.

These girls are the most important for us to know, these two. There is also little Sara Hughes, the daughter of "Baltimore" Bill Hughes, who caught for the Orioles for two weeks of heaven back in 1988. Caught for them and missed pitches. But what the hell, the man was in the Majors. We cannot be too exacting in our study. He has a chain of forty-seven convenience stores, Southerly Farms. They sell beer, mostly, beer and sundries and gasoline. It's a good business. He does it well, making sure that not a single clerk dips the till.

Sara is small and pale-complected. She loves Sugar Babies, her toy dachshund Oscar, her boyfriend Sandy Hecker, and yellow jackets. They push face and do yellow jackets. They really *work,* I mean, you feel *so good.* Sandy and Sara sit by the lake on pure nights, watching the stars and experimenting with drugs and each other. Daddy calls her Princess. She can imagine her family on a talk show, and loves to, like, think about what she would say. Sara Hughes could be only a short time from participation in an event that will gladden the hearts of many a media executive, including the producers of every talk show in the country.

But time is growing short, and there is another we must meet as well, Jake Blair—Jason Blair III—whose great-to-the-something-power grandfather was Colonel Jason Blair of the Georgia Zouaves. The Blairs lost Summerwell during Reconstruction, but Jake has been raised on family stories of the place, and of the great days of the Blair clan. Perhaps that is why he has fallen in love with Mikey, Summerwell's present young master. Mikey who has taught him things he wishes he didn't know; Mikey who is by turns so kind and so mean to him; Mikey who has made him be up cleaning this damn gun at seven o'clock in the morning.

Most times, Jake enjoys cleaning the gun. It's a beautiful

machine, one that he has known all his life. He first shot it at the age of ten, and with it got a nine-point buck. On his first shot. Later that afternoon he tasted of his first beer, a Dixie that made him sneeze.

He learned how to skin and dress a buck, a chattering little boy trying to control an enormous dressing knife. Jake is the kind of shot you read about.

By seven-thirty there is a smell of coffee in almost every house, the streets are full of cars and the sidewalks with children walking and biking to Edgewood Elementary, Memorial Middle School, and Rock County High. Yellow school buses flash their lights, demanding that all stop while their precious cargo enters. The possums and coons and bats are sleeping in cover, the flies and locusts awakening to have their days. Comes the lark rise. Butterflies flit almost everywhere.

In his bathroom, Mikey is rubbing a film of Neosporin on his contusions. He is thinking about the Three Gunches. In him there is something that feels good if it's mad. Good anger. Like hard blood, kind of. As if you had hard blood. He looks in the mirror. Not a blackhead, not a zit. Clear kiddie face. Pussy face, go on. He flutters his eyes, thinks of Jake whispering "oh, baby, oh, baby" like he would if he was a girl. Jake oughta be burned at the stake. Have a stake put through his heart. Be staked to the ground for the antz.

He covers his mouth with both hands, screws his eyes closed, and screams as loud as he possibly can. Even while he is doing this, he hears the tinkle of the dreaded breakfast bell from hell. He has exactly sixty seconds if he is not going to eat his breakfast on his goddamn knees. He throws on his clothes. Brush hair, swoop, swoop. Hears Becky's feet pounding on the stairs. Teeth, hands, run your ass, bo.

Just as the second hand on that big ol' clock on the wall gasps past the twelve, he hits the table.

Dad: "God thank you for our bounty. Bless this house and all who dwell within it."

Mikey: "Pass the Frosted Flakes, please, Mother."

He's gotta eat fast because there is a plan, a major plan that is gonna make this sucker go *down*. These bitches are history, man, and that is a fak! Okay.

"May I please be excused?"

Daddy lum lum looks over with his shit-green eyes and smiles his shit-faced smile. Daddy cum cum says, "Yes, son, you're excused."

Back upstairs get that video he was supposed to make for Mira, drop it in his backpack. Then go into Picture Perfect on his PC and totally shred the entire file marked "Jake." That'll clean it all out, no way even a hacker could get it back or tell that it had ever been here. Yeah, his dad is not stupid about computers, as he has learned to his own butt-blistering cost. His has a child guard on the browser. No sex sites. No Communist sites. No liberal sites. No Jewish sites. No UFO sites. No medical sites. No on-line bookstores. No PBS-kids'-show sites. No no no fucking *sites*!

Long honk downstairs. The bus!

Get into the file that conceals Picture Perfect, then into the file called homeworkmath97 that conceals the video of him plumbing Jake.

"Mike, get moving!"

Drag the file onto the Zippy Shredder icon, hit the yes button with the mouse.

Ho-o-o-nk!

It's a big file. It takes time to shred a big file.

"Michael!"

"Coming, Daddy!"

Come on you stupid file come *on*!

Ho-o-onk!

Third honk, the bus leaves in one minute.

Why won't the file shred? Please, file!

"Michael, you're fined one dollar!"

Mikey is seeing the images flash past in his mind as they are swept from his hard disk. And he thinks: Fuck Jake, man. *Fuck him!* I am gonna vomit, man! Shit, man!

I don't *like* it. He my fren and he *need* it. I mean, *shit!* He makes me makes me!

A note comes up on the screen: *Finished*. Okay! Turn off the computer, move your ass down the stairs three at a time. "Daddy I got diarrhea."

"The toilet didn't flush!"

Ho-o-o-nk!

"Yes it did!"

"We'll discuss this after school."

Oh, yeah, like you'll be remembering anything about this then! That's Columbo discovers America time, go on!

The bus: Kenny says, "Doughnut?"

He doesn't answer. Nobody answers Kenny. Nobody talks to him. It's social suicide to admit he even exists. He looks like something that lives in a swamp.

Mikey sits beside Claire Parker, she's a quiet bitch, you ain't gonna get no shit from her. And mainly, Mira is there right in the seat in front.

Frog Martin is across the aisle. "I hate people let their zits go."

"I ain't got no fuckin' zits."

"You piece a shit, you *are* a zit. Shit! Hey, that rhymes. Zitshit. Froggy's a zitshit from Zitsville."

"I gonna come upside a' your head," Jake says casually as he strolls down the aisle. He barely glances at Mikey. Sits behind him.

Now comes the cool part. Mikey gets out the tape and leans forward and says into Mira's ear, "You suck, but I got the friggin' tape done."

"Oh, thank—"

"Put it down, bitch!"

She stuffs the tape into her backpack and tosses her head. For the rest of the trip in, Mikey does math homework and tries to figure out where the hell Jimbo Routier learns to cuss: He's in the far back where little kids like Mikey ain't allowed, and he's goin' so fast it is, like, it is

awesome. I mean, you can't even follow it, it's like a rap.
An 'effing rap, man.

After the bus stops, Jake follows Mikey down the walk
just like he knew he would. Mikey ignores him like a good
boy should. But a guy is a guy wherever he may be, and
Jake says, "What the fuck you give the cunt, man? I thought
you hated that cunt."

"Our tape."

Jake laughs, shakes his head. He just cannot believe that
shit. It is too impossible, I mean, that tape is gonna get
them both landed in some kinda *home,* you know, it is so
totally sick that it is gonna make some goddamn perv doc
cream pure dee Cool Whip, man!

In truth, the tape that Mikey had transferred into his
computer and then so carefully eradicated contained a little
sexual acting-out of the sort that, in normal societies, is
typical for this age group. Even the vaguely sadomasochis-
tic overtones of some of their acts were of trivial significance, especially given the prevalence of corporal
punishment in their lives.

Jake grabs Mikey by the back of his collar and shakes
him so hard that pigeons standing in the walkway before
them rise, their wings sparking in the sun. "You are such
a profound asshole, Mikey. I mean, I am big enough to tear
your head off, man, and you tell me you done that. You
wanta get yourself killed? Murder most foul?"

Mikey stops him. He looks up. Their eyes meet. Mikey
says, very carefully, "Pop. Pop. Pop."

"Shit, I ain't gonna! You tellin' me to lose my *life*, man!
I ain't gonna."

"You ain't got a life. You a perv, man. Everbody gonna
know it. I mean, that tape is gonna be played at every
Memorial party and County party there be, bo. You go into
County with that on you, bo. 'Cept if you pop the bitches."
As Jake choked out demurral, Mikey paused. Then, as if to
test or savor the words, he repeated, "Pop the bitches."

"I'll go to Hofford."

"You ain't goin' nowhere lak dat, you go wit my plan." He gestured toward the recess yard. "Them trees a long way off, bo."

Jake turned on him, seized his thin shoulders. "Fuck the fuckin' trees! I ain't killin' nobody, not for you or nobody else." He plunged into his pocket, brought out his house key. "Here! You go get the gun, you do it. If it's so friggin' goddamn safe!"

The first bell rang. Melissa Smith went past going "smoke smoke," signaling that she had reefer and would be under the Sunshine Bridge after school.

"Fuckin' bitch, every time she heavy is a time I ain't got five bucks," Jake said. "Man, my old man docked me good. Ten-buck fine. The maid found a goddamn Jerry under my mattress. Thank you, Leroy, that moron left it there."

"You sleepin' wit 'im?"

Jake tousled his hair. "Only wit you, pretty child."

They went into the school. Jake did not see Mikey slide a note into a certain locker. Had he, he would have known that the locker belonged to Mira, and he might have guessed that not all was as it seemed.

And so to Science 3. Accelerated second-years took it along with normal third-years. Mikey and Jake sat side by side. "Students," said Hadley Cox, "how old is the earth?"

"Three thousand one hundred and fifty years," Jewel Brown said.

"Now, is that a fact or a theory?"

"Fact!" Mikey announced.

Against the far wall, Mira suddenly gasped. Her face turned crimson. Her eyes became tiny and bright.

"Mira?"

"Sorry, Miss Cox," she said. She darted a horrible glance at Jake. "I'm allergic."

"Mikey, that is one theory. Another theory holds that the earth is much older. Who can tell us about that theory?"

"The earth has gotta be really old or the dinosaurs' bones wouldn't have had time to turn to stone."

"No way," Clifton George said, "Jurassic Park is, like, on that island."

Nobody laughed. Everybody assumed that Jurassic Park had to be somewhere. Mrs. Cox closed her eyes, trying to hide her impatience. The state board of education had mandated that creation theory be taught alongside scientific theories that she personally regarded as proven. The result was that the children were now completely confused about the past. "Jurassic Park is imaginary," she said patiently.

"Mikey, how *could* the dinosaurs have existed three thousand years ago? That was when the Bible was being written. Surely Moses or somebody would have mentioned seeing a beast so fantastic."

Mikey hated this cunt. She was a smart cunt. He didn't care about dinosaurs or whatever. All he cared about was that he not get listed by the church monitor for heresy and he ends up having to get grace counseling. The church had all kinds of monitors all over the damn school. Becky was a monitor. They never said nothing about it, but if you were Christian, you better not spout out any funny ideas at Memorial, you gonna get stuck in Bible detention every Friday night for a month, go on.

"The dinosaurs weren't living in the Holy Land," he explained. "God wouldn't let them because it was holy."

So it went, across the reaches of the school, as the children were patiently and carefully taught a slightly skewed version of the past, in which creation theory was taken seriously. In its own way, Memorial science curriculum was as carefully edited as the one that had been taught in Soviet schools until the fall of the USSR. Belief and fact had clashed, and belief had won—at least, it had won the right to be disguised as something rational.

Mikey waited. He did not like science, geography, history, math, or English. He did not like Sunday school or Bible study on Saturday afternoon. He did not like baseball, which he had to play on the church team. He envied the kids doing school soccer. No soccer for Mikey. It wasn't an American game. So what, we got a German car and a Japanese car and an American pickup. So why can't I play an American game and a whatever game? No backtalk, which was what the adults in his life all said when they were defeated.

He gazed over at Mira, wondering where the bullet would enter her head. And what would it do in there? What was in your head? Some kinda brain meat, yeah. He threw his hand up. "What is the brain?"

"That isn't until the Science of Humanity Sequence, Mikey. But the brain is a collection of billions and billions of cells that work together to store your memories and engage in logical thinking."

"I mean, what's it made out of?"

"Tissue. Human tissue."

"Is it, like, hard?"

"It's very soft, Mikey. Very fragile." She went on with her lesson, while Mikey watched Mira. It wasn't that he hated the gunches, not really. Called him a dumbhead, at'un. But he didn't hate her, or her friends. Just had this thing needed to get done, that was all.

Ten-fifteen: morning recess. Out to the yard. Melissa Smith is going around, "smoke, smoke" until everybody at Memorial knows what is gonna go down under that bridge tonight. The church kids won't tell, nobody will tell. You tell a thing like that, you are gonna get like that dork Jimmie Landers, by accident run over by a car that somehow or another just happened to start, like, rolling.

There is this apocalypse going on among the three gunches. They are like, gagged. They are *beholding* Jake and he is sort of smiling and trying to—hey—get out of this problem. Then all of a sudden the gunches all take a big step back away from Jake . . . just like Mikey knew they would. And then Lenny Moore does it and Carrie and

Becky do it, and these real, like prominent kids who never talk to you even, Charles Shandy and Patricia Turner and Shultz, they do it, and that gets everybody doing it.

Jake is in the total meltdown situation of he is in a queer circle. Mikey goes walking in even though it is hard to move his legs. He goes walking right in and he stands beside Jake.

Jake is getting the most total rejection that you can get, that led that horrible gunch Kathie Breedlove to transfer out last year, and that black kid who got in here somehow to get back on out of here somehow, too. Jake lopes off, and the circle moves with him, speeding around the field like some kind of drill-team formation on steroids. He cannot get out. He has to stay in it till the bell.

He yells, "Why? *Why!*"

Mikey looks up at him. "They got a VCR in 112, man."

"You fucked yourself, too! You dumb-ass shit!"

"I blacked my face outta the tape, man. This circle ain't followin' me."

"Okay, let's see you get off it."

Mikey begins walking toward the edge of the circle, which indeed does not follow him. When he reaches the border, the kids unlink their arms for him. As he comes out, Melissa whispers urgently, "Smoke smoke."

"Okay," he says, "I heard it fifty times already!"

The note he had slipped into Mira's locker said, *I hate all you fucking gunch bitch cunts and I am going to shit on your face. Sincerely Yours, Jake.* The tape was an old Bible story. And there was no VCR in 112.

But Jake thinks he is totally owned doing a boof on some blacked-out boyfriend. Mikey sees the tears on his face, sees the wide eyes of a man just got convicted big time. He is so mad he is white like Kleenex.

The kids watch with indifference. They don't know what it's about, most of them, but they know the code. You don't circle somebody for fun. 'Course, what Jake thinks—I mean, that tape is gonna go on the Internet, like. I mean, every kid that knows how to read newsgroup code is gonna go to wherever they put it down, like behind some firewalled Web site run outta Finland or Greece or somewheres. Kid newsgroups will be full of coded messages about how to get to it. Jake thinks he is gonna get, like, very fucking famous for being the ultimate pervert of the world. Because Mikey stood beside his friend, he's, like, got some points now. You can feel it in the halls. Lotta kids going hi. You got a friend in trouble, you stand up.

Mikey passes Jake on the way into Soc. Sci. "Why, man?" Jake says.

" 'Cause you gotta take 'em out now."

He looks back and catches Jake staring at him like some kind of inhuman animal or alien, like. He is real far done, like, he sees now that Mikey is serious.

Tick, tock, soc. sucks. You gotta Listen to The Brain, which is what they call Miss Enderle. She is, like, real enthusiastic. She smiles. She thinks the people in the room know what she's talking about. She believes her own shit, Miss Enderle does. Who the hell cares about social ethics, whatever the hell they are. Mikey is not stupid. You can't say that criminals need compassion. That is horseshit. You commit a crime, you get your ass put in the fuckin' slammer, go on.

Comes the bell finally, and he goes into history, which he also has with Jake. He waits for Jake to come in, but Jake does not come in. Mr. Bitters calls the roll. No Jake.

It is the most total high that Mikey has ever felt in his entire life, it is like his blood has turned to gold or something. He feels like he has got wings all of a sudden, like he has reached the highest place in the world, and all the cities lie below him, the cities of the plain.

Then the bell rings and that is totally amazing because it feels like this class just started. He is beside Debbie now. "Hiya, Deb."

"Hey, man."

Fucking cunt! Fuck her in the face! She's about to goddamn well *die* and she don't know nothing about it.

Lunch. He looks at the clock. Twelve-fourteen. Jesus
God, in sixteen minutes they go out. Oh, Jesus, it's like
Great Adventure in Atlanta, you are going to the very tippy-
top of the coaster.

They got weenies and catsup and corn, today, that is
lunch. Billy Parker puts his weenie in his pants and unzips
in front of Claire and Wendy and Melissa and Sara and
they all scream. Mr. Witherspoon puts him on report.

Mikey eats with Sara and Mira and Billy and Joe Army.
He doesn't think about it. Then they go out on the field.
Beside them is the low west wall of the school. The eastern
edge is the chain-link fence. Beyond it, Montmorency has
traffic that Mikey never thought of. A FedEx truck. Then
Joe Paletta Farms. And all kinds of cars.

Sara flies off like she got angel wings all the way into
the wall of the school, must be fifteen feet. Most of the
kids, they don't notice. But Debbie has got blood on her
and she is opening her mouth to scream when there is this
snap like a brassiere getting popped and pieces of her
mouth come exploding out like some kind of geyser.

Teachers come racing like they are crazy out into the
yard. All of a sudden Mikey grabs hold of Mira and shields
her. He doesn't know why; it just happens.

Out in the street a car is honking continuously. It has
run into a fire hydrant, and water is shooting out from under
it and making spray rainbows in the noon sun. The driver
can be seen darkly huddled against his steering wheel. The
inside of the windshield is sprayed red.

Mikey yells, "Get down, get down," and all the kids that
aren't screaming go down like they were shot, and then
there is this silence that is the biggest deepest most important thing that Mikey has ever known. It is as if God is this
silence. *God* is.

Witherspoon and Hall have the doors open. They are
screaming, "Get inside, get inside," and the bell is going.
Miss Harlor comes up. "Get inside, honey!"

Sirens join the bell. Accompanied by wet whistling screams, Debbie is kind of humping along like a big caterpillar. Mikey screams, too, he's never had pain like this before. There are cops running around. "Get inside, get inside." They got their pistols out. Those things aren't gonna make a shit.

So they all get inside. The screaming is terrible to hear, the screaming of Debbie, who is now put down on the floor with all this meat coming off her face. Meat, Mikey thinks. He bursts out crying like most of the others, and half of them are running toward the front of the building, they want to get the fuck out of here and get home because they all know just what happened, dumbheads Mira and Debbie and Sara did the queer circle on Jake and he went home and got his rifle.

Suddenly Mikey is grabbed and thrown onto a stretcher, and he realizes that half the school has been yelling at him and he didn't even know it. He got hit, he's hit. What the hell, don't you *feel* these things?

Then the ambulance is rocking along, its siren is neat, he has this nurse with oxygen on his face and everything. Then they got cameras. He is sleepy but it is so neat. Christ, this is like, you are famous. Mom and Dad and Becky are running up in the outside world—the world outside of all these machines and stuff rolling along beside him.

They get him naked, about a million of them, and then there is this doctor and outside Mom is screaming and screaming like you set her on fire or something.

The child, having been discovered to have a surface wound where a bullet had brushed his back, was treated and administered a sedative.

Jake was picked up at his home. He was mistaken about The Age, and the police charged him as an adult and placed him in the maximum-security section of the county jail, not under juvenile detention. He was moved to Atlanta the next morning, having been charged with two counts of capital murder and one of assault with intent to kill.

He told them all what had happened. He told them everything he and Mikey had ever done, and all about the videotape the girls had and what was on Mikey's computer, all of it. Mikey's computer was examined by professionals, but not the least trace of anything about Jake was found. Certainly nothing like the lurid video he described. The Internet was searched, again without result. The videotape given to Mira Banks turned out to be a dub of *King Jesus*.

When Mikey was sitting up in bed, Mira and her mom and dad and two brothers came and thanked him for his heroism in saving her life. Had he not pushed her aside as he did, she would certainly have taken a bullet right in the side of the head.

The funeral for Sara was the next day. Mikey went in a wheelchair. He looked sadly at the coffin with her face inside all waxy. She was dead. Like Sim Eubanks, Jr., who had been driving along minding his own business. And Debbie has got no face. She has not got a face. So she sure ain't gonna have no open coffin tomorrow.

The thing's a long ho-hum. Mainly, he's wishing he could get to scratch his damn wound. Shee-*ut!* Wounds itch like hell, which they don't tell you on TV. Sara's mom screams and does this, like, major seizure. That slows things down even more. But she shuts up. Eventually.

Then the Rev. Collins says, "Lord, O Lord. Dear Lord, show us the way." He raises his eyes. "Lord, tell us why! *Tell us why!*" He looks from face to face. "Lord," he repeats, "show us the *way*." Again he says it and again, until everybody is saying it, praying it, asking it. You can probably hear them up five hundred feet, there are so many of them on this soft afternoon, so many of them packing the church. A tiny beetle—almost no bigger than a gnat, really—has climbed off the lily that is in Sara's hand, and gone onto her finger.

When Rev. Collins gets to mentioning Mikey, Dad wheels him up to the front. Rev. Collins smiles down at him. "Here is an example of Christian youth at its finest, this courageous young man who threw himself into the line of fire in order to save another!" He looks at the ceiling. "Show us, Lord, show us the way!" He waves his Bible at Mikey. "I say this to you and to the world: When you are asked, who among you would offer his life for another, you answer that it is young Mike. Who would stand up to the hate and the madness? Who would? Oh, this *boy* would!" silence. "This boy would."

Mikey looks out across the faces. He has never seen admiration before. They look like people do when they are being all sloppy about a cute puppy.

"Show us the way, young Michael," the Rev. Collins shouts. And with one voice the congregation repeats his trembling cry: "Show us the way!" Mikey doesn't say nothing. He don't need to, 'cause he is saved.

LOVE MYSTERY?

From cozy mysteries to procedurals,
we've got it all. Satisfy your cravings with our monthly
newsletters designed and edited specifically for fans of who-
dunits. With two newsletters to choose from, you'll be sure to
get it all. Be sure to check back each month or sign up for
free monthly in-box delivery at

www.penguin.com

Berkley Prime Crime

Berkley publishes the premier writers of mysteries.
Get the latest on your
favorties:
Susan Wittig Albert, Margaret Coel, Earlene
Fowler, Randy Wayne White, Simon Brett, and
many more fresh faces.

Signet

From the Grand Dame of mystery,
Agatha Christie, to debut authors,
Signet mysteries offer something for every reader.

*Sign up and sleep with
one eye open!*